FRIENDS DISUNITED

by Richard Ayres

To Pam
love from Dick
xx

New Generation Publishing

Dedicated to my school friends of the 1950s and 1960s.

We had it so good.

Acknowledgements

The author would like to thank Dave Roden, Martin Brayne and Darin Jewell for all their much-valued advice.

Thanks are also due to Gillian Conway for her advice on the procedures followed in an Intensive Care Unit.

FOREWORD

'Friends Reunited', the first British internet social networking site, was launched in 2000. The concept behind it was to give former school friends a means of searching for and reconnecting with each other.

At its peak the site had 23 million users. As a result there was a burgeoning of school reunions both official and unofficial, and the renewal of old friendships. It soon became evident that it was not just friendships that were renewed. There was a reported increase in the number of extra-marital affairs resulting from teenage passions being re-awakened. And there was sometimes a re-awakening of latent hostilities between former fellow pupils.

As the decade progressed, the rise of Facebook and other social networking sites began to erode the membership of Friends Reunited, and it closed down in 2016.

PROLOGUE

Staffordshire, 2002

When I wake up each morning, just for a second everything is all right. I am as I used to be. Then I remember what I've become.

To begin with, soon after my transformation, a feeling of well-being used to last for several minutes, the time it took to stumble to the bathroom for a piss. But, of course, the bathroom contained a mirror, and I was immediately confronted with myself. So I removed the mirror, and not just the one in the bathroom. My house is now a looking-glass-free zone.

Exercise goes some way to ward off depression. To attend a gym is out of the question, of course. So I've disciplined myself to do sit-ups and lunges and weight-lifting in my bedroom for twenty minutes every day, and my body's in reasonable nick for a near-sexagenarian, though I can't get rid of the roll of loose flesh that hangs over my belt. But so long as I don't tuck my shirt into my jeans it isn't visible. At least I assume it isn't – hard to tell without looking in a mirror. So I can't see myself as others might see me.

But indoor exercises are tedious. Walking is much more therapeutic. I do a lot of it, just as I used to back in the days when I had partners and friends and a Labrador to accompany me. But now I walk alone, and it has to be early in the morning or late in the evening so there's little chance of encountering others.

Of course this means there are many hours when I'm confined to the prison that is my house. My only company comes from the weekly visit of my shopper-cum-cleaner, and the monthly visit of my counsellor. The cleaner still can't bring herself to look at me, so when she's here I shut myself in my study. The counsellor, of course, is practiced in the art of insouciance and gazes into my eyes when she questions me. They're often questions to which I have no real answer.

Books should be my lifeline. Bookcases line the walls of my lounge and study, as would be expected in the house of an academic – well, a former academic. But I get little comfort from them, especially those which I wrote, for they remind me of a career cut short. I'd had the notion of continuing my researches, but found this impossible without the daily engagement with colleagues, and the stimulation of a very different kind provided by contact with undergraduates.

There are a few photograph albums on the shelves. I used to be an avid photographer, keen to document my progress through life and the friends and lovers who'd accompanied me on my journey. I've kept the snaps taken in my adolescence, though I can't bring myself to look at them. There are no photographs in my collection taken after 1995, because none had been taken. And I've binned the pictures of my former colleagues and partners, because I wished not to be reminded of my work-mates and lovers, for I'll never again have either.

Most documents relating to my recent past have met the same fate, all except for newspaper cuttings dating from the 1990s. I'd decided to keep those, because if I ever reach the point when I'd swallow the sleeping pills hoarded in a drawer beside my bed, my last action prior to that would be to post those cuttings, along with a letter, to the police.

PART ONE

May 2002

Staffordshire

It was this morning's walk that gave me the idea. Or maybe the idea was already there, lurking in my subconscious, planted by what Susie, my counsellor, had suggested, oh, must be a year ago now.

Back then, I'd persuaded myself I was reconciled to my social isolation, that life didn't make sense and couldn't be rearranged, that there was nothing for it but to be a passive observer of the world. Susie had kept pushing me to join a local support group, but I couldn't face that. It wasn't just the way I looked, but the way I sounded. My injuries had caused a speech impediment – when stressed I tend to slur consonants. So Susie had then suggested going on-line and making contact with others who were in my sort of position.

I'd never used email. In Universities, particularly in the Humanities Faculties, online communication had been in its infancy when I was forced to retire. I didn't even possess a computer. Susie was au-fait with modern technology, and arranged for a young man from the IT shop in town to come and install one, connect me to the internet and give me a quick lesson on how to use it. But he'd only stayed half an hour; couldn't look me in the face. He said he'd return sometime, show me what the internet could offer. But he hadn't.

In fact, I wasn't interested in other sad cases in situations similar to mine. What I wanted was the means to contact old friends without having to meet or talk to them. My isolation was such that the content of my life seemed to comprise solely what had once been, rather than what now was. Happiness was bound to people, times and

4

places in the past. Strange how happiness is acutely remembered, unlike sorrow, which, like pain, is never recalled with any acuity.

But which of my old friends should I contact? Not former colleagues: they would only remind me of a promising career cut short. Certainly not former lovers. Old undergraduate friends, perhaps? I realised I didn't want to: I'd enjoyed my student days, but looking back they seemed almost too surreal to allow reconnection. And then it occurred to me that in any case I had no way of finding anyone's email address. So I'd abandoned the idea.

Until my walk this morning.

***

I'm lucky in one respect. Less than a mile from my house are fields, woods and a hill, from the top of which is a panoramic view eastwards over to the edge of the Staffordshire moorlands, fifteen miles away on the other side of Stoke. Today was a perfect late spring morning, and from the top of the hill the Roaches were clearly visible, their jagged outline silhouetted against a sky which had started to redden with the approach of dawn. I turned to look to the west, where the view is much more restricted, the wooded horizon only a mile away across a valley, the intimate, man-made English landscape of all our imaginings – small pastures, hawthorn hedges dotted with ash and oak. That sort of scenery has a special resonance for me, because my academic discipline involved the study of the English landscape and how it evolved. It always evokes field visits to deserted mediaeval villages, where I was the only lecturer among a small group of receptive admiring students.

I try to seek solace from the sights and sounds of the countryside in summer, but the experience is always bitter-sweet. It was the same today. Wistfulness, sadness, anger and self-pity battled within me. Dispirited, I entered the wood that clings to the side of the hill.

And then it hit me. The smell.

Bluebells. I'd been aware of their purple haze on previous mornings, but today I was beguiled by their delicate fragrance. These days they're past their best in June. It's the warming climate we have to blame for that, I reckon. When I was a teenager living in the Chiltern Hills, bluebells weren't in full flower until the start of that month. Not that I paid them much heed at the time; what sixteen-year-old would?

But the scent took me back to my adolescence, to the seemingly endless summer of 1959. It was the year I took my 'O' levels. But I hadn't swotted for them: neither had my mates, because every evening we'd cycled along lanes bordered by bluebell woods to a field at the village of Lee Common, to play knock-about cricket. It was the first time I'd ever been in anything that could be called a gang. I distinctly remember riding the eight miles home, and every evening thinking 'I'm happy! I'm happy!' There are very few, if any, times in one's life when one is aware of being consistently happy, as opposed to merely content, for months on end. Joy such as that is usually fleeting.

I pulled myself back to the present. How long had I been standing daydreaming? I needed to hurry home before the first cohort of dog-walkers took to the hill. And in any case, I now had something to do at home. I'd have a look at those old photographs.

***

The photos taken at Lee Common were in an old shoebox. I'd removed them from an album at the time when I was trying to rid the house of all traces of the past, but couldn't bring myself to throw them away. They'd represented an era that seemed almost pre-historic, so alien that maybe they couldn't hurt me.

I was so impatient to see them that I didn't even make a cup of coffee, but went straight to the cupboard under the stairs. After a few minutes of frenzied scrabbling through accumulated junk I found the shoebox, and carried it up to my study to open it.

They were still there, a dozen or so small black-and-white contact prints. I'd taken them with my first camera, a Box Brownie. I rifled through them, memories washing through me. In most of them we were acting the fool, young bucks posing and posturing in the field where we'd played cricket. Some of them were of me: I think I'd entrusted my camera to Frank Grayson to take those. It was a view into another country, another world. I was wearing Buddy Holly spectacles, a check shirt, jeans, and had an Elvis quiff. My Elvis quiff was the envy of my mates, as was my new Raleigh bicycle with its three-speed Sturmey-Archer gears.

There were no girls in the photographs, even though our Grammar School was co-educational. But rock'n'roll, the soundtrack to our days, spoke to us of pleasures yet to come. As we cycled along we sang of Chantilly Lace and Great Balls of Fire and of being All Shook Up by our Livin' Lovin' Doll. But our own experiences were limited to surreptitious snogs on the back seat of coaches on school trips. For me, on one trip, had been the sublime moment I'd been allowed to unhook a bra strap. I'd had to wait another two years until, in a wood near that same field, I'd had my Cider with Rosie. It was she who had alerted me to the sight and smell of bluebells, before we got down to business.

I sat staring at the photographs for what must have been half an hour. Since the start of my isolation, I'd begun to think a lot about my schooldays, and the friends with whom I'd shared the delicious agonies of adolescence. Four of us had become close mates. We remained so, even though Jack Chapman and Pete Kennedy left school after 'O' Levels while Frank Grayson and I stayed on in the Sixth Form.

Later, though we were under-age, we'd started to drink in a pub in Chesham, the *George*, attracted by the young women who attended the meetings of the Young

Conservatives held there. They were way out of our league, of course, and Frank, the only one of us who shared their background, was too shy to try chatting them up. But we'd continued to drink there, and finally, after a lot of effort, I'd managed to persuade Judy Mason, a fellow 6th form pupil, to accompany me.

But no, I knew I mustn't start thinking about Judy. It was my old mates whom I'd try to contact. But how in hell's name would I go about it?

***

It had taken five frustrating days before the problem was solved. I concluded I'd have to resort to telephone directories. But how could I get hold of them, and which ones? I couldn't search through every directory in the country. How many of my friends, if any, had remained in my home town or nearby?

Once again it was Susie who came to my rescue. I asked if she'd mind going to the library and searching through the directory for my home area for the names of the three people for whom I was searching. They were Jack, Pete and Frank, of course.

'What did your last servant die of, Dave?' Susie had said. She'd been my counsellor for four years, and we'd developed the sort of relationship which allowed for banter. 'I won't be able to get to the library until Saturday, so you'll just have to be patient.'

But today, Saturday, my patience was running out. It was noon and she hadn't phoned. I'd begun to get twitchy. I often get twitchy when confronted with my total dependence on other people. I was alternating between feeling annoyed by Susie's lack of consideration, and worry that something might have happened to her.

But then there were three long rings on my front door bell, followed by two short ones. I jumped, but was relieved to hear the sound. It was the pre-arranged signal which Susie always used to warn me she was about to let herself in, to give me time, as she put it, 'to make myself decent.' This process saved me the worry of having to open the door to a possible stranger.

She entered, shut the door behind her and stood facing me in the hall. 'Thought it was easier if I gave you the list rather than reading it all out on the phone,' she said. 'I looked in the business directory as well. Would have taken me an age to dictate them while you wrote them all down. Don't say I'm not good to you.' She handed me two sheets of A4 paper.

I thanked her profusely of course, but I wanted her to leave immediately. Usually I made coffee for us both when she arrived for my counselling sessions, but I couldn't go through that performance today. I'd waited for this moment long enough.

'I'll be off then, Dave,' she said after a short pause. 'Our scheduled session's next week. See you then.'

'Yes, see you!' I shouted after her as I turned to charge up the stairs to my study.

I sat at the desk. Now the moment had come, I could hardly bring myself to read them, dreading that this might be all to no avail, that there'd be no names I'd recognise, that I'd be cast once more into the limbo of having nothing to anticipate, nothing to do, nothing to live for. Seeking the only comfort available, I groped behind the VDU, pulled out the ashtray hidden there, picked up the half-smoked roll-up lying in it, searched again behind the VDU for the lighter, extracted it, lit up and inhaled deeply. It helped, a bit.

I put on my reading glasses and examined the first list, the one taken from the residential directory. After the first entry, Susie had written – *All in this list are J. Chapmans. There were no F. Graysons or P. Kennedys.* I read each entry carefully. There were several possibles, but one stood out: J Chapman, living in Church Street in Chesham. I glanced at the list taken from the Business Directory, not expecting to find anything of significance. But amongst the entries for plumbers and builders and gardeners there was listed a company located in Aylesbury, the county town. It was only a small entry – *F. Grayson, Independent Financial Advisor.*

In neither list was there an entry for P. Kennedy. Still, two out of three wasn't bad. I decided to make myself a coffee and have a bite to eat before deciding whom to ring first.

***

My hands were trembling slightly as I picked up the phone. Worse than that, I was breathing heavily. This didn't bode well for the clarity of my speech. Talking to strangers on the phone was always an ordeal: being continually asked to repeat myself was so dispiriting that I often abandoned calls without having obtained the information I was seeking.

I keyed in the number. It rang three times, then 'Hello?'

Shit. Bugger. It was a woman's voice. I was on the point of switching off the phone, when it struck me – Jack was probably married. This might be his wife.

'Good morning. Hope I have the right number. I'd like to speak to Jack Chapman.'

Silence. *Oh Christ, please don't ask me to repeat that.*

'Jack Chapman, did you say? Yes, he lives here. This is his wife speaking. Jack can't come to the phone at the moment. Can I take a message?'

The voice had a trace of an old Bucks accent, but the delivery was very formal, as though the speaker were a secretary shielding her boss from interruptions.

'I'll hang on, if that's ok.'

'I'm afraid he's only just got in the shower. Who's speaking, please?'

The question unnerved me. If I told her, Jack might choose not to phone back. We hadn't parted on the best of terms. Also, there was something familiar about the woman's voice.

'Tell him it's an old friend of his. I'll ring back some

other time.'

'Sorry, I didn't catch all that. Old friend, did you say?'

'I said I'll … no, hang on. Does Jack have an email address?'

'An email address?' There was what could only be described as a chuckle, hurriedly stifled. 'No, he doesn't. We don't even have a computer.'

It was my turn to laugh, not with merriment but with shock, because the chuckle was unmistakable. I switched off my phone.

I sank back in my chair. Judy. It had to be Judy.

***

I spent the rest of the day in a state of agitation, buffeted by conflicting emotions. There was a kind of joy, of course, the joy which came from speaking to someone with whom I'd assumed contact had been forever lost. But it was tempered by frustration: an opportunity had been missed – why had I not introduced myself? Then disbelief: Judy, married to Jack? Jack, of all people! Yes, he'd been sweet on her, but she'd been beyond his reach, a vivacious, intelligent sixth-former, bound for university, whereas Jack … and this thought led to envy, which led in turn to a jealousy so griping that I could feel it in the pit of my stomach.

Judy had stayed on in the Sixth Form along with me and Frank. In the early years at Grammar School she'd been shy, hadn't participated in adolescent badinage, and made no attempt, unlike some girls, to modify her school uniform to display her budding assets. We discovered her father was a strict Baptist. But in the fifth form she'd begun to change – not her appearance, but her character and attitudes. I suppose she'd belatedly become a teenager. And after her father died, just after we entered the Sixth Form, her appearance began to change as well. It was this that had prompted me to invite her to *The George*. She only agreed to come if Frank was there as well. That first outing had been the first time I'd seen her not in school uniform. She looked amazing. As we used to say back then, she really gave me the horn. But she always refused to come out with me alone.

My opportunity came when she flunked her 'A' Levels. She'd been in need of comfort, so I took her for a drive (my dad had loaned me his car as a reward for my good results) and for a drink in the *Cock and Rabbit* at The Lee. We ended up in a wood close to the meadow at Lee Common where we lads used to congregate two years before. I provided the comfort she needed, but there was a lot of fumbling, and she told me, as she rearranged her clothes, that it must never happen again. It was the last time I saw her, for in the weeks remaining before my departure for university she never returned to the *George*. And because my parents moved to Yorkshire soon after, I had no reason to visit Bucks again – my vacations were spent with them.

Why the hell was I feeling like this? I'd soon forgotten about her. I was sucked in to the whirlpool of undergraduate life in the 1960s, had my first live-in lover during my postgraduate years, to be followed by other loves and lusts when I was a junior, later a senior university lecturer. Now, I knew that somehow I had to make contact again, but to what end?

I had to snap out of this – yes, do something constructive, telephone Frank Grayson's office. But all I got was an answerphone response, a female saying that the office was closed until Monday, and would I like to leave a message?

***

I just about managed to get through Sunday. In the morning I went for my usual walk, had breakfast, did a bit of gardening, mowed the back lawn even though it didn't need doing. I tried to read *The Observer*, but I couldn't concentrate. I could think of only one thing, how to handle the phone conversation I hoped to have with Frank Grayson on Monday. I mustn't cock it up like I had with Judy: but no, I mustn't think about Judy.

In the afternoon I resorted to what I often do when I can't settle: took a cup of tea up to my bedroom where I've installed an easy chair by the front window so I can sit and look out without being seen. The houses on my street overlook a large grassed area planted with trees. We residents call this 'the green', and at various times of the day it's used by dog-walkers, young mothers and their toddlers, tree-climbing children, lads who play football or cricket according to the season watched by giggling pubescent girls (whom I used to delight in teasing until I was harangued by one of their mothers, the stupid bitch), and, when dusk falls, snogging teenagers. But it's a transient population – the dogs walked when I'd first moved here are long dead, as are some of their owners, the original canoodling teenagers have married and moved away, the young mums are probably now grannies. All have been replaced by new generations of canines, toddlers, mums and teenagers. And pubescent girls, of course. Obviously, I can no longer go out to tease them: they'd run away screaming were I to approach them. But I like to watch them through the binoculars I always have to hand.

After dinner, a heated-up ready-meal, I went to my study and set about writing a script for my conversation with Frank. In fact, I wrote several scripts, each with variations to take account of the possible replies that Frank might make. Then I read them aloud, paying particular attention to enunciating the consonants. All this took over two hours, but I managed to restrict myself to one roll-up.

Feeling more relaxed than I had all day, I had a long soak in the bath, allowed myself three paracetamol, and went to bed.

***

The next morning, I'd returned from my walk and was having breakfast when my door-bell rang and kept on ringing. I peered out of my bedroom window and saw the top of a bald head, its owner peering into the porch. He wore a postman's red florescent jacket, but it wasn't John, my regular postman.

When John was off work sick or on holiday, his colleagues knew my situation and followed his procedure of leaving packages behind the rubbish bin outside the side entrance. The bald head probably belonged to a new postie, yet to be initiated into the arcane practices of John's round. The bugger rang the bell at least a dozen times before giving up and walking back down my drive, still carrying the packet intended for me. I cursed long and loud. It didn't take much to make me rant when I was alone. What for most people would be a minor hiccup in their morning routine was for me a reminder of what a pathetic bastard I'd become. The insistent ringing of the door-bell had jangled my nerves, emphasised my isolation, swamped me in a wave of self-pity.

I knew it would take at least an hour for me to recover from this disaster, two more cups of coffee certainly, and oh God, I needed a cigarette. More than that: what I really needed was the calming effect of a spliff. I hadn't indulged in those since I became a responsible Senior Lecturer, bloody hell, twenty years ago now. Of course it was now impossible for me to score, and it wasn't something I could ask Susie to do for me.

Did I really want to contact Frank? At school, it was only in the Sixth Form that we struck up a sort of friendship. He was what we called 'posh' (his primary education had been at a private school), but then so were many others – it was a Grammar School in the Home Counties, after all. Even when he joined us in our evening games of knock-about cricket, he was still a bit aloof. But he wasn't just posh, he was clever, cleverer than me, always beating me to become first in the end-of-year class rankings.

He'd been immune from what today would be called peer-group pressure. He didn't even pretend to like rock n' roll, his haircut was a short-back-and-sides, he made no attempt to adapt his school uniform to conform to the trends of the day – he was mocked because his flannel trousers remained un-tapered. And, unlike most of us, he seemed to have no interest in girls.

But the Sixth Form girls were interested in him. His gentle manner and politeness seemed to appeal to them, in particular Judy. I envied him that, of course, but if the price of having her company was to have to share it with Frank … well, so it had to be. Judy had insisted on Frank joining us when I invited her to visit the *George*, that memorable occasion when I first saw her dressed in something other than her school uniform. But Frank had seemed immune to Judy's charms. As our 'A' Level exams approached, his visits to the *George* became rarer. The Headmaster wanted him to sit for Oxford entry, but he'd set his heart on the London School of Economics.

The last time we saw each other was for a celebratory drink after we'd been accepted at university. Judy, of course, wasn't present. I was tempted to boast to Frank about how I'd been able to comfort her, but held back. I'd gone to Leeds, never to return to my home town, and Frank had gone to London. I think we exchanged two letters, then…. nothing. No doubt he, like me, had become totally immersed in undergraduate life.

***

It was nearly noon by the time I felt able to phone.

'Grayson Financial Services. How may I help you?'

Oh please God no, not another bloody woman.

'Would you mind telling me please if Mr Grayson's first name is Frank?'

'I beg your pardon?'

'Mr Grayson. Is his first name Frank?'

'Well, yes it is.'

Progress!

'Did he by any chance once work in the City?'

'Sorry, could you repeat that please?'

Oh, shit.

'Did he work in London, in the City?'

'I'm sorry sir, but I'm not party to Mr Grayson's CV.'

Pompous bitch. Typical of Frank to have a business that employed an oh-so-refined secretary.

'Well, can you tell me his home town? Or what school he went to? Did he go to London University?'

Silence. *Try again.*

I said, 'What school did he attend? Did he go to London University?'

'I heard you, sir. I'm sorry, but I'm sure you'll appreciate I can't divulge that sort of information. Who is it who's calling?'

Posh as well as pompous.

'Look, can you give me your company's email address?'

'Would you give me your name, please?'

'There's no harm in giving me an email address, surely?'

'Your name, please?'

Seething, I disconnected the call, reached for my coffee and spilled half of it down my shirt.

I tried reading the *Guardian*, but couldn't concentrate. I turned on the computer, only to realise there was nothing I wished to use it for. Went down to the kitchen, made a cup of tea, took a couple of sips, didn't want any more. Wandered into the back garden, sat for a while in the sun, but what use was a tan on what remained of my face? Back to the kitchen: it was time for lunch, but I wasn't hungry.

Went to the living room, slumped in the armchair. Oh, what was the point? What was the fucking point? Suddenly, to try again to make contact, whether with Jack or Frank, whether by more phone calls or by letters, was all too much effort. And what good would come of it if I succeeded? We had only the distant past in common. Look to the future, my counsellor had once said, but what future? Solitary morning and evening walks? Careful tending of a garden that no one but me would see? Investigate online pornography? Try to resume my academic research without the stimulus of colleagues?

Looming in front of me once again was the ghastly black pit of depression. I went up to my study, opened the filing cabinet and extracted the newspaper cuttings. Just to check they were still there, of course. No, I hadn't reached that stage yet. I got undressed, took two sleeping pills, and went to bed.

PART 2

May 2002

Buckinghamshire

Jack

Jack heard the phone ring in the kitchen. Oh Lord, mum always rang when he was taking a shower. She'd probably forgotten again what time he was coming to visit her.

The ringing stopped. No doubt Jude had picked it up.

There was no point kidding himself. Mum was beginning to lose it. He'd soon have to broach the issue of a care home, and he was dreading it. Mum seemed to think that because he lived close by he'd always be on hand to rescue her from whatever scrape her increasing forgetfulness had landed her in. Sometimes he regretted not having moved away from his home town. It was too late to consider doing so now. At the age of 59 he was too old to uproot. In any case, Jude would be dead against it. She loved living in the town of her birth, close to the people she'd grown up with and all the friends she'd made since.

As he towelled himself down, he could hear Jude's muffled half of the phone conversation, no doubt reassuring Mum. She was very good with his mother, far more patient than he was. But then Jude was very good with everyone. Everyone said she was a lovely lady. She was. He was lucky to have her, he knew that. She'd been a sexy, vivacious teenager when he first went out with her. He could still remember his elation when she'd accepted his invitation to go the flicks – it had been *Goldfinger* at the long-since demolished Embassy cinema. All his mates had been surprised: she could have had the pick of any bloke in the town. Surprise had turned to astonishment when they started going out regularly with each other – became an item, he supposed it would be called now – and when, a few years later, they'd married, in the local church, only a few hundred yards away from where they'd set up home and where they still lived.

He pulled back on his jogger bottoms and a sweater and entered the kitchen. Jude was replacing the receiver, a puzzled expression on her face.

'Mum, I suppose?' he said.

'No, it wasn't. Dunno who it was. He wouldn't give his name.'

'Probably a wrong number. D'you want a coffee? I'm having one.'

'No thanks, No, it wasn't a wrong number. He asked to speak to you. When I said you were in the shower he said not to trouble you.'

'Didn't you recognise his voice?'

'No. It was hard to make out what he was saying. His voice was sort of slurred.'

'Strange. Didn't you ask who it was?'

'Course I did. He just said he was an old friend of yours. He said he'd call back sometime. Then he asked if you had an email address. I told him you didn't even have a computer. He laughed. Then he rang off.'

'Sounds like a practical joker. Lot of 'em about, these days. Don't worry about it, Jude.'

She shrugged, moved over to the sink and began washing up the breakfast things he'd left before going out for his bike ride. Washing up was his job, but she often stepped in to forestall him. He wished she'd relax a bit, but she'd always been house-proud, and it had become obsessional when it transpired they could never have kids. It was then she'd started losing weight, drastically.

He boiled the kettle, made two cups of coffee, placed one on the draining board in front of her, settled himself at the table and opened the *Sunday Express*. He had to search through it to find any good news, but at least there were no plane crashes or riots in London or natural disasters.

But whatever the news, he always enjoyed this short period of relaxation between his bike ride and setting out for Morning Service. While he was there, Jude would prepare lunch. She never accompanied him: she'd rejected religion after her father had died. In the early days of their marriage she used to mock him gently for his attendance, but he'd explained he went just because he enjoyed the singing – he'd been a member of the choir – and she'd accepted that. She was a very accepting person, was Jude.

As he walked towards the church, the phone call suddenly came to mind. A practical joker, he'd told Jude, and when he'd said so he'd believed it. But now, he began to wonder. An old friend, the caller had said. What was meant by that? Someone he'd known since childhood, or an old school friend, or one of the many friends he'd subsequently made during his half-century in the town? It was a puzzler. But the fellow had said he'd call back sometime. If he did, all would be revealed. If he didn't, well, then it probably *had* been a joke call.

He went round to the side of the church and pushed open the vestry door. He was the organist and had a key, but he knew the vicar would already be in there. The Rev. Charles Barnes was the new, conscientious, enthusiastic young incumbent. He was a very young man indeed. He was full of ideas of how to make the church – what was the expression he used? – 'meaningful to people in this new century'.

Jack didn't like him. Oh, he was pleasant enough in a slightly condescending way, was respectful to Jack, called him Mr Chapman, but he had no regard for the history and traditions of the place. The old oak pews on which generations of Jack's ancestors' backsides had rested had been the first to go, to be replaced by plastic chairs which could be stacked away to provide space for what Barnes called 'communal expressions of joy in worship'. Next the ornately carved and decorated chancel screen, in place for over two centuries, had been ripped out because, apparently, there should be 'no physical manifestation of any division between the congregation and those in the chancel'. But what was really getting to Jack, the thing that made him grind his teeth when thinking about it, was Barnes' proposal to scrap Hymns Ancient and Modern because they 'disenfranchised the younger worshippers' and be replaced by songs for which there was no sheet music for organ accompaniment. 'You see, Mr Chapman, I'm hoping the youngsters will accompany themselves, on guitars and ukuleles perhaps.' He hadn't seemed to have noticed that, apart from those in the choir, there were few people under the age of thirty in the congregation, a congregation which was steadily diminishing in size as its members sought refuge in a church in the neighbouring town.

Jack knew his days as organist were numbered. He was resigned to this, and in any case he no longer enjoyed the sort of music he was required to play. But if he were to give up attending, he'd miss the worship – not so much what was left of the ceremonial, but the comfort of just being together with those who had faith. For Jack was a Christian. He always had been, but he kept quiet about it. He wasn't an evangelist, not one to trumpet his beliefs or opinions about anything, and he didn't care for those who did. He never discussed his faith with Jude. He was afraid she might be upset by being reminded of his belief in the merciful God who had nevertheless chosen to make them childless.

So he was looking forward to seeing Pete Kennedy after lunch and having a good old moan to him about the Rev. Barnes. It wasn't something he wished to burden Jude with.

Pete and Jack

Pete ill-temperedly threw his clubs into the back of the Range Rover. He was going to be late, and that meant Jack would be hanging about waiting to be picked up. His lateness was due to Marion having served lunch an hour later than she'd promised, the result of a protracted phone conversation with one of her Women's Institute friends during which she'd downed at least three glasses of sherry. The meal had been eaten in silence.

Pete always looked forward to his Sunday afternoons with Jack. Jack didn't play golf – he couldn't afford to buy the gear, let alone pay the Club fees, but he acted as Pete's caddy whenever he played at Ley Hill. The arrangement suited them both. Though neither had articulated it, both knew it provided a reason for them to meet regularly on neutral territory where the disparity in their respective incomes and lifestyles didn't impinge on their life-long friendship, so long as they didn't enter the club house, of course. Jack and Judy had obviously been uncomfortable on the few occasions they'd come for a meal at Pete's large detached house. And Pete felt equally ill-at-ease in Jack's poky terraced cottage in their home town, mainly because he was unable to converse with Judy in the relaxed intimate way in which he once had, even though the incident which had prompted his taciturnity had taken place years ago. That saddened him: he'd known her as long as he'd known Jack. She'd been at Primary and Grammar School with them, and later was one of the group who'd met every Friday in the *George*.

The ten mile journey to Jack's place took him from the Vale of Aylesbury into the Chilterns, along narrow lanes under a canopy of beech trees. The same thought always occurred to him – there was still a hell of a lot of countryside about. And it wasn't productive countryside either. None of the fields contained cattle or sheep, most farmers now let out their land for horses to graze in. The land was ripe for development. People needed houses, didn't they? And he could help provide them, if only the bloody local council would grant planning permission to the owners. But they always refused applications, always citing the same reason: the Chilterns were designated an area of Outstanding Natural Beauty. Bloody socialist claptrap. But at least after five years Blair still seemed to be relatively sane.

He never divulged his feelings about planning restrictions to Jack, not wanting a disagreement to come between them. Old Jack was a bit of a lefty and a bit sentimental, kept going on about what a wonderful part of the country it still was, how lucky they were to live there. He still had his bike, went for long rides along the lanes which radiated from the town. He said it always reminded him of his adolescence, and how comforting it was that the area had changed so little. He said it had been one of the happiest times of his life. He could be a soft old sod, could Jack.

But Pete was fond of him. They had been born in the same town, they'd both attended the same primary school, passed the Eleven Plus, left the Grammar School after 'O' Levels. The shared experiences of their youth had resulted in a bond that couldn't be broken, despite the subsequent divergence of their paths. Pete had been articled in a local architect's firm, had eventually qualified after years of part-time study. His career had taken off when investment from his father-in-law enabled him to set up his own practice. But Jack ... the silly bugger had got a job as general dogsbody in a Building Society, had never bothered to get further training, and was now what he had been for the past twenty years, a glorified receptionist. Pete thought he'd wasted his talents. But in the interests of their continuing friendship he never told him as much.

He pulled into Church Street, hoping for the chance to have a cigarette before Jack emerged. But Jack was waiting outside his front door, dressed in his usual summer weekend outfit, a short-sleeved shirt and baggy trousers. Not very suitable attire for the Golf Club. But Jack could carry it off. Strange, how Jack's physique had improved with age. At school he'd been skinny, gawky, uncoordinated in his movements, useless at sport. There

23

still wasn't an ounce of spare flesh on him, but he was well muscled, carried himself like a man half his age, and seemed more nimble on his feet. All that bike-riding, no doubt. Pete, who had high blood pressure, a spare tyre and was often short of breath after a round of golf, envied him that. And his full head of dark hair, only just starting to show the first flecks of grey. And his face, which though lined, still showed the fine bone structure with which he'd been blessed, in particular his straight narrow nose. Pete's nose had always been bulbous, and recently red blemishes had begun to appear on it. His doctor said it was rosacea and had put him on a course of antibiotics. While he waited for them to take effect, he'd secretly started investigating the contents of Marion's make-up bag.

'Sorry I'm late, mate,' he said as Jack climbed in beside him. 'Marion was a bit slow getting lunch.'

'No problem, Pete. Gave me a chance to help Jude with the washing up.'

Pete, just in time, stopped himself from saying they ought to get a dish washer. 'Judy okay, is she?'

'Yeah, fine. She sends her love.'

Pete doubted she had. He and Judith used to exchange kisses on meeting and parting, things that old friends of opposite sexes often do, but that had stopped after … well, after she'd started losing her looks. In her thirties she'd suddenly got very thin. And now, what with his red nose, they both shied away from displays of affection which might hint, however remotely, of a previous mutual attraction. It was probably worse for her, now she was no longer the stunning woman she'd been in her youth. He, on the other hand had never had stunning looks to lose.

'Give her my love back,' he said. He put the Range Rover into gear and they set off for Ley Hill.

Pete's game was never up to scratch when Jack acted as his caddy because he would keep chatting when Pete was trying to concentrate. Not while he was taking his shots, but between shots, not seeming to understand you had to remain focused for the duration of each hole. Today, he'd been going on about that new Vicar at his church. Pete managed to show sympathetic interest.

The round completed, they returned to the car. Pete knew Jack would be uncomfortable in the club house amongst the well-to-do clientele.

'Quick one in the *George*, then?' he said as they drove back towards the town. He said this at the same time each Sunday, and he could predict Jack's reply, word for word.

'Yeah, why not? Can't stay long though, Pete. Got to pay me mum a visit.'

Pete didn't like the *George*, not the way it was now. But Jack retained an affection for the place, and as the poor old bugger never seemed to go out for a drink with anyone these days Pete kept up the pretence that he enjoyed visiting the haunt of their youth. Yes, they'd had good times in there, but that was history now, wasn't it? Never look back, that was Pete's motto. Or at least, try not to look back.

***

Jack pushed through the door of the pub and headed for the bar. It was now an unspoken tradition that he bought the first round because Pete bought all the subsequent ones.

He carried the drinks over to where Pete was sitting in the window seat. Jack always asked him to sit there and Pete usually obliged. Jack liked to face him, so he could see the upholstered bench on which his friend sat, because the bench and the window behind it and the doorway to the side of it were unchanged since the time they used to drink here as teenagers.

He still thought about those times a lot, how he used to arrive here early every Friday evening, to be the first one in and to watch his mates one by one pushing through that same door and greeting him before they turned to the bar and ordered their pints of Watney's Red Barrel from Gerry the landlord, and then joined him in the cosy lounge waiting for the arrival of the girls with their bouffant or beehive hairstyles, who drank Babycham and responded to chat-up lines with giggles that became raucous shrieks as the evening progressed, and who let their wide skirts rise above their knees to reveal stocking-tops and occasionally a flash of bare flesh, and how the room became hazy with the smoke from Rothman's King Size and Player's Number 6 Tipped. And he would never forget the occasion when the door opened and Judy had made her first entrance alongside Tim Bailey and Frank Grayson, and how it had been the first time he'd seen her for ages because she'd stayed on in the Sixth Form and spent most of her free time with her fellow pupils, and what a gorgeous girl she'd become, tall, slim, with huge brown eyes, thick black hair which unfashionably but bewitchingly hung down over her shoulders, and a figure and legs which he'd always gawped at even when shrouded by her frumpish school uniform but which, on that evening, were enhanced by a tight skirt and high heels which made her seem … well… totally unobtainable. She'd sat down next to him, began to chat to him while Tim was getting her a light ale, but he'd been able only to stammer inane replies.

He could still envisage that scene, so long as he didn't turn round to see the remainder of the pub as it now was. The small bar against which old codgers used to stand chatting to Gerry had long been demolished to make way for an austere uncarpeted expanse which housed metal tables and chairs, a pool table and an assortment of slot machines. Behind these a garish bar extended the width of the room, service provided by a tattooed gorilla who communicated mainly in grunts. Thank the Lord it was too early in the evening for piped pop music and the sort of clientele who enjoyed it.

He jumped. Pete was talking to him.

'… I said, any news then? Apart from your bloody vicar, that is?'

'Sorry, mate. Miles away. No, no news. Work's the

same as ever. Mum's on the verge of going doolally. Clocked up nearly 100 miles on me bike this week. How about you?'

'Well, I've got the chance of a deal with a builder who's got outline planning permission for twenty luxury houses out Aylesbury way. If it comes off I should -'

'Oh, hang on a bit Pete. Sorry. Just remembered I *have* got a bit of news that might interest you.'

'What's that then?'

'I had a strange phone call this morning, well, Jude took it, but she - '

'What d'you mean, strange?'

Jack gave a brief outline of what Jude had told him of the conversation and ended by saying he couldn't imagine who the caller might have been.

Pete took a swig from his pint.

'Very old friend, you say he said? Well, that narrows the field a bit, doesn't it?'

'How come?'

'Well, it wouldn't be anyone who still lives in the town and you still see, would it? And you've never moved, so it's not someone you met somewhere else. So it must be someone who once lived here and later moved away.'

'But how would he know my phone number?'

'Think about it. There must be thousands of J. Chapmans in the country. But if he took a punt on you still living here, well, he could easily get your number from Directory Enquiries, couldn't he?'

'Suppose so.'

'I wouldn't mind betting it was someone we knew at school. Probably one of those buggers who stayed on in Sixth Form, then went off to university, and never came back.'

Jack considered this for a moment.

'You might have something there,' he acknowledged eventually.

After the usual agreement that they'd meet again next

Sunday, Jack left Pete outside the pub door, and started on the walk to his mother's bungalow.

Once Pete had come up with his suggestion as to who may have been the mystery phone-caller, he'd evidently lost interest in the subject and spent the next half-hour telling Jack about the antics of his business associates. Jack usually found this entertaining, but this evening he hadn't been able to concentrate: something had been nagging at him, but he couldn't get a handle on it.

Now, as he walked along in the balmy summer evening, it suddenly came to him. Tim and Frank had been in the Sixth Form with Judy, hadn't they? In fact, Tim, after his parents had started loaning him their car, had taken her out once, but, as she'd told Jack later, he'd tried to get fresh with her and she'd given him short shrift. That didn't matter now. But surely, if it had been any of the old sixth-formers who'd phoned, wouldn't Jude have recognised the voice? Voices didn't change that much, did they, not till you got really old and quavery.

So perhaps Pete was wrong, perhaps it hadn't been one of that crowd. Jack hoped this was the case. But he couldn't work out why he felt that way.

Pete and Marion

Pete, driving home to an uncertain welcome from Marion, was also thinking about the mysterious phone call to Jack. He was wishing now he hadn't said what he had, about it possibly being from one of the old sixth-formers. Old Jack was inclined to live in the past, and there was now a chance he might try to contact them. The last thing Pete wanted was to get involved in any attempts to renew former friendships.

'You're bloody late.'

That was the greeting Pete had been expecting. Marion was splayed on the lounger on the patio, an almost-empty bottle of Pinot Grigio beside her. The evening was now cool enough to have required her to cover up a bit. Pete could never understand why she felt obliged to get an all-over sun tan: it wasn't as if at her age she'd ever contemplate displaying her body to other people, surely? *He* didn't count: he assumed she didn't care what he thought about her appearance. He did, though.

He was tempted to remind her why he'd been late meeting Jack, but he hadn't the energy for the debate which would inevitably follow. He wanted nothing more than a shower, a light snack, and then a couple of gins and a fag or two while he watched mindless drivel on the telly. He had a busy day at the office ahead of him tomorrow.

'Give me a hand up, then' she said as she attempted, and failed, to rise from the lounger.

There was no getting away from it: she was on the verge of becoming obese. He felt the familiar flash of distaste. When they'd married she was … well, cuddly was the best way to describe her, but was able to carry it off by paying careful attention to what she wore. She'd begun to let herself go after Sarah was born. Sarah was the reason they'd married. Despite being in her late twenties at the time, Marion had still been in thrall to her parents and wouldn't agree to his suggestion of an abortion. He was glad now that she hadn't; okay, she'd found it hard bringing up Sarah while he was busy trying to grow his business, but Sarah had turned out well, and now he had the joy of grandchildren, though all too rarely. Grandchildren were fun. Fun wasn't something you had much of, in late middle age.

He hauled her to her feet, not receiving any thanks, and she lumbered towards the kitchen. He picked up the wine bottle and the glass and followed her.

'I'm going to get a quick shower,' he said.

'You'll get your own snack, won't you? I'm going to have a long soak.'

She had an en-suite bathroom next to her own bedroom.

Showered, revived by a ham sandwich and strong coffee, and with G&T and cigarette in hand, he entered the lounge. Its minimalist décor had been dictated by Marion – she said it made things easier for her daily, a treasure whom she didn't want to lose – but there were two triple-seater settees which he'd insisted on. He'd had to get angry with her over that. He turned on the TV and slumped in front of it. He flipped through the channels but as he'd anticipated it was the usual Sunday night crap. Perhaps he ought to go to his study, start preparing for tomorrow's meeting with the developers. Marion wouldn't like that, not after having spent the afternoon by herself, but bugger her. They never spoke much in the evenings anyway.

She pushed through the door, bearing a tray on which would be, he knew, a selection of biscuits or a box of expensive chocolates, a glass, and a bottle of wine. Another bloody bottle of wine. Over her nightdress she was wearing a full length dressing gown. He quite liked seeing her dressed like that: it covered a multitude of sins. But one's attention was drawn to her face, a face which had once been pretty but was now reaping the consequences of years of booze and cigarettes. And why did she spend so much time sunbathing? It did nothing for her. Her face was too brown, a bit like those deep-fried visages you saw on old women who'd just returned from two weeks in Majorca.

She placed the tray on an occasional table, poured a glass of wine, and subsided onto the settee next to it. Not his settee, of course.

'Anything on the box?' she asked, reaching for a chocolate.

'Not a lot.'

'So, what's new?'

'What d'you mean, what's new?'

'Any news from Jack? How is he?'

Her question amazed him.

'Jack? He's okay. Why the sudden interest? You don't

usually ask after him.'

'Because I've been by myself all afternoon, that's why. It would be nice to talk about something, even if it's only Jack.'

'What d'you mean, only Jack?'

'You know what I mean. Why do you keep on seeing him every Sunday? What do you find to talk about? I can't see what you two have in common.'

Pete's gorge rose. He was on the brink of shouting at her, telling her once again about the bond that came from growing up together and sharing adolescent rites of passage. But he didn't. Instead he turned up the volume on the TV.

'Turn that rubbish off, Pete.'

'What? But you always watch – '

'Not tonight. It's time we had a talk.'

Such was Pete's surprise that he obeyed, instantly.

***

Marion had wanted to have the conversation for months. No, if she was honest with herself, it had been for years, ever since Sarah had flown the nest. She'd been happy enough in the early years despite Pete's flashes of bad temper, content to stay at home and raise them while Pete worked to provide the sort of lifestyle to which she aspired and to which her parents believed she was entitled. Looking back, it was ironic that her happiest time had been when they lived in the modest house in Aylesbury, close to Sarah's primary school, outside which she'd made friends with the other mums delivering and collecting their offspring, despite the fact they were mostly lower-class and younger than her.

When, thanks to Daddy's help, Pete's business had taken off, they moved to the near-mansion in which they still lived, two miles from the nearest village. Her parents had suggested Sarah attend a private school near Princes Risborough, and though Pete was reluctant for some reason, he eventually agreed. But the school was a half-hour's car journey away and she'd begun to resent the amount of time she was spending ferrying them back and forth. 'Why can't she become a boarder?' she'd asked. 'Daddy will help with the fees.' Pete had been even more hostile about this suggestion, but eventually gave in after Daddy had persuaded him it would be wrong to deny Sarah a good start in life.

But it was then, she now knew, that discontent had begun to set in. She'd found herself lonely. Pete had become totally absorbed in running The Vale Architectural Services, and when he wasn't spending evenings in the office he was out seducing prospective clients or negotiating with builders, activities which, he claimed, were best undertaken in the informal setting of a pub or a hotel lounge.

She'd resorted to joining the local WI, an organisation she'd once derided. Although her new acquaintances weren't the most exciting company, she'd tried to immerse herself in the Branch's activities.

But it wasn't enough. She knew that the frantic day-time activities into which she threw herself were not just a means of staving off boredom, but of inducing the sort of tiredness which made her so sleepy that the edge was taken off the loneliness of those evenings when Pete was out, and the even greater loneliness when they sat in the same room but not together, exchanged banalities but never conversed, passed each other snacks or topped up each other's glasses, but never touched.

This evening, after another Sunday afternoon spent alone, she'd had enough. She knew Pete might lose his temper, but it was a risk she was prepared to take.

'What's this all about, then?' said Pete.

'How long are we going to go on doing this?'

'Doing what? What d'you mean?'

'Doing nothing. At weekends and in the evenings. We never do anything together.'

32

'But we're both tired in the evening. I am, anyway. Totally knackered. You've never mentioned this before. But if you really want to go out, we could go for a meal on Saturday nights, if you like. Or just to a pub for a drink.'

A vision came to Marion of them facing each other across a table in a restaurant, or side by side in a pub: silent, nothing to say to each other, just observing the camaraderie of others.

'You know what our problem is? We haven't got any mutual friends.'

'But you've got your friends at the WI – '

'You never listen, do you? Mutual friends, I said. You don't know any of the women at the WI, and I don't know any of the blokes you work with. And as for their spouses, well … '

'But you know I don't socialise with my colleagues. Don't have time for that, do I?'

'But one day you will!' She heard her voice go shrill with exasperation. 'You'll have to retire sometime, won't you? And then what? What will you do with your time? You'll be friendless. *We'll* be friendless. A lonely old couple, sitting around waiting for visits from Sarah.'

'But for Christ's sake, I've often suggested going out for a drink with Jack and Judith, but you – '

'Oh *fuck* Jack and Judith.' Marion knew that swearing would have the effect of shocking Pete and maybe stop him from shouting at her. 'I've got nothing in common with them. I'm not spending evenings listening to you three go on and on about your schooldays.'

'But Jack's an intelligent bloke. So's Judy, she stayed on into the Sixth Form, got an 'A' level, and – '

'There you go again! It always comes back to your schooldays, doesn't it? If they're so bloody clever, why haven't they achieved anything?

'So, what are you suggesting we do? Join a bridge club? Or a rambling group maybe? Or the University of the Third Age? You might have time to do that sort of thing, but I haven't.' He ground out his cigarette, then lit another immediately.

Marion steeled herself to broach the topic Pete always shied away from. They hadn't discussed the matter for … God, it must be well over ten years: he always clammed up, or went into a rage, when she mentioned the name.

'No, of course I'm not suggesting anything like that. Look, Pete, there *is* one of your old school friends who I always liked. Liked his wife as well. We had some good evenings with them.'

She noticed his brow furrow, his body tensing even as he remained reclining on the settee. He'd got there already. But she was determined to carry on.

'You know who I mean, don't you? Frank. Frank Grayson. I'd like to see him again, and Angela. They were fun.'

He said nothing, drained his glass, stared straight ahead.

'Oh come on, Pete. Whatever it was caused you two to fall out, it was years ago, wasn't it? I know it was something to do with business, but you never really explained what it was all about, did you? But why can't you try and make it up? Tell you what, if you can't bring yourself to make the first move, why don't I phone Angela, say we're going for a drink near their place, suggest they join us?'

He stood up, walked over and stood in front of her, raised his arm. She cowered. But there was no slap. He was silent for a moment, then said, 'You can do what you fucking want. But I tell you now, there's no way I want to see Councillor Grayson again. And he won't want to see me. I'm going to bed now. Goodnight.'

Judith

It was Monday, and Judith was walking along the High Street, on her way home from work. She was distracted. Her boss had been consulting personnel records. 'Good

Heavens, Judith!' he'd said. 'You've only got another year before you retire!' She knew that only too well, but it was always a shock when someone else voiced something you'd begun to worry about.

She'd been working at Saunders and Parsons for forty-one years. Forty-one years! Her 'A' Levels hadn't been good enough to get her into university, so she'd taken a secretarial course at the technical college in Wycombe and on completing it had immediately obtained the post of junior shorthand-typist at the long-established firm of solicitors in her home town.

She never imagined she'd spend her entire working life in the same company. Of course, if she'd had children … She tried not to think about that, but the sorrow was always there, lurking in the recesses of her mind, ready to spring out and attack her without warning, usually when her friends cooed over the winning ways of their grandchildren.

She always sought comfort herself by reminding herself it was her earnings which enabled her and Jack to live, if not exactly in comfort, but at least without major financial worries. Jack earned a pittance.

Poor old Jack. There were times when she felt for him a deep, protective love. He was one of those people who somehow aroused guilt. But these days he seemed quite content. He had his weekly choir practice, never missed Morning Service, went for his bike rides, visited the library for his family history researches. Other than that he rarely went out, apart from the Sunday golf sessions with Pete, and she didn't begrudge him that. Pete had been a good friend to him, apart from that time when … no, he *had* been a good friend, still was. But Pete's visits to the house to collect Jack were now all too brief, and she missed his company but … well, perhaps it was for the best.

She found she had stopped walking and was staring into the window of a newly-opened shop that sold computers. It reminded her that they didn't possess one. If only Jack could be persuaded …

Damn. Day-dreaming again. And she'd forgotten to call in at the Tesco mini-store to purchase their evening meal. She retraced her steps along the High Street, entered the store, picked up a quiche, and was on her way out when she was bumped into by a woman making an entrance. The woman looked familiar.

Good heavens, could it be? Yes it was. It was Maureen.

'Judy? It is Judy, isn't it? How wonderful! I was only thinking when I parked the car, wouldn't it be strange if I ran into an old school friend after all these years! How are you?'

'Maureen! What are you doing here?'

'Long story. Look, I've only got to get a few things in here. Fancy a coffee? Does the old place have a decent café? It would be nice to catch up. Christ, it must be over 30 years since I last saw you. You haven't changed a bit.'

'Neither have you,' Judith replied, though of course she had. They both had. She was about to add that she really had to get home, but then thought, what's the harm? There's no hurry, we never eat till 7.30. Jack wouldn't mind me being a bit late.

'Well, there's a Costa just down the street, doesn't close till six, but I mustn't be long because – '

'Great! Just give me a few minutes.'

Maureen insisted on buying the coffee and told Judith to grab a table. Sitting at it, she watched Maureen waiting for the drinks to be served. Her body language demonstrated extreme impatience. She always had been impatient, even when she was a teenager. They'd been in the same class at Grammar School, but were never close friends. Judith's mum had said Maureen was common, and advised Judith against mixing with her.

Maureen had been blonde and pretty with a voluptuous figure which wasn't entirely disguised by the school uniform because she rolled up the waistband of her skirt so the hem was above her knees, and left undone the top two

36

buttons of her blouse. But she'd soon lost interest in the boys at school: she'd cast her net further afield, and this resulted in possibly the greatest scandal to hit the school since its foundation, for she did not return after the 1959 Easter holiday. The reason for her absence was never announced, but when the news of her hurried engagement to Fred the Ted leaked out, it became the focus of delicious outraged gossip in the changing rooms.

'Here you are Judy. A large latte, and I thought you might like a chocolate brownie. I can't resist them. I know I ought to. Have to watch my figure these days. You're still slim though, aren't you? A bit too thin, if you don't mind my saying. Have you got any kids, or grandchildren? I've got three kids and four grandchildren. I quite like being a granny, so long as I don't have to see them too often. Do you know, I sometimes ...'

Judith was reminded that when with Maureen you never had to grope for conversation, and in that respect she hadn't changed. But her way of speaking had. As a teenager she'd had a sub-cockney accent, Estuary English she supposed it was now called, but now she spoke with Received Pronunciation, well, almost: there were lapses when she started to gabble, and she did a lot of gabbling.

Judith managed to interject that the last time she'd seen Maureen must have been in the High Street in the early sixties because she was with her toddler and ... and then she'd stopped, conscious this was something of which Maureen might not wish to be reminded.

But it didn't seem to bother Maureen at all. She launched into another monologue about her son Johnny, Fred the Ted's son, and then about how her marriage had broken down so she'd gone to live with her parents who'd moved to Berkhamsted, and how this turned out to be a blessing because there she'd met Martin, who was a businessman, well off, and they'd got married and ...

Judith felt breathless just listening to her. It was only when Maureen took a sip of coffee that she managed to ask what she was doing in the town, and it seemed she'd been early setting off to return home from Wycombe where she'd been visiting her son, so she'd decided to call in and have a look at the old place, because since the inner by-pass had been built you never got to go along the High Street, did you?

'*I* do,' said Judith, 'I walk along it every day, I work in a solicitor's office just by the – '

'It's a bit strange now it's been pedestrianised, isn't it? I'm not sure I like it; seems a bit empty somehow. It used to be a really bustling town, didn't it, everybody crammed together on the pavements? Remember when we were teenagers, how we used to walk up and down the street on Saturday mornings, eyeing up the boys? I think we started doing that when we were about fourteen, that was when we started wearing those dirndl skirts with net petticoats, oh, and tight blouses and wide belts, remember? That was when rock'n'roll started, wasn't it?'

'I wasn't allowed to wear those sort of clothes, Maureen. And I never used to parade down the High Street, either. My dad was very strict, don't you remember? He always – '

'We used to chat to the blokes who were in our class, didn't we? Well, the ones who were with it, you know, like Pete Kennedy and Tim what'sisname. You never saw the squares in town on Saturday morning, did you? There were quite a few squares at Grammar School, weren't there? Real swots. Remember Frank Grayson? All he talked about was politics. And Jack Chapman, and his bloody classical music; spent all his time practising in the school choir. And there was – '

'I married him, Maureen.'

'Sorry?'

'I married Jack Chapman. He's my husband.'

This had the effect of stopping the flow. Maureen had the grace to look embarrassed. She fished in her handbag and pulled out a packet of cigarettes, extracted one, lit it, inhaled deeply, exhaled expansively, and then held the pack out to Judith.

'I don't, thanks.'

'Bloody hell, Judy, I'm sorry. How did you come to … I mean, Jack left in the fifth form, didn't he? And didn't I hear you stayed on in the sixth? What made you … how did you come to get together?'

'Well, Dad died just after you left school and Mum gave me a bit more freedom. And when I got to eighteen she even let me go into pubs, so long as I wasn't alone. I used to go to the *George*; it was quite a respectable place back then. It was there where I came across Jack again. ''

She noticed Maureen was staring at her, appraisingly. Her eyes were narrowed, but that might be because she was peering through smoke. Seen at close quarters, she wasn't ageing well. Although her face was chubby, it was criss-crossed with deep lines, especially round her mouth, and her heavy make-up, which was beginning to crack, served to emphasise them. She looked rather as though she'd had Polyfilla applied to her.

'I'll let you into a secret, Judy. I was always a bit jealous of you at school. You were bloody attractive, weren't you? Fantastic figure, long legs. We only saw it in PE, 'cos you kept it all under wraps with those horrible long skirts we had to wear, and those ankle socks! But the boys fancied you – you must have known that, surely? Pete Kennedy was always trying to chat you up. And so was Tim – oh what was his bloody surname? You know, he wore Buddy Holly specs. But you never seemed interested. Proper ice maiden, you were.'

'I told you, Maureen, it was the way I was brought up. Dad drummed it into me that – '

'Hang on a bit, though. There was one occasion when you were a bit of a naughty girl, weren't you? That time we were taken to see 'Midsummer Night's Dream' in London, remember? In the coach on the way back you sat with Tim, didn't you? We were all amazed when you started snogging. He was a good snogger, was Tim. Oh! Just remembered his surname, it was Bailey, wasn't it? Tim Bailey.'

Judith was not happy about where the conversation was heading.

'Just a silly teenage cuddle, Maureen. Did you know, I've been working at the same firm since I – '

'Oh come off it Judy, it was more than a cuddle. A bit of a grope, wasn't it? That's what Tim told everyone.'

Judith looked at her watch, jumped up from her seat. 'Heavens, Maureen, I've got to go. Jack'll be wondering where I am.'

'Oh, so soon?' Maureen rose. 'We must do this again! So much to catch up on.' She made to kiss Judith's cheek.

Judith dodged the puckered lips. 'Yes, we must. Goodbye, Maureen.' She hurried out, vowing never to see her again.

She walked briskly in the opposite direction to the car park which she assumed would be Maureen's destination, then stopped to draw breath. She was angry, of course, but it wasn't because of the nonsense Maureen had been talking about what happened on the coach more than forty years ago. It *had* only been a cuddle, she was sure of it.

No, what was annoying her was Maureen's total lack of interest in her life. She hadn't even bothered to ask after Jack, hadn't waited for a reply when she asked if they had a family, though of course Judith was relieved about that. But she might at least have asked her about her job, no, her career. Judith was proud of her career, proud of how she'd progressed from such lowly beginnings to being Personal Assistant to the Managing Director.

It wasn't something she could discuss with her friends; it would sound like boasting, or trying to justify having to work until she was sixty. She'd thought she'd reached her peak when Mr Parsons had made her his secretary, but, encouraged by him, she'd kept up with all the developments that had transformed life in the office. She'd seen golf-ball then daisy-wheel typewriters, bulky word-processors then slim personal computers; she'd mastered Wordstar, Word, spreadsheets, databases, the intranet,

Compuserve, websites, emails, voicemail. She'd become so indispensable that when Mr Parsons retired, his successor relied on her expertise: she was given the title Personal Assistant, with general responsibility for management of the office and the training of junior operators. Not bad for someone who'd only passed one 'A' Level. She would have loved to have told Maureen all that.

Assuming Maureen had by now reached her car and driven off, she began retracing her steps. She'd tell Jack about her meeting with Maureen, of course. But there was now something else she needed to talk to him about. Her thoughts of how she'd become something of an expert in information technology had stiffened her resolve to tackle him over his reluctance to buy a PC. It was nonsense: she was missing out on the opportunities to chat to friends, many of whom were doing so online. She was digitally disadvantaged. And the amusement of the mystery telephone caller when she'd told him that Jack was without a computer had got to her.

And there was something else. That mystery phone call. As she'd told Jack, she couldn't recognise the voice: in fact, the caller had something of a speech impediment, seemed to have difficulty in pronouncing his consonants. But the laugh he'd given before he'd hung up – there was something familiar about it.

And now, after her conversation with Maureen, she had an idea whose laugh it might have been. But it wasn't something she'd tell Jack.

Frank and Angela

It had been a fractious meeting of the Council Planning Committee, and Frank wasn't happy.

He no longer knew where he stood on planning issues. He was a Tory, wasn't he? So surely he ought to be in favour of encouraging private enterprise? But he was pulled in two directions. He wanted to save the countryside he loved from further development, but on the other hand there was a desperate housing shortage. This sort of dilemma had begun to haunt him recently. He'd never been a gung-ho Thatcherite, even in in his younger days. Now he saw himself as an old-fashioned one-nation Tory like Harold Macmillan had been. That generation of Tories had been gentlemen, of course. Some of the young Conservative members of the council were little more than yobs, wealthy yobs of course. Sometimes he felt he had more in common with the Liberal Democrats, and the one fellow-councillor he really liked was the sole representative of the Green Party.

He left the committee room and walked to the lift. Damn, it was out of order. He carefully eased himself down the stairs towards the foyer of the council offices, and was overtaken by the younger members of the committee taking the steps two at a time while he clung to the bannister rail and hesitantly lowered each foot towards the next tread. Angela was always telling him, affectionately of course, to lose weight, and she was right. She usually was.

He moved as quickly as he was able towards the foyer doors, his progress impeded by councillors and council officers milling around or standing chatting in groups. Not only were a large number of them younger than him, but many were women, something else he was finding it hard to adjust to. Some of them, he supposed, could be described as lookers, but he had never had the slightest inclination to stray. He only ever had eyes for Angela, ever since he'd first met her when he was working in London in the 1970s.

Frank's office was fairly close to the council building, but he had to use his car to get there. To have walked through the town centre would have exhausted him.

He sank into the driving seat and allowed himself a few

minutes rest before he set off. The car, a Golf Cabriolet, was no longer as comfortable as it once had been. The seat was pushed back to its maximum extent, but the steering wheel still dug into his belly and the safety belt chafed his shoulder and chest. Perhaps it was time he bought a car more in keeping with his age and size.

He started the car, acknowledged the half-salute of the council car-park attendant as he drove under the raised barrier, and turned onto the ring road. Driving along it at rush hour was a fraught experience and he was relieved to reach his office. It was located on the edge of the town centre and housed in a Victorian terrace, one of the few which had survived the redevelopment of the area that had taken place in the 1960s. The discreet sign on the front door announced *F. Grayson, Independent Financial Advisor*. Frank had set up a development company to utilise the expertise he'd gained in the City in the years before he moved back to his home county, but had downsized in the 1980s. It was now just a hobby, really. He had only one employee, his secretary Brenda.

'Sorry I'm a bit late, Brenda. Just leave any letters for signing, and any other guff that's come in, and you get off. Nothing urgent, I assume?'

'No, Mr Grayson. It's been very quiet.'

Frank wished she'd call him by his Christian name, but she resolutely stuck to Mr Grayson. Brenda was one of the old school, and had both the appearance and the efficiency to be expected of the type. That was why he'd appointed her.

'Any phone calls?'

'I've made a list.' She passed it to him. 'All pretty routine stuff, but there was one rather strange one.'

'Strange? In what way?'

'Well, it was a man who seemed to have some sort of speech impediment. I found it hard to understand what he was saying at first. He asked me if the Christian name of the company owner was Frank. I was a bit taken aback, and said yes it was. Sorry, Mr Grayson, I shouldn't have divulged that. Most unprofessional of me.'

'Don't worry about it, Brenda. What else did this fellow say?'

'He asked me if you used to work in the City. By that time I'd recovered myself, so I said I wasn't party to your curriculum vitae.'

'Nice one, Brenda!'

'But he kept on asking questions. He asked where you grew up, where you went to school, which university you went to. By then I was getting annoyed so I just kept asking him to give his name. He wouldn't give it. Then he asked for your email address. I told him I wouldn't answer any more questions until I knew who I was speaking to. Then he rang off.'

'Speech impediment, you said he had?'

'Yes. Hard to describe. Sort of slurred.'

'Sounds to me as though it was some sort of nutter, Brenda. Don't worry about it. You get off, now. I'll see you tomorrow.'

He started signing the letters.

It was only when he was driving home that he remembered the phone call. It probably *was* some sort of nutcase, there were a lot about these days, but one thing was a bit strange – the caller had asked if he'd worked in the City. Frank had, for a few years, worked there in a junior capacity after leaving university. Could it have been one of his former colleagues? He searched his memory for someone who'd slurred his words, but could call no one to mind. In any case he could remember very little about the people he'd worked with. He hadn't socialised with them. Most of his free time in London had been spent with Angela and her friends.

Thoughts about the caller evaporated when the lane along which he was driving twisted to the left, and the Chiltern escarpment came into view. On the summit of Coombe Hill, the highest point of the Chilterns, was the monument to those who fell in the Boer War, lit up by the early evening sun. It never failed to uplift him.

It always reminded him of a former school friend, Jack Chapman, whom he hadn't seen for years. Jack often used to recount the story of how his grandfather had been present when the monument was unveiled back in 1904, and how the old boy used to tell Jack of how he'd marched up the hill in full military uniform as a member of the County Yeomanry to attend the ceremony. He'd been an enthusiast for family history, had Jack, even as a teenager.

But the downside of thinking of Jack was that it brought to mind Pete Kennedy, because Jack and Pete had been friends when they were at school. Frank hadn't been close to either of them, and after they'd left in the fifth form he saw little of them except occasionally in the *George*, even less when he went to university, and not at all once he'd started work in London. But after he'd returned to live in Bucks he ran into Pete one day in Wendover: he lived only a few miles away. They were in a similar line of business, so had taken to socialising: indeed he and Angela had begun to see a lot of Pete and his wife Marion, until Pete had threatened to do the dirty on him, the bastard.

He found he was gripping the steering-wheel tightly, still, after 16 years, outraged by the way Pete had behaved. Best not to think of him: concentrate instead on the evening to come. Angela had invited to dinner a couple whom they'd recently met at the bridge club and whom they liked. He was looking forward to getting to know them better.

He drove through the main village street and turned into Hampden Close. Mock-Tudor detached houses, built between the wars, were set back from the road behind carefully tended front gardens. Frank lived in the one at the end of the close. It was quite modest, only four bedrooms, but Frank, despite being well-off, had never been one for ostentation or conspicuous consumption, and it had been spacious enough to raise three children in it without being them all being too cheek-by-jowl.

Angela had chosen the house when they'd moved out from London. At the time Frank would have preferred to have returned to live in the Chilterns, but Angela found the deep valleys and dense beech woods claustrophobic, so they opted to settle in the Vale. Frank was now glad they had. The village was close to the county town, which made his role as first District, then County Councillor, easier to perform. Angie had made the right choice. She usually did.

He parked the car in front of the garage. The front garden bore witness to Angie's main hobby: roses, hydrangeas, fuchsias, buddleias in the beds, geraniums spilling from tubs and stone urns on the drive. Frank's forays into horticulture were confined to the back garden where he mowed the lawn once a week and, at Angie's behest, planted and tended runner beans in the vegetable bed.

As soon as he opened the front door, he could smell the cooking – a casserole perhaps? Or maybe coq au vin? The latter, he hoped. Frank enjoyed his food. Too much, he knew. Whenever Angela told him he should lose weight his response was always that his size was her fault for being such a brilliant cook.

He entered the kitchen. 'Sorry I'm late, Angie.'

Angela was lifting a casserole dish out of the oven. 'It's okay, all under control.' She pulled off her oven gloves, came over to where he was standing by the door, and kissed him.

'Good meeting? You look a bit tired.'

'I'm okay. How's yourself?'

'I'm fine now I've got all this nearly prepared.'

And she looked fine, despite being dishevelled from her labours. Frank still couldn't believe his luck in successfully wooing and marrying such an attractive woman, and one who remained attractive, sexy even, in her fifties. She'd retained her slim figure, her elfin features had only a delicate tracery of fine lines around the large brown eyes, her hair was still thick and only just starting to grey. She was effervescent, entertaining, popular with their friends. But beneath the bubbly exterior was a determined, feisty woman, one who had consistently bolstered him when he'd encountered problems in his work, encouraged him to keep going, not to give up. And she had supported him up to the hilt over that ghastly business with Pete Kennedy. Frank didn't know how he would have survived without her.

'Need any help with anything?'

'Well, you can lay the table and maybe tidy up the lounge a bit. But it's not urgent. I've got something to tell you. Sit down, Frank.'

'Why? What's happened? Is it one of the kids?'

'No, not bad news; well, I don't think you could call it that.'

Frank subsided onto a kitchen stool.

'What is it, then?'

'I had a phone call this afternoon. From Marion.'

'Marion?'

'Marion Kennedy.'

'*Marion Kennedy*? Sweet Jesus Christ! What the hell did she want?' Frank began to sweat, feel dizzy. Angela put her hand on his.

'It's all right, Frank. Look, why don't we go and sit in the lounge and I'll tell you all about it. Would you like a drink?'

'Too bloody right I would.'

***

Angela had been anticipating Frank's reaction to the news, but couldn't think of any other way to break it to him other than to state Marion's name at the outset. It obviously came as a much greater shock to him than she'd expected. She noticed his hand shaking slightly as he poured himself a large measure of Scotch. He took a swig before sinking down on the settee next to her.

'Come on then. Spill the beans.'

'Actually, there isn't all that much to tell. She phoned early this afternoon. When I said "Hello", she said "Is that Angela?" and of course I recognised her voice immediately. I was amazed, didn't know what to say. She asked me how I was and how you were, and then about the kids, so of course I went through the same ritual. But I couldn't bring myself to ask after Pete.'

'I should hope not.'

'Anyway, after a bit more aimless chatter, she suddenly said how much she missed seeing us, and how we'd had good times together, and how nice it would be if we could meet up for a drink –'

"*What?*'

'Hang on, Frank. At first I thought she meant just me and her, and I was trying to think of an excuse not to, but then she said it was about time you and Pete … oh, what were the words she used? *Put aside whatever silly business disagreement you had.* So I said I didn't think you'd be prepared to do that.'

'Good. And I bet that bastard Kennedy won't be prepared to, either.'

'But don't you see, Frank? From the words she used I reckon she has no idea of what actually happened. 'Business disagreement'- that doesn't get near to it, does it? I bet Pete never told her the truth about it.'

'I bet he didn't. So, what are you saying?'

'I don't know, really. I suppose it means that after all this time nothing's ever likely to come out. I mean, the last thing Pete would want would be for you to spill the beans, would he?'

'So, nothing's changed then, you reckon?'

'So it seems. Eventually, she seemed to accept it wouldn't be a good idea to meet up. Actually, when she said goodbye she sounded a bit sad.'

'I'm not surprised, married to a sod like him.'

Frank drained his glass and stood up. 'I'm going to get a bath. I wish you hadn't told me about this, Angie. It's spoiled my evening, and I've been looking forward to it.'

And now *I* wish I hadn't told you, Angela thought, as he left the room. But that was the problem in a marriage where both parties had promised never to have secrets from each other. Perhaps she should just have been economical with the truth.

She returned to the kitchen and began clearing up the detritus. To an extent the evening had been spoiled for her, as well. She didn't like seeing Frank upset. Though managed to disguise it from his business associates and, she assumed, from his fellow Councillors, he was a sensitive soul. She'd soon realised this when they'd started going out together – he used to rail about the arrogance of his colleagues in the City, call them barrow-boys. It had endeared him to her. And he'd been quite a good-looking man.

Only once had he let his standards slip, when as a County Councillor he'd been rather more helpful to a business associate than was appropriate. Privately, she'd been shocked, but was reassured by his remorse. And when Pete Kennedy had started making his loathsome hints, she'd supported Frank's threat to retaliate, even though it would have involved an innocent third party.

After that incident he'd started to age. It had been sad, to see him grow fat, go bald. It never bothered her, but she knew he worried about it, not because he was vain, but because he feared she might be tempted to stray. He'd admitted that to her, and it had resulted in the only serious row they'd had – how *could* he think that of her? Hadn't she told him about every single attempt other men had made to get her into bed, and how she'd rebuffed them all because he was the only man for her?

She'd managed to make Frank understand that, for a woman, remaining physically attractive into middle age could sometimes be a burden.

Jack

'I'm off in a minute, Jack. See you this evening. Oh, could you peel some potatoes? Sausage and mash tonight, if that suits you.'

Jack, sitting at the breakfast table – he was taking a day's leave – glanced up from his newspaper. 'Yeah, that's fine, Jude.'

'What are you doing with yourself today?'

'Library. Got an idea about where to look for stuff about great-grandad. Might have to go over to the County Records Office sometime, though. Just want to check here first.'

'Just think. Your research would be so much easier if you had a computer and went on-line. There are lots of family history websites, I hear.'

'So you said last night. I'll think about it.'

He turned his attention back to the newspaper. Then he started: a kiss had landed on the back of his neck. He turned; Judith was crouched over him.

'What was that for?'

'Just to remind you I'm still here. We could afford a computer, you know. Right, I really am off now. Ta ta.'

'Yes … right. Bye.'

She left the kitchen. He heard the door to the street slam and a few seconds later, through the open window, the click of her high heels on the pavement, getting fainter as she walked away.

He swallowed the dregs of his coffee, carried the crockery and cutlery over to the sink and began washing up. Okay, they might be able to afford a computer, but shouldn't a dishwasher take precedence? That would be more helpful to Jude – but even as he thought this he realised that as chief washer-upper it would be more to his advantage than hers. He often experienced twinges of guilt about the division of domestic duties: it was Jude who did most of the shopping, cooking, laundry and cleaning even though she had a full-time job which was, he had to admit, more demanding than his.

But he never claimed to be a new man: blimey, he wasn't sure he knew what a new man was. He was all in favour of gender equality, of course, but Jude always insisted in taking charge on the domestic front, said she'd do things more efficiently than he would, said she knew where items were located in the supermarket, said he'd only make a mess of the ironing. By the same token, he was better at organising their money, paying the bills, doing maintenance on the car, and … well, he was sure there were other things but he couldn't bring them to mind right now.

It was because of his responsibility for the household budget that he'd never contemplated buying a computer, wasn't it? Too expensive. Jude sometimes tried to tell him about the I.T. she used in her job, but it all went over his head. There were computers in the Estate Agents where he worked, of course, but his menial duties didn't extend to using them. And as for this Internet malarkey, well … sometimes he felt like a throwback to a bygone age: all this dotcom stuff was everywhere, in shops, on the back of tradesmen's vans, in adverts on the telly, even in the library. He supposed that if they'd had kids he'd have learned about it all from them, only it wouldn't be his kids teaching them now, it would be grandchildren … no, don't go there.

He dried the dishes and put them away. Have a shower and wash his hair, maybe? Yes, he always liked to look spruce on his trips to the library, wear a white shirt and the smarter of his two pairs of jeans. You never knew who you might run into in the High Street, and in Costa which he always visited after his researches were completed. Costa was usually full of young mums: well, he supposed they were young, it was hard to gauge the age of people under 40 these days, but they were all fresh-faced, attractive, and he was on nodding and smiling terms with some of them. When he'd told Pete this, Pete had laughed and asked if he fancied his chances with a Milf. Jack didn't know what he was on about, but ever since then Pete had referred to Costa as the Milfcafé and it was now too late to ask him what he meant by the term.

It wasn't a satisfactory morning in the library. He'd drawn a blank on finding any information about his great-grandfather in the records of the local newspaper, and two hours of squinting at microfiches had given him a headache. A visit to the County Records Office would be needed. But what he needed now was coffee.

On his way out of the library, he passed through the room that housed the computers. Every workstation was occupied, and the heads leaning towards the screens were all grey-haired or bald. Of course, you wouldn't find young folk here on a work day, would you? But the sight of old geezers tapping at keyboards and fiddling with - what were they called, mice, was it? – discomforted him. Most looked older than he did, but then they would, wouldn't they, because they were probably all retired. He hurried out, eager to seek refuge in Costa.

He didn't need to place his order. The girl at the counter knew exactly what he wanted, a latte and a slice of carrot cake. It was comforting, being a regular, just like it used to be in pubs. He sat down in his usual seat by the window and glanced round the café. Even though it wasn't Saturday there were a few familiar faces, a few nods and smiles in his direction. There was one young lady in particular whom he couldn't help watching. She was so like Jude had been in her youth: completely different clothes and hairstyle of course, but the same features and figure, the same vivacity as she talked to her friends.

Jude sometimes still showed her old vivacity, particularly when she'd met up with her mates, and she often chatted to him with a degree of animation, admittedly mainly about her job, TV programmes and recipes. But last night when she'd returned from work she'd seemed unusually distracted, and their dinner had been eaten in near silence. He'd asked her if anything was the matter.

She'd told him she'd run into Maureen Hearn and had had a coffee with her. Jack remembered Maureen very well. A bit of a goer, so his classmates had said. Jack had always been in awe of her. Jude had said meeting her had brought back a lot of things she'd forgotten. But then she'd stopped talking about Maureen, and said it was time they bought a computer – and even if he didn't want one, she did.

Sitting alone with his latte, it was suddenly though he were at odds with the world he inhabited – a job which made no demands on him, cycle rides, Saturday mornings in the library, attending church, Sunday afternoons with Pete. He felt … what did he feel? Hard to analyse, but this café, the latte and carrot cake, the chattering young mums, all seemed to represent something that he wanted … to escape from? No, not exactly, but something that should just be a merely a backdrop to a more fulfilling life. He wolfed down his cake, took a gulp of coffee, and got up to leave. He didn't even smile his usual goodbyes to the young women.

He didn't walk home at his usual brisk pace. Jude had said meeting Maureen had brought home to her that they were the one of the few from the Grammar School who hadn't left their home town. This didn't worry him, he loved the familiarity of the High Street down which he walked. Of course the place had changed over 50 years, but it was full of associations. The *George*, of course, but so much more than that. The shops he used to visit – all gone, but the buildings mostly still stood. Here used to be Gutteridges, the gents' outfitters who stocked the Grammar School uniforms, now a charity shop. Over there, the estate agent's premises where he worked: it used to be the Primrose Café, where, daringly, he and his mates used to go on Saturday mornings for tea … tea! when they were twelve or thirteen, before they progressed to espresso coffee at the Kwela, which had a juke box and a complement of the local Teds – wasn't it there they'd seen Maureen Hearn being chatted up by Fred the Ted, the one who'd got her pregnant?

It seemed his memories were so strongly linked to this town that they were something more than just personal associations, they were in some way the reality of the place. Was it the same for others, he wondered? His old school friends, for example – was their reality the same as his?

It might be for Pete. After all, he'd worked in a local architect's office in the town after leaving school and stayed there until he qualified. But those who'd gone to university: okay, most of them returned to the town in their vacations to take holiday jobs, had resumed their drinking at the *George,* but then their careers had taken them away. As for Tim Bailey – well, he'd visited the *George* when he was in the Sixth Form, but once he'd left for university he'd never been seen again, had never returned in the vacations. Jack had been told by someone that he was a real high-flier, had done research, become a university lecturer.

So he, Jack, was the only one who was trapped in the past. He needed to consider some life changes. Perhaps Jude was right – yes, he'd get a computer, go online, broaden his horizons. He found his pace had quickened, he was eager to get home and tell her about his decision.

PART TWO

July–August 2002

Staffordshire

It was Susie who once again dragged me from the pit. It was one of her regular visits, something I always looked forward to, but such was my self-absorption I'd forgotten all about it.

I was still in bed when I heard the three long and two short rings on my doorbell, and in the two minute hiatus that followed I managed to pull on a tee-shirt and jogger bottoms and scramble down the stairs. She was already in the kitchen when I entered it.

'Have you only just got up? Naughty boy! It's half-past ten.'

When she first started visiting me she'd adopted a very formal, if sympathetic approach as befitted a Cognitive Behavioural Therapist. I suppose it was my background in academia, where informality was the name of the game, which made me find this irritating. My responses had been flippant. If she'd resented this she hadn't shown it, but after a while she dropped the formalities and began to speak to me as though I were – well, a naughty boy. She was young, in her late thirties probably, and attractive. Too bloody attractive: dark hair, brown eyes, trim figure, long legs. Any attempt I might make to flirt with her she'd doubtless find distasteful. Distasteful? Repugnant, more like. But with each successive visit I'd warmed to her ways, began to respond jokily as though I were a child who expected to be chastised. I'd begun to look forward to our banter. She seemed to enjoy it as well: sometimes she stayed a bit longer than her allotted hourly session. She'd become the nearest thing to a friend I had.

'Coffee, Susie?'

'Please, darlin'. Make it a strong one. I've just had a bloody awful session with my supervisor.'

Did she call all her clients 'darling', I wondered? Probably. In a way I hoped so. Though I liked to hear the endearment, it had crossed my mind that it might be an indication of her pity for me. I allowed myself self-pity, but didn't want pity from others, and certainly not from a young woman with whom, back in the day, I would have fancied my chances.

I handed her the coffee and sat down at the breakfast table opposite her.

'Why are you so late up, Dave? Not on the booze last night, I hope.'

'No booze. Only sleeping pills. Having problems nodding off at the moment. Wake up early as well.'

She peered at me over her coffee cup. 'Anything troubling you?'

'Troubling me? What's always troubling me? Bloody life, of course. If you can call it a life.'

'Come on, Dave. It's something more than that, isn't it? You look awful.'

I slammed down my mug. 'Awful? How can I possibly look more awful than I always do? What a fuckin' insensitive remark. Call yourself a counsellor?'

She leant across the table and touched my hand briefly. She did that, sometimes. It was no doubt intended as a comforting gesture. She probably didn't know how unsettling I found it, how starved of touch I was, how I would have liked to grab her hand, hold it for a few minutes.

'Something's happened, hasn't it? You've not been in this state for ages. Tell me about it, Dave. It's what I'm here for, to listen. It's my job, isn't it?'

Remorse. 'Sorry. Didn't mean what I just said.'

'Remember what I said when we started these sessions? You don't have to apologise for anything you say to me. Did you try phoning those old friends of yours? Didn't it work out? Is that what's upset you?'

There was nothing to be gained by keeping it to myself. So I told her how I'd tried phoning two of them and how that had failed. I went into great detail – once I get an opportunity to talk there's no stopping me. It's a distinctive trait of lonely people. I'd learned this when I was a lecturer, when the loners among my students seized every opportunity at the end of one-to-one tutorials to stay behind and rabbit on about things of little relevance to their studies. I'd given them short shrift. I regretted that, now, and often wondered if I would have been more attentive had they'd been attractive, the girls of course. But the lonely ones never were.

Susie listened to me, encouraging me with nods and smiles and interjecting only to ask the occasional question. When I'd finished she looked pensive, took a few moments before she spoke.

'Yes, I can see why you found it frustrating. But there is a way to find some email addresses. But didn't your man from the computer shop tell you about search engines?'

'Search engines?'

'Yes. Yahoo? Or Ask Jeeves? Or better still, Google. That's only been going for a year or so. We use it at work quite a bit.'

'How would it help?'

'It wouldn't help find people's personal email addresses, people like that Jack fellow you mentioned. But if someone has a business you might find the business has a web-page, and that might give a contact email address.'

'So you think Frank Grayson – '

'Well, you know the name of his business, don't you? And where it's located. So it's worth a try.'

She gave me one of her grins. I could have kissed her – no, I couldn't. Stupid idea. But my spirits lifted. I wanted to get to my computer, straight away. I stood up.

'Another coffee would be nice, Dave. I've only been here half an hour. Don't see my next client till twelve.'

'Oh, right, yes. Sorry, Susie. And thanks very much for

listening, and for the advice. Don't know what I'd do without you.'

'All part of the service.'

I filled the kettle and turned back to the table to pick up the mugs. She was sitting with an elbow on the table, her hand cupping her chin, staring out of the window. It occurred to me she looked rather sad. And thinking about it, there'd been occasions on her previous visits when her usual cheery demeanour had slipped. I have so little contact with people I'd forgotten that others might have sorrows. I knew nothing of Susie's personal life.

Perhaps I'd upset her. Maybe my body language had appeared to dismiss her. For the second time that morning I felt remorse. Then I had an idea.

'Here you are.' I placed her mug of coffee in front of her. She started. 'Susie, could I ask you a favour?'

'What sort of favour?'

'Well, I wondered … well, if you could help me with this Google thing? If you've got time, that is.'

'Course I've got time, you silly boy!'

Normal service had been resumed.

'Let's take our coffees up to my study, then.'

It was the first time Susie had been anywhere in the house apart from the hallway and kitchen. As soon as I opened the door I was ashamed: my study was the one room my cleaner wasn't allowed to touch. Magazines, books, box files, CD cases, unanswered letters, final demands, all were scattered randomly over every available surface. Everything was covered by a layer of dust. On the desk top were littered writing pads, pens, pencils, markers, a Pritt Stick, Post-it notes, a staple gun and a hole-puncher, all fighting for position with the computer keyboard, screen and mouse. The one piece of bare wood still visible was stained with the brown rings of a hundred coffee mugs. And then I noticed, half hidden behind the VDU, the ashtray containing the stubs of half-a-dozen roll-ups – shit, and I'd told Susie I'd given up.

'Obviously, a hive of industry in here, Dave.'

I glanced at her: she didn't usually employ sarcasm. But she was grinning amiably.

'Good idea to restrict your smoking to one room: helps you cut down. Where shall I sit?'

My office chair was positioned at the front of the desk. The only other seat in the room was a battered wooden chair by the window, draped by a pair of jeans, an old sweater, and several shirts which I'd forgotten to transfer to the washing basket in the bedroom. I hastily swept the clothes onto the floor.

'You sit in the office chair so you can use the keyboard,' I said. 'I'll perch on this.'

She sat, turned to me. 'I can't show you what to do with you sitting over there, can I? Pull up your chair next to me.'

I obeyed. As I sat down the realisation came to me: this was the first time we'd sat beside each other – in all previous encounters the kitchen table had been between us. Then I was suddenly hit by her smell. Delicate, fragrant. The long-forgotten scent of a woman.

'Shall I log on, then?'

I could only nod, afraid of what my voice might reveal. It wasn't just her scent, it was – could I be imagining it? – it was the warmth that seemed to emanate from her body.

'I'll get you into Google,' she said, 'It's simple. 'Watch what I do, then next time you'll find it easy-peasy.'

She began tapping at the keyboard, manipulating the mouse. I knew I should be paying attention to what she was doing, but how could I? Her arms on the desk top – smooth skin, slightly suntanned, all the way up to her shoulders, for she was wearing a top which exposed them. The swell of her breasts under it. And, glancing down – her legs, her skirt ridden above her knees, no tights, the flesh as flawless and brown as on her arms. Did she have any idea what she was doing to me? Even if I hadn't been a freak, I was late middle-aged, though no doubt she saw me as an old man, old enough to be her father, someone who'd cause her to recoil in horror if I so much as … no, don't even think of it, you pathetic bastard.

'There you are, then. I'll log off now, and you have a go.'

She didn't move from her chair. I had to lean towards her to reach the keyboard. As I did so, my knee grazed against hers, my hand brushed her forearm. My fingers were trembling slightly

'Okay. Done it.'

'Right. Now, now enter the name what's-'is-name's company. Come on, fumble-fingers! There you are, a list of websites. Only one with that precise name. Click on it.'

The webpage came up. *F. Grayson. Independent Financial Advisor*. A lot of print, and a photograph. Bloody hell! Could that really be Frank? Bald, bloated cheeks, double chin? But it was. I found the sight of an aged Frank very comforting.

'Look, there, at the bottom. It's the company email address. You've got there, Dave!' She beamed at me, then stood up. 'Up to you, now. You can take it from there, can't you?

I stood up as well. 'Susie, that's great.'

And I *felt* great, elated. It had been years since I'd experienced the delicious pleasure of looking forward to something. The glow inside me was a sensation long forgotten. But it wasn't just the anticipation of making contact with Frank; there was something else, a feeling, no, a hope, that Susie might - well, might become someone of even more importance to me than she already was.

We stood, facing each other.

'Susie …'

'Yes? What?'

'Can I ask a very great favour of you?'

'Try me.'

'Would you … could you possibly…'

'Spit it out, Dave!'

'Would you give me a hug?'

She said nothing, but stood looking at me, her face

serious. My elation evaporated in an instant, the inner glow turned to ice. Oh Christ, what the fuck had I done? Ruined everything, hadn't I. She'd leave, never to return. Would I even get a new counsellor? If I did, it would be a male. The NHS would now see me as a potential risk to their female staff.

But then she stepped towards me, stood beside me, put one arm round my shoulder, gave me a squeeze. It wasn't the embrace I craved, and it didn't last long. But when she let go, she put her hand to my face, kept it there a few seconds. A simple action, but one I'd not experienced for years. The effect was more than overwhelming, it was mesmerising.

She stepped back but maintained eye-contact with me, her expression hard to read.

'It's time I went, Dave. I'll see you in a month, unless … well, unless you need to see me before then, if you get depressed again, I mean.'

She turned and left.

I sank down in the office chair. It was still slightly warm from its contact with Susie's arse. I groped behind the VDU, found my tobacco pouch and Rizla papers, and rolled up. When I took the first delicious drag I knew this wasn't a comfort fag, it was a celebratory one.

No, don't day-dream, attend to the job in hand. I logged in to my email account, entered Frank's company address.

Hello Frank. You won't recognise my email address. You don't know me as Dave Turner, but that's what I'm known as now. It's a long story. We were at school together. I'm Tim, Tim Bailey, remember?

Buckinghamshire

Frank

'Anything of importance come in, Brenda?'

61

'Not much, Mr Grayson. I've put it all on your desk in the order I assumed you'd like to deal with it. Mr Beddows has paid what he owes, but he's enclosed a letter with the cheque. Not a very polite letter, I'm afraid. He's still complaining our fee was excessive.'

'Just so long as his cheque doesn't bounce I don't give a damn what he thinks. I thought the fellow was trouble after our first meeting. Anything else?'

'All pretty routine stuff.'

'And any emails to deal with?'

'Only a few. But there's one which seems to be personal. I only read the first few lines, of course, so I don't know if it's important.'

'Okay Brenda. I'll have a look. It's time for your break, isn't it? If you're making coffee, would you be so kind as to make me one as well?'

'Of course, Mr Grayson.'

'And no sugar please. I've got to try and give it up. My wife says I'm well on the way to a heart attack.'

Frank eased himself into his chair, loosened his belt, and opened the file which Brenda had put on his desk. He rifled through it – the contents were indeed pretty routine. Brenda had called the letter from Beddows impolite, but in fact, it verged on the abusive. It was ungrammatical as well. Frank experienced the familiar wave of depression as he was confronted again with the declining standards of behaviour and literacy which, it seemed, were beginning to characterise business dealings in the twenty-first century. The codes of conduct which had applied in his youth now seemed to be obsolete. Politeness was often misconstrued: a few weeks ago in the Council offices he'd held open the door for a young woman and smiled at her: she'd shot him a look of pure malevolence, as though he were a potential rapist.

He turned on his computer and logged into his emails. He recognised the names of all the senders except one. It was from a *d.turner@hotmail.com* – probably the personal one to which Brenda had referred. Who the hell was D.

Turner? He didn't know anyone of that name.

He opened the email.

Christ! Tim Bailey! Why D. Turner?

He scan-read the contents – *Over 40 years since we met: see you're in business: I'm long retired: was a university lecturer: had a bad accident from which I've not really recovered: feel the need to make contact with old friends: lots to catch up on –*

'Here's your tea, Mr Grayson.'

His office door had been ajar and Frank was so engrossed he hadn't registered Brenda's entry.

'Oh, thanks, Brenda.'

'You've got two ginger biscuits as well. Is that allowed?'

'What?'

'Would your wife approve of your eating biscuits?'

'No. I mean yes. Thanks, Brenda.'

She left, leaving the door ajar. He got up and shut it, wondering as it closed why he was doing so.

He continued reading the email. It was short. Tim asked what Frank had done since they'd left school, if he was married, where he lived, how it would be good to start a correspondence. He asked if Frank was still in touch with any of the others of their school-friends, and did he have any email addresses? Judy Mason's, for example? And those two fellows who left after the Fifth Form, Pete Kennedy and Jack Chapman? He concluded by asking Frank not to tell any of them that he'd been in contact – he wanted to surprise them.

Frank turned off the computer. He wondered what sort of emotional reaction he ought to be feeling at the restoration of contact with someone to whom he'd hardly given a thought for half a lifetime. Excitement perhaps? Nostalgia? But no: just mild interest, rather as one might on stumbling across a book one had not read since adolescence. He and Tim had never been bosom pals, even in the Sixth Form, though they'd come to respect each other's intelligence. They used to go to the *George* together, but always accompanied by Judy Mason – in fact, come to think about it, it was she who always insisted on him, Frank, being present. And now he remembered why – Tim had fancied her, had made his intentions only too obvious, and it hadn't taken Frank long to realise his presence was required by her only as a chaperone.

Frank rarely dwelled on the past. Thanks to Angela, he'd always been content to live in the present, still was, even as he approached his sixties. It amused him to observe those of his contemporaries who were obviously affronted by the prospect of old age, those who fought against it, dressed too youthfully, adopted modern speech idioms, frantically set out to acquire new interests, younger acquaintances.

He wondered if Tim might be like that. He'd been a good-looking fellow, and he'd known it. Was successful with the girls – at least he claimed he was. It must be hard for him to accept his philandering days were over, assuming they were.

Then he remembered the first part of Tim's email. He'd said he'd suffered an accident, hadn't fully recovered. It had been Frank's intention to send a polite reply, so polite as to discourage further exchanges. But perhaps the poor chap was lonely. Why else would he set about trying to get in touch with former friends? So he decided he might reply, eventually. But of course he'd discuss the matter with Angela first.

'Hello? Angie? I'm home!'

Angela was usually in the kitchen when he arrived home.

Not today though. And there was no appetising smell, the usual sign of a meal having been prepared. Perhaps she was having one of her migraines? If so, she'd no doubt retreated to bed. Poor old Angie. It was best just to let her sleep them off.

He went through to the lounge – and there she was, sitting on the settee.

'Angie? Didn't you hear me? Are you all right?'

'Yes, I'm okay.'

But she obviously wasn't. She hadn't got up to greet him with her usual kiss, hadn't asked him what sort of day he'd had.

'What's for dinner, then?'

'I haven't cooked today. Don't feel hungry. There's a quiche and some salad in the fridge. Or you could always do yourself some pasta.'

The remarks weren't made dismissively. She sounded tired – no, not tired exactly, but vague, as though her thoughts were elsewhere. She hadn't looked at him while she was speaking.

'Are you sure you're all right, Angie?'

Then she did turn to face him.

'Yes, I said I was, didn't I? Don't fuss, Frank.'

Frank knew better than to push her further. She was rarely brusque, and when she was it was usually an indication that she was either recovering from a migraine, or starting one. She always hated admitting she was feeling unwell, and didn't like being questioned about her health. It was best to carry on and act as though she were her usual cheerful affectionate self.

He dumped his briefcase on the floor and sat down next to her.

'Something interesting cropped up at work today. I had an email from an old friend who I haven't seen since we were at school together. Have I ever mentioned Tim Bailey? Probably not. Anyway, he's had a bit of bad luck. He …'

He continued giving an account of Tim's email, but it soon became apparent Angela wasn't listening. Or wasn't interested. There were no expressions of surprise, no questions, no comments. His account began to falter, and then she turned to him.

'Frank, listen, I've got something to tell you. I have a confession to make.'

'What have you done –scraped your car?

'No, no. Look, I haven't cooked because I went out to lunch today.'

Frank wondered what was coming. Out to lunch? Not alone, surely. Then who with?

'So?'

'I met Marion. You see, she – '

'Marion? *Marion*? But … but when she phoned you told her you thought it wasn't a good idea to meet, didn't you? What made you change your mind, Angie?'

He got up, began pacing round the room. It wasn't just the fact of their meeting that distressed him, it was what might have transpired.

'Frank, calm down. It's all right, I promise. Listen to me, please. And sit down, won't you?'

He sat. Sat and listened. Listened to how Marion had phoned again, why Angela had agreed to meet her, why she hadn't told him because she knew he'd be upset, why Marion was so lonely. And when they'd met, she'd hardly mentioned Pete at all.

She reached out and touched his hand, the first touch since he'd arrived home. He wasn't comforted, either by her touch or by the news about Pete. He didn't give a toss about Pete. Why hadn't Angie told him of her intention to meet Marion? They could have sat and discussed the matter like they always did it when potential disagreements loomed. There'd never been any secrets in their marriage.

He felt betrayed, betrayed by the wife he adored, the wife who, he assumed, always told him everything, not just what she'd done, but what she intended doing. He was about to ask her if she intended meeting Marion again, but realised he didn't want to know. The present and the future were now full of uncertainties.

He decided, for the first time in his life, to seek comfort in the past, the past that existed before Angela entered his life. He would reply to Tim's email.

Judith

'I'm off, then, Jude. See you later.' It was Saturday and Jack was off to the library.

'Will you be back for lunch?'

'Course I will.'

'Well, don't go stuffing yourself with carrot cake in Costa.'

Jack didn't reply. He picked up his shoulder-bag and left.

Why had she said that, Judith asked herself? For some reason Jack was sensitive about the visits he made to Costa after he'd been to the library. He'd never mentioned it to her, and Judith had only discovered it was his regular haunt when one of her friends had said her daughter often saw him in there. When she'd told Jack this, he'd muttered that he liked their coffee and carrot cake. And he'd blushed. Anyone would think he was having an illicit liaison. In the local Costa, of all places!

Judith had assumed that once they bought the computer Jack wouldn't need to go to the library for his researches. Indeed, he'd greeted its acquisition with some enthusiasm. When it had been installed, she'd sat him down and started instructing him on how to use it. But he'd seemed uncomfortable, couldn't remember the essential keystrokes, was clumsy with the mouse, hopeless at the keyboard. She'd become impatient with him. Eventually, he'd said it was no good, you couldn't teach an old dog new tricks: he'd go back to visiting the library.

Part of Judith was disappointed he had given up so quickly. She'd hoped that going online would broaden his limited horizons, give him something to think about other than his cycle rides, choir practice and his Sunday meetings with Pete.

But another part of her was relieved. With Jack out, she could settle down to an uninterrupted hour or so online. During the week she had little opportunity to use the computer – it wouldn't be fair to be engrossed in the evening when Jack needed her company. In any case the computer was in the lounge and, for some reason she found hard to explain to herself, going online seemed to be an act requiring privacy. It reminded her of how she felt as a teenager when her mother barged into her bedroom while she was writing her diary – no matter how innocuous the entries, there was always a sense of shame that she'd somehow been caught in a questionable act.

She was enjoying being part of the digital world and using the expertise she'd accrued at work. All her friends who were online had given her their email addresses, and it was fun being part of a community which exchanged gossip and jokes and used it as a means of complaining about the peccadillos of husbands. In fact, it had been in an email from her friend Penny that she'd learned about Jack's visits to Costa.

But it had also been frustrating, for there was no way of finding the email addresses of those with whom she'd lost contact – old school friends, of course. Google was no help there. She'd entered their names, but it just came up with a string of websites containing so many possibles that she'd given up investigating them. She'd tried to convince herself it wasn't anyone in particular she was seeking, but she was still, after two months, haunted by the laugh of the mystery telephone caller.

Why not admit it? Before the phone call she'd managed not to think of him much. But since hearing that laugh, his face – well, the face of the teenager she remembered – occasionally loomed up to interrupt her in whatever routine task she was undertaking. It floated in front of her at work when she sorted through the mail, was seen on the shoulders of a young lad in front of her in the check-out queue in Tesco, was superimposed on the surface of the kitchen table as she ate her breakfast so she sat in a trance, her cornflakes untouched. She wasn't sure she enjoyed the sensation.

She'd told Jack, shortly before they got engaged, that

nothing had happened between them, that yes, they'd gone out together once, but that she'd told him where to go when he tried to get fresh with her. And that was how it was, well almost, wasn't it?

Now, sitting at the computer, she was about to embark on a new voyage. Yesterday, one of her work colleagues had told her about the *Friends Reunited* website. Enter the name of your old school or former workplaces, she'd explained, and you'll be amazed at who you might find. So she was preparing herself for amazement.

She found the website, logged in, entered her name and a password. It was confirmed she was now a member. She was instructed to enter the name of the school or workplace to which she wished to connect. She typed in *Dr Penn's Grammar School*, then clicked on the search button, realising as she did so that she was breathing heavily.

She was confronted by a list of names, in date order of when they joined the school. Scrolling down to the 1950s, she found some that were instantly familiar, some long forgotten. Swots, bullies, the handsome and pretty, the unfortunate-looking, the skinny ones, the few fat ones (how times had changed!), the clever, the dim, the naughty, the prefects, the house captains. There was Maureen! No, she didn't want further contact with her.

But there was no Tim Bailey. She scrolled up and down the list again, and there – how could she have missed him? Peter Kennedy. Oh my God. Why did the one name from the old crowd have to be Pete's?

She got up, went to the kitchen, put the kettle on. But she didn't want a cup of coffee. She didn't know what she wanted. This was silly. She saw Pete on some Sundays when he came to collect Jack, though admittedly they were fleeting meetings, and more often than not Jack went to wait for him outside. So why was it so disturbing to see his name on the website? It wasn't him for whom she'd been searching.

She made her coffee and carried it into the lounge. She

nudged the mouse – the computer screen still displayed Pete's name. It had the effect of reminding her how much she missed his company. He'd remained in close contact with her and Jack after he'd left the town, even after he'd married Marion. He'd given her cheerful comfort during that bleak time when she found she could never have kids, comfort which Jack was unable to provide, comfort which had led to the incident which she, and probably he, had immediately regretted. But they'd still remained friends until suddenly, about twenty years ago now, he'd became distant, polite, as though he were a mere acquaintance. He'd stopped greeting her with a kiss.

But now she had a means to renew their friendship, assuming he wanted to. To be just old friends exchanging memories – not all their memories of course – via a website, something that needn't concern Jack. And if her overture was rejected, nothing would have been lost.

Her coffee remained untouched. She came to a decision, clicked on Pete's name. A prompt came up – *Enter your message in the box below, and include your email address. The message will be forwarded. Should your contact wish to reply, he/she will do so by email.*

She didn't give herself time to think. *Hello Pete, it's Judith. I've just discovered Friends Reunited and thought I'd try it out. I'm not sure I'm doing this correctly, so could you reply, just so I know you've received it? Judy x*

She clicked on the 'send' icon. Only when it had gone did she wonder if he might read too much into the kiss. And then, when she logged off, it occurred to her that he might tell Jack about it when they met tomorrow.

Pete

Pete hadn't spoken all through breakfast, despite Marion's attempts to re-open yesterday's discussion. He'd remained largely silent at lunch except to thank her for the meal, thanks delivered with the sort of scrupulous politeness that

70

indicates contempt. As far as he was concerned all that needed to be said had been stated yesterday afternoon when she'd arrived home. That conversation had been far from polite.

'Lunch with Angela? *Angela*? Jesus Christ, woman, what the hell do you think you were doing? Didn't I spell it out clearly?'

'What you said was, since you've obviously forgotten, that *I* could do what I wanted, but that *you* didn't want to see Frank again. And Frank wasn't there. So fuck you, Pete. Why should I have to abandon an old friend just because you took against her husband years ago?'

'Come out of the blue, this meeting did it? Just a chance meeting in a pub, I suppose? Come off it, you stupid … what do you take me for? How many times before this have you met her?'

'Not at all. Only phone conversations. Then last week I asked her to meet for lunch, and she agreed. And don't call me stupid, you selfish bastard.'

'And what did you talk about? If you can remember, that is. You were pissed out of your brains when you got home.'

'Can you wonder why I have drink now and then? Life with you is shit. And I *can* remember what we talked about – children and grandchildren, if you must know. You and Frank weren't mentioned except in passing. What the hell is it with you two?'

'How many more times? He did the dirty on me! Get it? Christ almighty!'

'Temper, temper! Your nose is getting redder. Going to raid my make-up bag again, are you?'

Bellowing expletives, Pete had charged up to his study. He couldn't stand to be in the same room with her.

Still seething, he'd lit a cigarette and sat down in front of his computer. There would be business to attend to, there always was, but there'd be no way he could concentrate on it. But he'd logged on, seeking other diversions in the cyber world. Mostly business emails of course, but there'd been an alert from *Friends Reunited,* which he'd joined last year but had never used. He'd entered the website, and had then been shaken by the second thunderbolt of the day.

When he'd woken this morning, there'd still been a residual anger, but it was tempered by an emotion he was unable to identify. He hadn't been able to reply to the email, because he wasn't sure what his response should be.

He'd pulled back the curtains to find it was raining. Not the sort of day for a round of golf. An omen perhaps? Some sort of warning that it would be unwise to go and see Jack? No, he didn't believe in that sort of crap, did he? And in any case, underlying all his misgivings was curiosity, and something else – hope, perhaps, but he wasn't certain what he was hoping for.

Now, with a silent lunch over, he rose, grabbed his car keys from the sideboard and made for the door.

'You're not playing golf in this weather, surely? Now I know you're mad.'

'No. Phoned Jack earlier. We're just going for a drink. I fancy some masculine company.'

'That's how I feel all the time.'

He chose not to reply and, slamming to door behind him, ran through the rain to the garage.

He couldn't remember ever having driven to Jack's in this sort of weather. Travelling through the Chilterns was usually a pleasant precursor to the afternoon's golf, whatever the season. Pete wasn't sentimental about landscape, knew little and cared less about the natural world, but was often cheered by the fresh green of the beech leaves in spring and their spectacular range of colours in autumn. But today the scenery was obscured by rain beating against the windscreen, lashing so hard that the wipers were barely able to cope. The lowering clouds reflected his mood, and he was still unsure whether what he was doing was wise.

He pulled up outside Jack's house. It was still pouring, so Jack wasn't waiting for him outside. At least that gave him a chance to have a quick fag. He still wasn't certain about how he should act, what he should say, if the door were to be opened by Judy.

He only took a few drags before he was seized by a fit of coughing. Christ, he ought to cut down. He extinguished the cigarette, ran through the rain to the door and rang the bell.

Jack opened the door.

'Watcha, Pete. You're early. I need a few minutes: come in.'

They entered the lounge. There was the sound of running water from the kitchen.

'Jude's washing up. Jude! It's Pete! Come and say hello!'

A few minutes elapsed. Taking off her apron, perhaps? Checking the mirror to see if she looked okay? Or even taking deep breaths, steeling herself for their meeting? Bullshit, Pete told himself. It had only been a few weeks since they'd last seen each other: nothing had really changed, had it? So why this sense of apprehension?

'Hi, Pete. How are you?'

'Fine, Judy. And you?'

'Can't complain.'

'Just going to the bathroom,' said Jack. 'Won't be a sec.'

A short silence, then -

'How's Marion?'

'Same as ever.'

'And Sarah?'

'She's fine, I assume. Haven't seen much of her recently. How's work?'

'Okay. Only a year to go before I retire.'

'Looking forward to it, are you?'

'Not sure.'

Another silence, broken by Jack returning. 'It's still raining, Pete. Are we going to walk?'

'No, we'll be soaked. Let's take the car to the carpark and leg it from there.'

'Right, let's go. See you later, Jude.'

As they walked to the door Pete turned to look at Judy. She gave him a quizzical glance, half raised her eyebrows. It was a silent question. He nodded in affirmation, then turned to follow Jack.

They sat in their usual seats in the *George*. Jack was treating him to the latest episode in the saga of the growing antipathy between himself and the Rev. Barnes, and Pete could just about concentrate sufficiently to be able to respond with occasional sympathetic interjections. It wasn't only that he had Judy on his mind, he found he needed to talk about her – even to her husband, of all people. And there was something about which he needed to be certain.

'So how are you getting on with your computer, then, Jack?'

'Eh?'

'Your computer. Are you using it for your family history researches?'

Jack grimaced. 'Can't get to grips with it. Jude's tried her best to teach me, but … oh, I dunno, there's too much to take in. Trying to type's bad enough, but all those symbols – I keep forgetting what they mean. And as for this internet malarkey – I'd much rather be dealing with something on paper.'

'So you're not using it at all?'

'Nope. It's not for me. I reckon I'm too old to learn.'

'But Judy uses it, I suppose?'

'Too right she does. She's used to it, of course, uses it all the time at work.'

'Uses email, I suppose?'

'I'll say. Spends a lot of time exchanging them with her mates. God knows why – she sees them often enough.'

'You know women. They can talk for hours. It's probably the same with email. Does she tell you what they talk about?'

'She used to, when she started. But to be honest I got tired of listening to her. I think she got the message – she never mentions emails now.'

Pete felt himself relax.

'Fancy another pint, Jack?'

'Won't say no. Cheers.'

Waiting at the bar to be served, Pete found himself looking at Jack – or rather at the back of Jack's head, because he was sitting in his usual position, back to the bar and facing the window. He always insisted on that seating arrangement, God knows why, but then old Jack had always been a bit of a stick-in-the-mud, set in his ways, reluctant to try anything new. His attitude to Judy's computer – Pete now found himself regarding it as *her* computer, not a shared acquisition – was typical of Jack, as was his evident reluctance to persevere in learning how to use it.

Pete had come to realise that Jack was one of those people who had low self-esteem. Perhaps subconsciously he'd always been aware of this, but his image of Jack had been forged when they were teenagers, and in youth one accepts flaws as part of a person's character. Jack's adult persona had been veiled by memories of when they were both caught up in the intimacy of being young in the same place and at the same time, an association so intense that it eclipsed their later friendship. But he now viewed him with a more critical eye.

The two pints were placed on the bar, but Pete didn't pick them up. He was still thinking about Jack. If Jack were a young man today, he'd already be identified as one of life's losers, passed over for advancement, someone with whom he'd unlikely to be friendly. Pete considered the young men, and women, in his profession – they all spoke well of themselves, pushed themselves forward, asserted they were 'passionate' about the business, would give it 110%. Pete supposed he'd been a bit like that, though he'd never used that sort of language. But he'd had to promote himself to ensure his business thrived.

So why, he asked himself, had he and Jack remained friends? Sentiment could only go so far. Was it because of Judy? Was remaining in contact with her the only reason he'd continued seeing Jack? And what did Jack think of him? The thought occurred to him – *bloody hell, perhaps I annoy him, perhaps he sees me as pushy and loudmouthed.* But Jack would never say as much, of course. He lacked the assertiveness.

He noticed Jack turning his head towards the bar. Pete picked up the pints and carried them over, wondering how much time he could decently spend with him before heading home and answering Judy's email. And he was gasping for another fag.

Judith

Judith was proud she had her own office. It confirmed her status in the firm, something she still found hard to believe. It was also a sanctuary, for she sometimes found the junior staff irritating. She wasn't interested in their gossip and in any case she often found it hard to understand what they were talking about – their slang was sometimes impenetrable, they couldn't string a sentence together without the interjection of words such as 'sort of' and 'like', and on being confronted with anything out of the ordinary their response was usually that it was 'awesome'. Judith hated that word. Even some of her contemporaries had started using it.

She sometimes wondered what the juniors thought of her. They were polite enough, carried out her instructions without demur, smiled when she made a joke, asked her to sign cards when any of them had a birthday. But there was no hint of deference - not that she wanted it - but she couldn't help but remember the subservient manner which she'd adopted towards Mrs Edwards, who'd been the office supervisor when she'd joined the firm as a seventeen year-old.

Did the juniors see her as she'd first seen Mrs Edwards? An old woman to be humoured, someone whose views and experience (other than those relating to work) were of no relevance to the young? But, in fact, Judith had soon learned to appreciate Mrs Edwards. Soon after she'd joined the firm she'd begun to find the attentions of the senior partner, Mr Saunders, unwelcome. She'd never invited them, had taken pains to dress demurely, had stopped applying make-up, but it had got to the point where she'd been considering handing in her notice. Mrs Edwards had evidently noticed her distress, had called her into the very office in which she was now sitting, and told her not to worry, Mr Saunders always tried it on with attractive girls, he never took it too far, and if it carried on she, Mrs Edwards, would have a quiet word in his ear. So Judith took pains to ensure she was never in the same room with him alone – this meant her visits to the print room required careful timing – and indeed after a few weeks he transferred his attentions to a new girl, Stephanie Jeacock, who, it was noticed, began to spend rather more time in his office than the simple delivery of a typed-up letter required.

None of the junior girls had ever needed to seek Judith's support for such incidents. In that respect, times had changed for the better. These days such behaviour by a man would be countered with a slap round the face or a formal complaint, or both. But Judith wasn't so ardent a feminist as to believe that the likes of Stephanie Jeacock no longer existed.

Today, she had even more reason to appreciate the privacy her office provided. She was about to break the company rule – never to use the firm's telephone for private calls. She wasn't going to make the call, but she was waiting to receive one. It was permitted to receive them in cases of emergency – that was how she'd learned her mother had died – but calls from friends were frowned on. Not that this restriction bothered the juniors: they all received text messages. Judith was beginning to wonder, given the new situation in which she was finding herself, whether she should purchase a mobile phone.

She couldn't settle to work. She picked up documents from her in-tray, tried to read them, found she wasn't taking in what was written, and replaced them. She started drafting an email, but the words wouldn't flow, and in any case she seemed to have lost her facility with the keyboard. There was no denying it, she was nervous. Apprehension battled with guilt, guilt conflicted with excitement.

Last night, during the one hour she allowed herself on the computer, she'd received a reply from Pete. The email was short. He'd said what a pleasant surprise it was to hear from her, how sorry he was they no longer saw much of each other, how that was all his doing, how one day he hoped to explain what had happened. He'd said he hated using emails for personal conversations, he'd much prefer to phone her but he supposed it wouldn't be a good idea to ring her at home, and did she have any suggestions? He'd signed off with love and added two kisses.

Judith had emailed back immediately, giving the company phone number, and suggesting it was best to phone in the afternoon. Then she'd shut down the computer, just as Jack came in from the kitchen. After two hours spent with him looking at the TV but not watching it, she'd gone to bed, only to spend a sleepless night.

When the phone rang, she started.

'It's a call from Vale Architectural Services,' said Kirsty the switchboard operator, 'The caller wouldn't say what it was about. Do you want to take it?'

Judith knew this was a pivotal moment. She could stop this nonsense now, tell Kirsty to say she was unavailable.

'Yes, put it through.'

'Hello? Judy?'

'Yes.'

'It's me, Pete.'

'Hello, Pete.'

'Can you talk?'

'Yes, but not for too long.'

'Judy … God, I don't know how to start. This is bloody ridiculous. I see you practically every Sunday, but – '

'But Jack's always there. That's what you were going to say, wasn't it?'

'Yes. Look, Judy, why did you contact me on *Friends Reunited*? Don't get me wrong, it was great to get it, but … well, why now?'

'Oh, I was just trying it out. Yours was the only name on it I … I knew. Apart from people I'm not interested in, I mean.'

'So it was nothing more than that?'

'Pete, I just wanted to be sure we were … we were, well, still friends.'

'Of course we are. A bit more than that, I hope – oh, don't get me wrong, I wasn't referring to …'

'But you haven't really acted like a friend for years, have you? Not the way you used to. And I don't mean – '

'I know what you mean. Look, Judy, I want to tell you why I've been, well, keeping you at arm's length for all this time. I'm so sorry about how I've behaved. I just didn't know how to go about telling you. Jack's always there. I'd thought a lot about phoning you at work, but it wouldn't have been right, somehow. And then I got your email. And now, here we are.'

'Yes. Here we are. So, why?'

'Why what?'

'Why the cold-shoulder for nearly twenty years?'

'It's not something I can explain on the phone. Too complicated. Is there any way we can meet?'

Judith had been anticipating this question ever since getting his email the previous evening. Trying to think of an answer was one of the reasons for her sleepless night.

'I can't get away during the week. At weekends Jack's around for most of the time, apart from Saturday morning at the library, and if he's not there he goes for his bike ride. Wouldn't give us long, would it?'

'Not long enough.'

'There's one thing, though. In September, Jack'll be attending his annual church organists' get-together. It's held on the third Sunday of the month, in the afternoon, and this year it'll be in Turville. Could you make it then?'

'That's a month away. But, yes, of course. I'll wait. Where shall we meet? Shall I come to your place?'

'No!'

'Okay, okay. We'll meet in a pub, maybe? Plenty of time to sort that out.'

'Yes. Contact me at the office, not by email. Pete, I really have to get on with some work now.'

'I know the feeling. See you, Judy.'

'Goodbye, Pete.'

'Just one thing. I've missed you, Judy.'

The line went dead.

Staffordshire

I was sitting in front of my computer, and I couldn't get Susie out of my mind.

Her last visit had re-awakened those parts of my psyche I believed had been consigned to an endless sleep. It had also had a strange effect on the way in which I perceived time. I'd grown used to the way in which my time was now consumed, how I'd carefully parcelled it out – morning walk, reading the newspaper, preparing lunch, afternoons reading a novel or gardening, preparing a dinner, watching TV or walking or playing on the PC in the evening. My days were long and each one resembled the other, distinguished only by the weather, subtle changes in the seasons, and visits from my cleaner. And from Susie, of course.

And now Susie had re-introduced unpredictability into my life. I used to thrive on unpredictability. Yes, of course there'd been structure to my days – my lecture timetable, regular tutorials, departmental and faculty meetings – but there was the perpetual buzz of being on the university campus, the stimulation provided by colleagues, the parties, and of course the frisson that came from contact with students, students who seemed to be younger with each successive academic year.

Back in the 1970s and 1980s the concept of a 'duty of care' was vague in Higher Education. It certainly wasn't illegal to have sex with students because they were over the age of consent, eighteen or older, so one could give way to temptation. I wasn't always the seducer, not by any means. In fact, I'd been told by one of my bed-mates (in fact, we were in bed when she'd said it) that there were many in the student body who thought there was cachet in screwing a lecturer. I obtained my first lectureship, at Leeds, in 1967 – the Summer of Love. I was only twenty-four, young enough to participate in the explosion of hedonism of that year. I'd always been a hedonist, well, since my late teens, and it seemed society had at last caught up with me. The music, the drugs, the sex – they'd defined me, especially the sex, which for me became something of a *raison d'etre* and continued to be, even after I'd obtained a Senior Lectureship at Keele.

Then, when my life changed, I'd tried to blank out all thoughts of sex. It had been easier than I expected, for I'd known the chances would never come again. It was a bit like being a smoker in a no-smoking zone – when lighting-up is forbidden, the urge for a cigarette is diminished. And there was no escaping the truth: it had been one particular sexual adventure which had eventually led to my drastically altered circumstances.

But now, after Susie's last visit, my libido was stirring again. Part of me was upset, even angered by the re-emergence of an urge which I knew could never be satisfied and which would therefore probably result in another slide into despair. But, try as I might, I couldn't extinguish the faint flickering of hope engendered by the remark Susie had made when we parted last week: that she'd see me again in a month unless I needed to see her before that.

But I'd resisted the temptation to phone her lest my request for a visit, even if granted, would lead only to rejection and the smothering of the hope to which I was clinging. It seemed that whatever I did, or did not do, would condemn me to hopelessness.

I turned on the computer. I'd been tempted by Internet porn, but hadn't succumbed. That would be the ultimate degradation. So I logged on to my email account.

Christ! A reply from Frank! So mired had I been in my introspection that I'd forgotten I'd emailed him.

Tim! How amazing! A blast from the past, as we used to say. It must be over 40 years – yes, it was just after we left school when we last saw each other. So much to catch up on! What have you been doing with yourself? Last I heard, you were doing a Ph.D. As for me, well, where do I start? As you'll know from my website, I run a small business. But more of that later. I'm married to Angela – we met when I was working in London, got married in 1970, moved back to Bucks in 76. As for family ...

There then followed a long account of his children and grandchildren, extolling their virtues of course, as all parents and grandparents do. That sort of doting pride in progeny always annoyed me. Even my university colleagues used to indulge in it. But now, it made me ... yes, depressed. Yet another bloody thing to depress me. If I'd had children, they might now be a comfort, but grandchildren? To them I'd be a freak, someone to be avoided, just as I'd avoided visiting my grandfather when he'd been reduced to drooling senescence after his stroke.

I skimmed down the email – would Frank ever get to the point and answer the important questions I'd asked? Perhaps I'd phrased them too casually. But then –

You asked about our old school friends. Not much to tell, I'm afraid. I can't remember the last time I saw Jack

and Judith, You did know they got married, I assume?
Don't know if they have an email address. Sorry, can't
help you there. Neither do I have an email for Pete
Kennedy. I may as well tell you - I don't want any contact
with him. We had a major falling out, years ago now.
Quite honestly, Tim, he's a bastard. Angie and I used to
see a lot of him and his wife, but not now. If you want to
try and contact him his company's name is The Vale
Architectural Services. But look, Tim, please don't tell him
I told you. In fact, don't mention me at all. I want nothing
to do with him.

What about you, Tim? Why are you known as Dave?
Sounds fascinating – tell me more! And I'd be interested to
hear about your career. I suppose you're married? And do
you have ...

There followed lots of questions about how I lived my
life. I'd have to consider carefully what I'd tell him. I
needed to encourage a degree of intimacy in our
exchanges, because what he'd said about Pete Kennedy
had intrigued me. A bastard? The Pete I remembered had
been a bit abrasive and quick-tempered, and I was never
sure I liked him much, but he could be fun, not someone
you'd call a bastard. What had happened between them?
Suddenly it was important that I knew. I'd need to gain
Frank's confidence, get him to open up a bit. The prospect
of observing the lives of others was enticing, and who
knows, I might be able to participate at a distance, even
influence the course of events. Wider horizons beckoned. I
googled Pete's company, found his email address and sent
him an email, telling him that Frank had given me the
name of his company, and saying it would be good to hear
from him.

It was only after I'd made myself a coffee that I
realised I hadn't thought about Susie for over an hour.

PART THREE

September – October 2002

Staffordshire

The forecast was for another warm, dry day. But with clear skies and the sun yet to rise, the morning air was distinctly chilly.

I'd always enjoyed early autumn. When the weather's kind it's possible to believe it's still summer, and September always used to bring the hopes and expectations of a new academic year – new challenges, the renewal of contact with colleagues, gossip in the common room, and of course the arrival of a new cohort of fresh-faced eighteen year-olds ready, and for the most part eager, to participate in their new-found freedom from parental oversight. Second- and third-year students called the first few days of the new semester 'Fuck-a-Fresher-week', and no doubt some of them took full advantage of it. Not that I ever indulged, tempting as teenage flesh was: too risky. Most of the Freshers were still little more than school-kids, naïve, interested only in their peer group, prone to indiscretion. No, it had been better to wait until they matured a little, learned to appreciate the sort of wisdom a friendly lecturer could bestow, came to realise an older man could offer the sort of experience not to be found amongst their peers. Those entering their final year were the best bet. They still had the bloom of youth but had learned discretion, were aware that any gossip or scandal was to be avoided lest it distract them from the approach of finals.

But now, September no longer heralded hope or anticipation. Leaves were still green, meadows still lush, warmth still in the sun, swifts not yet departed, but there was a hint of what was to come – tractors ploughing up the stubble, the shortening days, advertisements for warm clothing on the TV. Soon would come those endless dreary days when short walks in the dark, and winter tasks in the garden when the weather permitted, would be the only escape from my prison.

But today my autumn mood was lighter than usual. Susie would be making her monthly visit later this morning, and the pleasure this always brought was heightened by excitement mixed with foreboding, though quite why the latter I wasn't sure. And I had something else to contemplate – the email I'd received from Pete yesterday evening.

It didn't begin with any expression of pleasure at my making contact with him, nor with any surprise at my changed name. Instead, the opening sentence expressed outrage that the name of his company had been given me by Frank Grayson. I'd deliberately chosen to disregard Frank's request not to mention his name in the hope it would elicit some sort of response from Pete, and the ploy worked beyond all my expectations, for Pete had launched into a tirade which went on for two expletive-laden paragraphs in which he cursed Frank and all his works.

It seemed that Frank had once owned a property development company as well as being a County Councillor, and had used his influence on the Planning Committee to ensure the rejection of a rival company's application to build on a green-field site near the county town. Pete had a contract with the rival company to provide architectural services for the proposed development, and had invested heavily in design-time in the expectation of a share in the profits once the houses were built and sold. 'Bastard', 'Corrupt shit', 'Backstabbing Judas' were some of the milder epithets used to describe Frank, the last term used because apparently Pete and Frank, together with their wives, had become friends after Frank had moved back to Bucks.

But there was more. More of even greater interest. I could still remember, word for word, what Pete had written – *I hinted I'd spill the beans to some of the other councillors I knew about what Frank had done. Corrupt practice. That would have ended his days as a councillor and wouldn't have done his business any good either. But that shit threatened me with blackmail. Personal stuff I'd confided in him about. It would have ruined my marriage. And that of a mate. Okay, so I'd been a naughty boy on occasions. Who hasn't?*

Only at the end of the email had he enquired about my welfare, as though he'd suddenly remembered his manners. He had concluded, almost as an afterthought, by saying he saw Jack about once a week, but not very much of Judy.

I was still mulling over what he'd said as I walked home. What had intrigued me most in Pete's email was his revelation about what had obviously been an extra-marital affair. With the wife of a mate, it would seem. Pete had lived in Bucks all his life. Was the mate, or his wife, someone I might have known when I lived there? The chances were pretty remote, but it was a matter worthy of further research.

I was certain of one thing. I bet Pete now regretted saying what he had. It was all too easy, so I'd been told, to divulge things on-line and then click on the 'send' button without giving thought to what the repercussions might be. Something to bear in mind now I'd begun my campaign.

Back home, I set about making myself presentable for Susie's visit. Presentable! As if! But at least I could dress for the occasion. From the neck down I was in pretty good shape. I chose slim jeans and a roll-neck sweater. It would be the first time Susie had seen me in these: usually I was slobbing about in track-suit bottoms and a frayed shirt when she came in.

There was still an hour to wait before she arrived. I'd read all I wanted to in the morning paper, so went up to my study, now dusted and tidied, and turned on the computer. No emails. I sat staring at the screen, at a loss to know what to do next. I wandered down to the kitchen: all in order there. The coffee percolator stood ready: she might appreciate being offered the real thing instead of the usual cup of instant. Then, an idea. As usual, two chairs were placed opposite each other across the table: I moved one so they were side-by-side. Too obvious a ploy perhaps? But she could always return one to its usual position if the new arrangement displeased her.

At last – three long rings on the door bell. I went into the hall, could see her outline through the frosted-glass front door. Two long minutes, then the two short rings. Her key in the lock. The door opened.

'Dave! How long have you been standing there?'

This was the first time I'd met her in the hall: usually I was in the kitchen when she entered, or hurrying down the stairs.

'Only a few seconds. Thought I'd surprise you.'

And she'd surprised me, because it was like seeing – well, not exactly a stranger, but someone who was subtly different from the Susie whom I had in my mind's eye. Then it came to me. She wasn't wearing make-up, and her hair was tied back. And she was wearing trousers, not her usual short skirt. Was this intended to convey a message? If so, it was an unwelcome one.

'How are you, then?'

'I'm okay, Susie. Better than the last time you came.'

'You're looking very smart. Expecting a visitor are you?'

'Chance would be a fine thing. Just felt like a change.'

'Well, that's a good sign.'

'Come into the kitchen. Coffee?'

'Please.'

She must have noticed the changed seating arrangements, but sat down without comment.

'Thought you might like a real coffee instead of the instant stuff I usually give you.'

'Oh, yes. Great.'

There was silence while I busied myself with the

percolator. This was unusual: she normally chatted about her day or her supervisor and asked me about my morning walk before she started her counselling routine. Glancing at her, she looked – not sad, exactly, but serious.

I carried over the coffees and sat down. As I did, I saw the disadvantage of the new seating plan. When we sat opposite each other we were in almost continuous eye contact. Now, she'd have to turn her head to look at me. And she wasn't doing so.

'Mmm, nice coffee. Now, Dave, what do you think are the reasons for you feeling better?'

I was struck instantly by the formality of her question. Normally, it would have been something like 'Great you're feeling better, Dave. Why d'you reckon that is, darlin'?'

'Well, I've made email contact with two of my old school friends, thanks to you Susie. And I might have some leads so I can contact a few more.'

'And how does that make you feel? Other than being pleased, I mean.'

'Not sure what you mean.'

'Do you want to build a new relationship with any of them? Or just chat about old times? Do you reckon they'll become an important part of your life again?'

These were questions I'd already begun to ask myself, and for which I had few definite answers. So my reply was non-committal. But that didn't deter Susie. She continued to probe, adopting the low, measured, confidential tone of the professional counsellor, her most frequent question being 'And how did you *feel* about that?' all the while not looking at me. I'd always been irritated by people who constantly engaged in self-analysis and who expected me to do the same. I remembered telling one intense young lady to 'Lighten up, for Christ's sake', which had resulted in the evening not ending in the way I had hoped.

Susie had adopted that sort of analytical approach when she first became my counsellor, but had long abandoned it in the face of my flippant responses. Now, it was as though the last few years hadn't happened. It was like being at a first appointment with a consultant psychotherapist.

It was obvious what she was about. The absence of make-up, the tied-back hair, the trousers, the formal approach – all were designed to tell me, without having to articulate it, that she regretted the intimacy of our last meeting. But I wasn't prepared to let her forget it. Her hand was resting on the table, only inches from mine. I touched it.

It was as though I'd hit her. She jumped up from her chair, grabbed her coffee mug, carried it to the sink and began rinsing it. I was stunned by her reaction to a simple touch: hadn't she often touched my hand during our sessions?

She turned away from the sink and stood facing me. It seemed appropriate that I should stand also. I rose and positioned myself beside my chair, the kitchen table between us.

'Susie, what's the matter? Why are you so … distant?' I was slurring my consonants, something which happened now only when I was stressed.

'Dave, I owe you an apology. I shouldn't have behaved the way I did when I was last here. It was most unprofessional. And most unfair to you.'

Did I detect a slight tremor in her voice?

'No need to apologise. We're old friends, aren't we?'

Her response was to ask me to place one of the chairs on the other side of the table so we could continue the session as normal. I obliged. She sat down, as did I. But even though we faced each other, she avoided eye contact.

'Look, Dave. What you just said. About us being old friends. We can't be. Anything other than … than a professional relationship would be detrimental to the process of helping you to come to terms with your situation.'

'I understand that up to a point. But can't we go back to the way things were before … the last time? You don't need to be so formal, surely?'

'Yes, I do. I've let myself become too matey with you.'

For the first time, she looked at me. Perhaps it was the absence of make-up, but her face was care-worn, sadder than I'd ever seen it.

'Are you all right, Susie? You look sad. Sorry if I'm the cause.'

'No, you're not. I've got a few problems at home. Shouldn't bring them to work with me. And I shouldn't even have mentioned them. Let's get on with the session, shall we?'

Her formal questioning resumed. A wave of weariness engulfed me – it was like having to act out a minor role in a badly written play. My replies were monosyllabic. Then, suddenly –

'This isn't getting us anywhere, is it, Dave?'

'Doesn't look like it. We're just going over old ground.'

'So what do you suggest as an alternative?'

'I haven't the slightest idea. You're the counsellor.'

She stared at me. She began drumming her fingers on the table, almost as though she were agitated. It was something she'd never done before.

'Dave. D'you remember way back when we started these sessions, we went through a list of the things from your former life you missed the most?'

'I'm not likely to forget it. I hated it. Made me feel desperate, but you said it could be cathartic.'

'You said it was the simple things you missed most, like driving out into the country with a friend, then going for a long walk, calling in at a pub.'

'And I still bloody miss it. My morning walks cover the same ground every day. Anyway, I can't do it can I? Don't have a car, for a start. And no friend to take me.'

'But I've got a car, Dave.'

'What?' My question wasn't rhetorical, I genuinely assumed I'd misheard her.

'I think you'd benefit from a change of routine. Email contacts are all very well, but your horizons need broadening, and I'm not speaking metaphorically. Seeing different places, trying new walks, things like that would take you out of yourself.'

'But ... did I hear you right? You're offering to take me?'

'Yes, I might be. But there's a condition attached.'

'What's that?'

'You'll have to have a new counsellor. It's against our protocols to engage socially with clients, so I'll have to request that your case is handed over to someone else.'

'But ... but how often would you be able to take me out?'

'Let's not get ahead of ourselves. We'll have to see how it pans out. And you need to give it some thought before deciding.'

'I don't need to. Let's do it.'

'There's a lot to consider first, Dave. Confidentiality for a start. As far as my supervisor is concerned, I'm handing your case over because ... because I can't be of any further help to you. Not as a counsellor, anyway.'

'So you *could* be a friend?'

For the first time today, she grinned.

'Of course I'm your friend, you silly bugger!' She grabbed my hand, gave it a squeeze. Then she glanced at her watch. 'Bloody hell, I've overrun. I must go.'

She stood up. I escorted her to the hall, and stood behind her as she half-opened the door. She turned round.

'I'll be in contact, Dave.'

Then she was gone.

Buckinghamshire

Pete and Judith

Pete was waiting for Judith in the station car-park. As far as Marion was concerned, he was meeting Jack for golf as usual. The meeting place was Judith's suggestion, because she didn't want her neighbours to see her climbing in to the Range Rover. Silly of her, he thought: after all, his vehicle stopped outside her house every Sunday when he collected Jack, so the neighbours were used to seeing it there. What could be more innocent than her husband's friend making an appearance? It wasn't as if they were about to embark on a torrid affair, was it? In any case, this morning he'd woken to find a fresh outcrop of rosacea had erupted on his nose, enough to repulse anyone. Marion had been a constant presence in the house and he'd had no opportunity to visit her make-up bag. He'd tried dabbing talcum powder on his nose, but it had made him look like a clown.

He'd been looking forward to today for what seemed like months. How long it had been since he'd experienced this delicious feeling of anticipation? It was like being a young man again. The internal glow was a sensation almost forgotten. It might all end in disappointment of course, but all he wanted to do was to explain and apologise, wasn't it? And for her to accept his apology and forgive him.

Christ, he was dying for a fag. He hadn't had once since he left home. But he couldn't smoke in the car and get it all fugged up. Judith hated smokers, according to Jack. But he was getting twitchy. Bugger it, he'd get out and have a few drags.

He was just putting a cig in his mouth when Judith appeared at the entrance to the car park. She evidently spotted him immediately and waved. He dropped the fag and kicked it under the car, and watched as she walked towards him – bloody hell, she was dolled up: tight grey skirt, white shirt, high heels. From a distance she could be in her early forties. She still walked like a young woman. She may have lost her looks, but her figure was pretty good. A bit thin, perhaps, but … he found himself, not for the first time, comparing her favourably with Marion.

'Hi, Judy.'

'Hello, Pete.'

There was a fraction of a second's hesitation. Should he kiss her, revert to the habit of nearly twenty years ago? The decision was made for him: she stopped more than an arm's length away. He opened the passenger door for her. As she got in he caught a whiff of her scent – fresh, delicate, not like the musky stuff Marion drenched herself with.

'Jack got away okay, I suppose?' he said as he climbed in beside her. Silly question: she wouldn't be here if he hadn't, would she?

'Yes. One of his chorister friends is taking him, straight after morning service.'

'What time's he due back?'

'About five. But I must be home well before that. I'll need to get him something to eat. He'll only have had a snack lunch.'

Why, Pete wondered, did he find the reference to the Chapmans' domestic arrangements unwelcome? It had never bothered him before.

'Where would you like to go, Judy?'

'Oh, anywhere so long as it's out of town. I haven't been out in the country for ages.'

'I thought about having a pub lunch and then going for a bit of a walk. It's too nice to be indoors.'

'Yes, that sounds nice. Can't walk far in these heels, though.'

'Okay, let's go to the *Cock and Rabbit* at The Lee. They do –'

'No! Not the *Cock and Rabbit*!'

This was said with startling vehemence. He glanced at her: she was staring fixedly through the windscreen.

'Well, there's a good pub in Cholesbury, can't remember its name, if you'd prefer that.'

'Yes, that'll do.'

He started the engine and drove out of the car park, wondering what she'd got against the *Cock and Rabbit*. Maybe the place held associations for her and Jack. Bloody hell, if all reference to her life with Jack was to be avoided it would be even harder to talk about events in the past, and his confession would be all the more difficult to make. The glow of anticipation was almost extinguished, and for the first time he wondered if he'd set out on a fool's errand. Christ, he could murder a fag.

Conversation was desultory as he drove through the lanes. A bit about his job, a bit about hers and her impending retirement, then observations from her about the beauty of the countryside and how the beech leaves hadn't even started to turn, then how they both hoped it wouldn't be a cold winter. It was almost as though they were voicing the platitudes of a long-married couple, but Pete was all too conscious of what was being unsaid. Judith's voice lacked animation and her expression, whenever he glanced at her face, was deadpan.

Only once did she show some vivacity, when two large birds swooped low over the lane ahead of them, then soared aloft and hovered almost motionless over the field beside the road.

'Look! Red Kites! Aren't they wonderful! Stop the car, Pete. I'd like to watch them for a minute.'

'Oh, is that what they are?' he said as he applied the brakes.

'Do you mean to say you didn't know? How long have you lived round here, Pete? You must drive round with your eyes closed.'

'I've seen them, course I have. And I've heard people mention Red Kites. Just didn't realise that's what they were.'

'But all the publicity they've had! They were introduced around here, oh, over 30 years ago. Wonderful creatures!'

Pete wasn't impressed. To him, a bird was a bird.

'Have you seen enough?' he said, after several minutes had elapsed.

'I could watch them all day. But yes, you can drive on now.'

As he started the engine, Pete tried to think of some observation about Red Kites which might redeem him in her eyes. They were big birds, weren't they? And they hovered – probably watching out for prey.

'I suppose they're killing off all the other wild life. Did they think about that when they introduced them?'

'Rubbish, Pete! They feed on carrion. Don't know much about the countryside, do you?'

Well, that's told me, he thought. Their exchange didn't bode well for the conversation he was hoping they'd have over lunch.

In fact, once in the pub and with their meal in front of them, it was Judith who broached the topic. She was very matter-of-fact about it.

'So, Pete. What is it you want to tell me?''

'I told you on the phone, Judy. I want to say how sorry I am for being so … distant with you for the past twenty years.'

'Distant? Cold, I'd call it.'

'Judy, if only I could make amends. Once I'd started in that vein, I didn't know how to stop. I'm so sorry.'

'So you keep saying. But you haven't explained why. No, no more wine for me thanks.'

Pete poured himself a glass. It should be easy to explain, shouldn't it? After all, he'd been the potential victim as well as she. As was Jack, of course. Oh, and Marion as well. But he felt unable to do so while there was this constraint between them. It was as though their exchange of emails, each signed with kisses, had never happened. What could he say to break through her reserve?

'Judy, how long have we been friends? Must be over forty years.'

'Something like that.' She began to pay unnecessarily close attention to spreading butter on a bread roll.

'And we were a bit more than friends once, weren't we?'

She dropped her knife. He noticed her hand clenching and unclenching. He sensed her body had tensed – oh Christ, he shouldn't have said that.

'I don't want to talk about it. It's all in the past. I've always regretted it and you told me you did too.' This was said without a hint of emotion, and without so much as a glance at him.

'Yes, yes, I did regret it. I didn't mean … I wasn't referring to that … incident. I meant we still stayed good friends afterwards.'

'Yes, until you went distant on me. Are you going to tell me why, or not? If not, you may as well take me home now.'

Now the moment had come, Pete was unsure what to say. He'd rehearsed *ad nauseam* various versions, but now they all seemed to give too much information.

'There's no easy way to tell you this, Judy. I discovered someone I knew was engaged in a dodgy business deal, at my expense, and I told him I was going to make it public. The bastard said if I did, he'd tell Marion about … well, about us. I panicked, I suppose. Felt guilty as well, even though it … we, had happened years before this. That's why I suddenly went cool. And once I'd done that, I didn't know how to go back to the way I'd always been.'

She seemed to be taking a long while to digest this information.

'Judy – '

'No, wait. How did this person know about us?'

It was the inevitable question, of course, the one he'd been dreading. He'd have to be honest, there was no other option, but God, what would she think of him?

'I'm so bloody ashamed, Judy. You see, this … person: we were business associates of a sort. We got to be, well, friends, I suppose. Used to go out drinking together. One night we both got pissed, really pissed, and it was, well, boys' stuff. Started talking about women we'd … been with. I told him about us. Said it was a one-off. I'm so sorry. It's something I've – '

She scrambled to her feet, knocking her plate and cutlery to the floor. The pub fell silent.

'Take me home, please, now.' She started to walk to the door.

'Judy, wait.'

She didn't. He went to the bar to pay the bill. The process seemed to take years. The pub was still hushed and he knew he was the focus of attention. When he finally got to the car she was standing behind it. He unlocked it, got in, but she stayed standing. He opened the passenger door. But she got in the back.

'Judy – '

'*Just take me home.*'

***

The *bastard*. Judith rarely even thought in such terms, but that was what he was. And she'd always believed he was kind and thoughtful underneath all his brash ebullience. Had it all been a ploy for all those years, just to give him an opportunity to have his way with her when she was down and needed comfort, the sort of comfort Jack was unable to provide? And then, despite his promise never to mention it again, to boast about it to someone else? Boys' stuff, he'd called it. Was that what men did when they were together, compare notes about the women with whom they'd had one night stands? Jack, she knew, would never do such a thing, would have been unable to. To her shame, she remembered telling Pete about Jack's problem, at the time when she was at her lowest. Had he seen her revelation as an invitation? Had she been partly to blame for what had happened?

All she wanted now was to get home, to be alone, to compose herself before Jack returned. She was sitting directly behind Pete, squeezed against the window so there was no chance of eye contact in the rear-view mirror. That way he'd find it hard to try to talk to her, and in any case

97

she didn't want to see his face. She never wanted to look at him again.

She was accustomed to friendships fading, to the gradual growing apart when once-common interests began to diverge. It was the lot of a childless woman to experience a distancing from those contemporaries who'd reared a family and spoke of little else but the progress of their offspring, and whose lives now seemed to revolve around their grandchildren. She'd learned to cope with this: her work had brought her into contact with new people, people whose acquaintanceship was unencumbered by a shared past. But the sudden death of her friendship with Pete had come as a body-blow. It was worse than if he had died: she might have got over that. But now she was faced with the knowledge that he'd betrayed their trust, and that she could never forgive.

Deep in introspection, she'd paid no attention to the passing scenery, but glancing out the window she realised Pete was taking her home by a different route. What the hell was he playing at? Then, she recognised where they were. It was Lee Common.

He stopped the car outside the old village school.

'Why have you stopped?'

He turned and tried to look at her. She shrank back in her seat, peered out of the window.

'Judy, I know I've upset you, but I can't keep on apologising. I'm trying to make amends. I thought you might like to see where me and Jack, and the others, used to come and play cricket when we were still at school. I know Jack's fond of the place, he cycles out here sometimes, and maybe –'

'No! *No!* How many times do I have to say it! Take me home!'

'All right. Okay.' His tone was no longer appeasing. 'But now we're here, *I* want to have a look at the old place. I won't be a minute. Then I'll take you back to your precious Jack.'

He got out, slammed the door, and crossed the lane,

heading for a stile. He clambered over it and disappeared between two high walls, on one side the old village school, on the other a cottage.

Was this another ploy, she wondered? Surely he couldn't know the significance of this place for her? Was he hoping she'd follow him? Damn him. Damn him to hell. She scrambled out of the car, opened the driver's door and pressed the horn, keeping her fingers on it. The front door of the nearby cottage opened: an old man stood staring at her. She continued pressing the horn. Pete leapt back over the stile, ran across the lane.

'You crazy bitch! What the fuck d'you think you're doing? Let me in!'

His face was puce with anger. She didn't move, kept her hand on the horn. He grabbed her arm, none too gently. She resisted. He to seized her by the shoulders and roughly pulled her away. She staggered and fell in the road.

'Here, what you be doin'? That's no way to treat a lady.' The old man had left his garden and was standing facing Pete.

'Mind your own business, you interfering old git!'

She began scrambling to her feet.

'Here, let me give you a hand up, miss. Are you hurt bad?'

'Just grazes. I'm all right.'

Pete grabbed her free hand. 'Get in the car. I'll take you back, though God knows why I should after that performance.'

Her shock and outrage was replaced by an icy contempt. She shook off his hand. 'There's no way I'm getting back in that car with you.'

'And how are you going to get home?'

'Bus, taxi, whatever.'

'From here? Now I know you're mad.'

'Miss, my son, he lives in the village. He'll give you a lift to where you wanner go. Me missus'll come with you if you like. But I reckon them grazes could do with a seeing to first. Come in to the house, the missus'll wash 'em and put a dressing on 'em.'

'You're very kind. Thank you.'

She clung on to his arm as he led her to the cottage. Behind her she heard the car door slam, a furious revving of the engine and the scream of tyres as the vehicle was driven off.

She'd managed to change her clothes and rehearse her story by the time Jack got home: she'd gone for a walk in the park, slipped on a discarded plastic bag and had been quite shaken, but she was okay now and would start getting his supper in a minute.

But after cursory expressions of sympathy Jack evidently lost interest. He began to tell her about the events of his day, how much he'd enjoyed it, how it good it had been to talk to people from other choirs, how he'd spent a lot of time with a chap from the church in Wendover comparing notes on their respective vicars and how annoying trendy young clergymen could be, and how there was another chap from Chalfont whose vicar was a woman but she was okay, quite a traditionalist in fact, and how …

She listened with half an ear as she peeled the potatoes, scraped and sliced the carrots and put them on to boil. His monologue continued as she fried a steak, laid the table and eventually served the meal. It was a long time since she'd seen him so animated, and she was relieved he was: it saved her from having to make conversation when her mind was elsewhere, in a place where she'd never thought it would be.

She sat at the table beside him.

'Aren't you having anything, then?'

'Sorry?'

'Aren't you eating?'

'No. I'm not hungry. Think I'm still a bit shaken up after falling over.'

He stopped eating, put down his knife and fork, and

peered at her.

'Are you all right, Jude?'

'Yes. I said, I'm a bit shaken up.'

'You've been very quiet ever since I got in. Don't think you were listening to me half the time. Nothing worrying you, is there?'

'No, of course not. I just feel very tired. In fact, I think I'll have a long bath and go to bed.'

'You do that, Jude. I'll wash up. I'll watch a bit of telly before I come to bed. I'll try not to wake you.'

She got up and made to leave the room, throwing a 'Goodnight, then' over her shoulder.

'Don't I get a goodnight kiss?'

She turned to face him. He remained seated. She kissed him briefly on the back of his neck, squeezed his shoulder, and managed to reach the bathroom before the tears came.

Her bath wasn't relaxing her as she had hoped. It wasn't helped by the water being lukewarm, this the result of Jack's insistence that the boiler was turned off after six o'clock as an economy measure. She'd forgotten to turn on the immersion heater, and it was too late now: she'd have to wait an hour for the water to heat up. A familiar gloom enveloped her, brought on as it always was by the bathroom's antiquated fixtures and the stains on the porcelain. And the toilet was the only one in the house – please God let Jack not need to use it. After a lifetime of work she deserved better than this, surely?

But these thoughts were a minor irritation. Cinematic re-runs of the events of the day flashed in front of her. Her anger at Pete hadn't diminished, but questions had arisen, and with them nagging worries.

Would he continue to call for Jack as usual on Sundays? If he came inside, would he expect her to go through the charade of pretending nothing had happened? She knew couldn't behave normally because she wouldn't be able to look at him, let alone engage in pleasantries. Jack would be bound to notice.

And if he decided never to come again, what reason would he give to Jack? Would it mean the end of Jack's trips to the golf course and his drinks with Pete in the *George*? Jack would be devastated, for Pete was the only real friend he had. Now she was not only worried, but guilt-ridden.

But, most worrying, why had Pete suggested going to the *Cock and Rabbit*, and then taken her to Lee Common? Was he wanting to see her reaction? Did he know this was where she and Tim had gone, just that once? Surely Tim wouldn't have told him? No, that was impossible. The two had never been friendly. Tim hadn't liked Pete at school, said he was a bit of a yob. And in any case Tim hadn't been back to Bucks since he'd left for university.

The bath water had gone cold. She got out, towelled herself down, put on her nightdress and went to the bedroom. She took two paracetamol before climbing into bed, dreading the prospect of a sleepless night. But she drifted off almost immediately.

She woke with a start from a nightmare in which Pete had been hitting her – had she cried out? But Jack was snoring beside her. She turned to look at the bedside clock: one-thirty. Too soon to take more paracetamol.

She lay on her back. The events of the previous day began yet another cinematic performance, but this time she found she was paying attention to the dialogue rather than to the scenic effects, in particular to what Pete had said concerning his drunken revelation to the fellow who'd then threatened to tell Marion. There was something niggling her about this account: something didn't ring true.

It came to her. He'd said he'd felt guilty, that his guilt was the reason for his coolness towards her. But why? If he'd had any guilt it would be about Marion, not her. There was only one explanation. He must have told his drinking partner her name. Why? There could only be one reason. The drinking partner must have known her. Perhaps it wasn't only Marion the fellow had threatened to tell, but also Jack. *Whoever it was, he must have known both of us. Oh God.*

She made a mental inventory of the people who had known all three of them: her, Jack and Pete. But that was just conceptual displacement activity. She knew there were only two possibilities.

She reached for the packet of paracetamol.

Frank

They'd finished their evening meal and were sitting in the lounge when the telephone rang. Angela picked it up and glanced at the display.

'This might be a long one,' she said. 'I'll take it into the kitchen.'

'Who is it?' said Frank.

'Marion.'

Frank swore under his breath as she left the room with the phone. This was beginning to irritate him, because it was the third time that bloody woman had phoned since Angie had met her for lunch, well, the third time while he'd been present – who knows how many other occasions there'd been when he was out? Angie always took the phone into another room when he was around. She never divulged what they spoke about beyond saying Marion was depressed and needed someone to talk to.

Frank was beyond being merely irritated: he felt a growing sense of disquiet. For the first time in their marriage the calm, mutually supportive contentment of their life together had been contaminated by the intrusion of a third party with whom Angie was willing to engage, but with whom he wanted no contact. There was now a gulf between them, for something must be going on which she was unwilling to discuss. She'd never kept secrets from him before.

Angie had left the kitchen door ajar, and he could hear her talking – her voice was raised. Intrigued, he went into the hall to listen.

'Why don't you go and stay with Sarah tonight…'

'Well, if not at Sarah's, go to a hotel ….'

'I know, I know, I understand. We'll sort something out, try to calm down, please …'

'Yes, tomorrow, I promise. Let's meet for lunch … no, not in a pub. How about the Café Nero in Princes Risborough? It's …'

'Yes, about twelve. And Marion, please don't have anything to drink before setting out …'

'Okay, yes. Look, I have to go now. I'm thinking of you …'

The conversation was evidently ending. Frank retreated into the lounge.

After a few minutes Angie entered, replaced the phone on its stand, and sat down in an armchair opposite Frank. She looked abstracted, said nothing.

'Well?' said Frank.

'Well what?'

'What was all that about? Still depressed, I suppose?'

'Not depressed. Distressed.'

'I don't suppose you're going to tell me about it?'

'Yes, Frank, I *will* tell you. It's serious. Pete's been knocking her about.'

'Both drunk, were they? Mind you, I wouldn't put anything past that bastard. He always did have a temper.'

'Aren't you even going to ask how badly she's been hurt?'

Frank was momentarily ashamed. 'Sorry. Well, how badly?'

'It sounded pretty nasty. Apparently it's not the first time he's done it, but before it was always slaps. This time he used his fist.'

'When did it happen?'

'Yesterday. Apparently Pete got home from golf earlier than usual, and he was in a foul mood. Didn't say a word. You know Marion, she wouldn't let a thing like that rest. She kept asking him what the matter was. Then he blew his top. Started ranting about Jack. Said he never wanted to see him again. Called him all names under the sun.'

'Jack Chapman? Wonder what happened? I haven't seen Jack for years, but he was always an inoffensive soul. What did he do to get under Pete's skin?'

'That's what Marion kept asking him. He wouldn't tell her, but she kept on at him, and that was when he lost it. Thumped her on the face, knocked her down. Started ranting about her being useless, being drunk all the time.'

'Bloody hell.'

'I told her to lock herself in a spare bedroom tonight. Said I'd meet her tomorrow. Just hope to God Pete's calmed down by then.'

'So what are you going to suggest when you meet her?'

'Frank, I haven't the slightest idea. I'll need to see what sort of state she's in first.'

Frank didn't want to hear any more. There'd been too much information already. Jack and Pete at loggerheads? What could have happened? Might Jack have found out about Pete and Judith? After all these years? Would Pete assume it was he, Frank, who'd told Jack? And if so, what would Pete do?

But Pete had always been a boaster. Frank was unlikely to have been the only person in whom he'd confided about his conquests. It could have been anyone who'd told Jack, couldn't it? This thought brought some comfort. But not much.

When he got up the next morning, much earlier than usual, Angie was asleep. He'd been conscious of her restlessness during the night: he'd also had difficulty sleeping. He decided not to disturb her by taking up her usual cup of tea in bed. In any case he wanted to leave for work before she woke, to avoid the constraint he knew there'd be between them. But he couldn't just leave her like that, could he? To depart without their usual farewell kiss and expressions of hope that each would have a good day would only add to the situation he realised was verging on estrangement. So he scribbled a note – *Darling, you were sleeping soundly so I decided not to disturb you. Got a busy day today, so left early. Have a good day. Love, Frank* – and left it on the kitchen table.

He had an hour to himself in the office before Brenda arrived. The post had yet to be delivered, he'd cleared his in-tray and checked for emails before leaving on Friday. There were no outstanding matters needing urgent attention. He found himself at a loss to know how to occupy himself, something which was occurring with increasing frequency because he was allowing the business to wind itself down in preparation for his retirement. He'd never been one for marketing the company, preferring to rely on old contacts and their word-of-mouth recommendations, a method which was becoming ever less effective as the contacts themselves retired, or in a few cases died.

But today, it occurred to him that he'd miss one of the benefits arising from work. He'd been looking forward to retirement, to spending more time with Angie at the Bridge Club, to them joining other societies, having longer holidays, just being together more. Unlike some of his business contacts, he'd never needed the office as a place of refuge from the strains of married life. Not until this morning.

There would have been no business emails sent over the weekend, nevertheless he logged on for want of anything else to do. In fact, there *was* an email in his inbox, and it was from Tim.

It had been several weeks since Frank had replied to Tim's first message, and he'd begun to think that despite the restoration of contact there might be no further interchanges. Given the way he was feeling this morning he was glad of the distraction. He opened the email.

His first reaction was one of disappointment, for a cursory glance revealed the message to be contained in only a few lines. But they referred him to an attachment and said that he, Tim, hoped Frank would give sympathetic consideration to what was said.

Intrigued, he downloaded the attachment and opened it. Bloody hell, it was four pages. He started to scan-read it. After the first few paragraphs he realised the contents were so personal and revelatory that they required careful concentration and re-reading, not something that could be done by peering at the computer screen, which in any case always resulted in his getting a headache. But the printer was in Brenda's office, and he'd never taken the trouble to learn how to operate it. He thought about having a try, but was worried he might bugger up the machine, or worse, somehow lose the attachment. The operation of office technology had never interested him: he left that to Brenda.

He glanced at his watch. Another half hour before she arrived. Despite the electronic version of the attachment being in front of him, he decided against reading it. Better to wait until after Brenda's arrival. He logged off and went into the small scullery adjacent to her office to make himself a coffee. Only after he'd poured boiling water into the mug did he remember there'd be no milk until she arrived.

Brenda placed a mug of coffee in front of him. Frank had noted her quizzical glance when the first task he'd asked her to undertake was to print out the email attachment, and her ill-concealed look of surprise when he'd stood over the printer extracting each sheet as it emerged. But, ever the professional, she hadn't commented when he'd taken the documents into his office instead of giving them her to peruse.

'Is there anything you'd like me to get on with while you're looking at the post, Mr Grayson?'

'Eh? Oh, not really, Brenda. All this might take a bit of time for me to prioritise.'

'In that case I'll do a bit of filing.'

'Righto.'

She didn't turn to leave, but remained standing beside

his desk.

'Are you all right, Mr Grayson?'

'Me? Yes, of course. Why?'

'It's just that … well, I hope you won't think I'm speaking out of turn, but you don't seem yourself this morning. And if you don't mind me saying so, you look very tired. Did you have a bad night?'

'Well, since you ask, Brenda, I didn't sleep too well. But I'm okay, nothing to worry about.'

'Good. At our age we need to look after ourselves, don't we? I'll get on with the filing.'

As she left the room, Frank realised, for the first time, how much he'd miss her when he retired. He took a swig of coffee and started reading Tim's document. When he'd finished he read it again, more slowly. There was a lot to take in.

The first part started almost as a confessional. Tim gave an account of his career, but the detail was not about the life of academic, more that of a Lothario, and one who'd taken pride in his seductions. Then the tone changed abruptly to one of self-pity, how he'd been forced to take early retirement, how he lived alone, without friends, mostly confined to his house. There were several paragraphs of this before he revealed why – that he was severely disfigured.

The second part was even stranger. It took the form of an impassioned plea for Frank's continued online friendship. He seemed obsessed by what Frank had previously told him about his estrangement from Pete. There were long recollections of their time together at school: how he'd always considered Pete to be a bit of a yob, how he was sure Pete had deserved his come-uppance. He went on to say how he'd be most interested to know who the woman was with whom Pete had dallied (he actually used the word 'dallied', a strange euphemism given the explicit account he'd given of his own affairs) and how Frank could tell him who it was, surely? He ended by saying Frank could be certain he'd treat the matter in the strictest confidence, how he would receive the revelation as confirmation of Frank's friendship.

Frank had always despised the term 'gobsmacked' which everyone now seemed to use, but now he found it entirely appropriate. It was as though he had, literally, been smacked in the face. He deleted the attachment, then gathered up the document, marched into Brenda's office and began feeding the pages through the shredder, glad it was one the few pieces of office equipment he knew how to use.

He left the office early, unable to settle to any work. He'd told Brenda to take the afternoon off, but she'd insisted on staying while he was still there. They left the office together, and on parting outside the front door she said 'I do hope you'll be feeling better tomorrow, Mr Grayson' and laid her hand briefly on his arm.

As he drove home, his thoughts were not only of Tim's email, but whether he should tell Angie about it, and if so, how much. She'd never met Tim, but would be interested in what he'd had to say about Pete. But then the familiar outrage he felt towards Pete overwhelmed him, heightened by Angie's obsession with counselling Marion, because bloody Pete was the cause of that.

Still racked by indecision, he reached his house and turned into the drive. There was a car parked in front of the garage, one he didn't recognise. As he walked past it on his way to the back door he noticed dents and scratches on the bodywork even though the car, an expensive one, was this year's model. It offended him: he scorned the growing tendency of the well-off to be cavalier about their possessions. No doubt it belonged to a young person. Who the hell was it? Apart from the kids, he and Angie had little contact with the youth of today.

The back door opened before he inserted his key. Angie stepped out, blocking his way in.

'Frank, we've got a visitor.'

'So I see.'

'Listen Frank, don't fly off the handle. It's Marion, she –'

'Oh Lord, no! What's she doing here? How long'll she be here?'

'Ssh, keep your voice down. She's in the lounge. She's very fragile.'

'Drunk, you mean.'

'No, she's not. Don't be so insensitive, Frank. Look, come into the kitchen. I've got something to tell you before you go in to see her.'

Frank refrained from saying that the last thing he wanted to do was see her, and followed Angela into the kitchen. She turned to face him and began to whisper.

'Angie, please speak up. Can't hear a word you're saying.' This was becoming a growing problem for him: people these days all seemed to mutter. Recently he'd begun to find it necessary to ask Angie to repeat herself when she spoke with her back to him.

'Marion will be staying here tonight.' She spoke with exaggerated slowness.

'*What*?'

'You heard. And *please* keep your voice down. She can't go back to Pete. She's terrified of him.'

'But why here? Why can't she go and stay with her kid? How long's she going to be here? Bloody hell, Angie, we're not social workers.'

'No, we're friends. At least, *I* am. She can't go to Sarah's because she doesn't want her to see her in the state she's in. When you go in and see her you'll see what I mean. She'll phone Sarah when she's fit to go. It could be a few days. Now, Frank, go in and say hello to her. And be nice to her, won't you.'

'Yes, all right, but I don't feel nice. I'm doing this for you, Angie. Okay, okay, I'm going.'

When he entered the lounge, he saw a woman sprawled on the settee whom he hardly recognised. It had been seventeen years since he'd last seen her, but even so her deterioration came as a shock. She'd put on a lot of weight, but then so had he. It was her face that had changed the most: once pretty, it was now bloated and plastered with badly applied make up.

'Hello, Marion. It's been a long time.'

'Hello, Frank. Don't I get a kiss, then?' They used to greet each other thus, back in the day.

He bent over her. At close quarters the make-up failed to disguise the cut on her cheek and the purple swelling round her eye. He pecked at the undamaged cheek and stood back.

'Sorry you've been in the wars.' God, what an inane remark.

'That's one way of putting it.'

He struggled to find anything more to say.

'Frank, I – '

'If you don't mind, Marion, I'd like to go and get changed and have a bit of a rest. Had a hard day. See you at dinner.'

Up in his bedroom, he paced around. He gave little thought to Marion, nor even to Angie. He was thinking only of himself. He was experiencing a strange emotion, one he'd never felt before. Alienation, perhaps, now it would seem he'd be a stranger in his own house for a while? Worry about how he'd manage in retirement without the distraction of work? It was both of these things, but something much more, a sense of loneliness. For the first time in his life, there was no one in whom he could confide. The people at the Bridge Club were only acquaintances with whom he and Angie occasionally socialised. His business associates were just that, associates. His fellow councillors were no more than political allies or adversaries.

There was only one potential confidante. Tim. Tim's expressed desire for online friendship now, suddenly, seemed to offer a refuge. He would reply to his email, provide the information he sought. If nothing else, their exchange of confidences would provide a distraction from his sense of isolation.

He didn't want to do it while Marion was in the house. It would have to wait until tomorrow. Probably for the best: it would fill the empty hours now so little work was coming in.

Jack

'Wotcha Jack!

Jack, walking to the library, looked up. It was Terry Baines.

'Oh, watcha Terry. Haven't seen you for some time. How are you, mate?'

'Doin' all right. How about you? Retired are yer?'

'No. Still working. Some time to go before I retire. Taking a day off. How about you?'

'I'm retiring next year, mate. About time our Dick took over the business. I'm gettin' too old to clamber up and down ladders. I'll be leavin' the firm in good shape: just hope the young bugger makes a go of it.'

'What will you do with yourself all day?'

'Well, for a start, me and the missus are thinkin' of buying one of them time-share villas in Spain. Be good to get a bit o' sun in winter.'

Terry Baines in a villa in Spain! Jack was bemused by the incongruity of the idea. Terry still had vestiges of his Teddy Boy past: what remained of his hair was greased back in a feeble quiff, though the greying sideburns were still luxuriant. Jack glanced at his cheek, yes, of course the scar was still there, the result of a knife-fight with Fred the Ted more than forty years ago. Maureen Hearne was the cause of the dispute, in which Terry had come off the worse. The incident had merited a small column in the *Bucks Examiner*. Both had been bound over to keep the peace.

After a few more exchanges they parted, Jack saying they ought to have a drink together sometime and Terry agreeing. Jack continued walking down the High Street, thinking about Terry and comparing the different paths they'd followed.

He'd been at Primary School with Terry, but Terry hadn't passed the Eleven Plus. He'd left the Secondary Modern at the age of 15, and taken a job as a painter and decorator in a local firm. Jack had seen him occasionally in the High Street, a member of a gang of Teds that used to march aggressively down the pavements jostling people into the road. Jack had taken care to avoid him – Grammar School boys were often selected as the gang's prey – and had been amazed to discover some twenty years later that he'd started his own decorating business. The business had prospered: vans bearing the legend *T. Baines and Son* had become a common sight in the town, and Terry had moved from the terraced house in Red Lion Street to a large detached along Chartridge Lane. And now – a villa in Spain, for God's sake!

Where did I go wrong, Jack wondered, me with my Grammar School education and five reasonable GCE 'O' Levels? Might it have been better to have failed the Eleven Plus, to have leaned a trade and maybe prosper as Terry had done? But had he not gone to Grammar School he would never have got to know Jude in those days before she transformed herself into the seemingly unattainable beauty who'd walked into the *George* that unforgettable evening. If he hadn't been friends with her at school he would never have had the courage to talk to her, would probably never have married her.

Over recent weeks, he'd been thinking a lot about their marriage. It hadn't been a bad one in most respects. He doted on Jude, and she was usually affectionate and caring, though he'd suspected from the outset that her feelings for him didn't quite match the passion he felt for her. But passion wasn't really the right word, was it? It had erotic overtones, implied things such as lust, seduction, an active libido. He'd failed her in that respect. She'd been very sweet about it, and had continued to be, though there'd been that period when she'd withdrawn from him, when she found she could never have children and that it was her problem as much as his. So, with something akin to relief, he'd stopped trying. But the one good thing about growing old was that the physical side of marriage became unimportant, and they'd settled into a quiet contentment, each solicitous of the other's welfare.

Until recently. Over the past few weeks, she'd begun to withdraw again, be less affectionate, less interested in the things he had to say. It had taken him a while to grasp the reason for this. It was that bloody computer. She spent hours at the thing, emailing her mates, though why the hell she needed to when she saw most of them quite frequently he couldn't understand. She never told him what they spoke about – spoke, was that the right word? He'd considered challenging her about it, but held back, conscious that she'd tried her best to teach him to use the bloody thing before he'd admitted he couldn't grasp it.

But last Sunday he'd had enough. Okay, she'd fallen over, hurt herself a bit, but she was in such a strange mood he might as well not have been there. She was still, after three days, behaving strangely, almost jumpy, as though she was expecting bad news. This couldn't be anything to do with her accident: he reckoned it might be something which had cropped up in her email exchanges.

So he'd come to a decision. If he couldn't beat her, he'd join her. See what this internet malarkey was all about. But he couldn't ask her to try and teach him again. He'd noticed the library offered computing classes for Senior Citizens on Saturday mornings. He wasn't quite a Senior Citizen, but he used the library so frequently he reckoned the librarian could be persuaded to stretch a point.

This was why he was taking a day off work. One good thing about he and Jude being unable to afford long holidays – he always had plenty of days leave owing to him.

PART FOUR

October-November 2002

Staffordshire

I'd started to read Frank's email when the telephone rang. I was already so engrossed that I only just picked the phone up in time: if it was another bloody junk call I'd give whoever it was a mouthful. British Telecom's so-called telephone preference system was worse than useless.

'Hello. Who's calling?'

'That sounded very aggressive, Dave. Hope nothing's upset you. It's me, Susie.'

'Susie! Sorry. I was concentrating on something.'

'Not too busy to speak to me, I hope?'

'Of course not. Didn't expect to hear from you so soon.'

'Would it be okay if I called in later this morning?'

'Yes, of course. It would be great to see you.'

And it would. Fascinating as Frank's email promised to be, it would come a poor second to a visit from Susie. Perhaps she'd already cleared things with her supervisor and she was coming to take me out on the promised trip to the country.

'I'll be bringing someone with me, your new counsellor. He's called Robert. He's a nice fellow: reckon you'll get on with him.'

The glow of anticipation I'd felt was extinguished. Frank's email was now a far more inviting prospect. I hated meeting new people, whoever they were.

'Dave? Are you still there?'

'Yes. I was hoping you'd be coming alone.'

'Can't do that yet, Dave. This meeting is part of the formal handover. My supervisor has okayed the idea, but I need to be present when you and Robert first meet, just to oil the wheels. It'll be easier for both of you if a third party's present. If everything goes well, the changeover will be signed off when I get back to the office.'

'And that'll mean you'll no longer be my counsellor?'

'That's right.'

'And we can then – '

'Don't get ahead of yourself, Dave. There's something you need to know before you meet Robert. He's been brought up to speed about your case; he knows as much about it as I do, which isn't much, is it? So he won't be going over old ground. But that doesn't mean you can't tell him things you've chosen not to tell me, if you want to, of course. You might find it easier to divulge things to a man.'

When she'd first become my counsellor Susie had told me that all she knew about my case was that I was the victim of an assault, that my assailant hadn't been charged. Maybe some NHS manager, several career rungs above Susie, knew all the details, but these weren't divulged to practitioners? Susie had said that counsellors were required to approach their clients with an open mind but that when we got to know each other better, if it would help me to tell her more of what had happened, then I could do so.

But I never had told her more, because she was a woman and I doubted a woman would be sympathetic to my case, however professionally disinterested she might claim to be. But I certainly wouldn't confide in this Robert guy. He'd be a stranger.

'Would eleven be a good time to call then? We'll only be there about half an hour.'

'Yeah, that's ok. It'll be instant coffee, though. Not wasting the proper stuff on this Robert fellow.'

'Ever the gentleman, Dave! See you at eleven.'

As Susie made the introductions in the hall, my first impression of Robert was one of overwhelming hairiness and height. He must have been well over six feet: his hair was ginger, as was his luxuriant beard. He looked me in the eye as we shook hands, and his grip was firm.

'Good to meet you, Dave.'

His accent was Scottish, the sort of Edinburgh lilt I always associated with *The Prime of Miss Jean Brodie*. His size, his hair and his brogue immediately suggested a private nickname for him: Robert the Bruce.

'And you, Bru-… Robert. Come through.'

As I ushered them into the kitchen, I appraised Susie for the first time. She'd reverted to her usual look – short skirt, hair untied, make-up. A signal to me that our accord was fully restored, perhaps? Of course there was always the possibility she was dolled up to impress Robert the Bruce. No, nonsense. It was her usual look, known to, and no doubt appreciated by, all her colleagues and clients, the male ones at least. After years of self-imposed purdah, I'd forgotten the heightened awareness of the possible delights and disappointments that came with a developing relationship, and I was reading too much into things which of course had no significance.

We sat with our coffees on three sides of the kitchen table. When I'd arranged the chairs I'd wondered what the seating arrangement would be – would Susie sit opposite me as usual? But no, she indicated she and the Bruce would face each other and I should sit at right-angles to them. I had to stop myself from once again reading too much into a situation. The seating arrangement was probably in accordance with a Counsellors' Manual, a protocol for the handover of clients.

We chatted. There was no other way to describe the conversation; nothing about my case history, nothing about my state of mind. The Bruce seemed interested in my career: where had I been an undergraduate? What was my subject? Where was my first lecturing post? When did I start lecturing at Keele? Was it a rewarding profession? At first my replies were monosyllabic, but prompts from Susie encouraged me to open up. The Bruce maintained eye contact with me throughout except when he addressed a remark to Susie. There wasn't a hint of his eyes flickering over my face: he'd obviously been well briefed. I found myself talking animatedly, without so much as a single stammer, about university politics, former colleagues, students, my research. Susie had heard it all before, of course, but she kept nodding encouragingly.

I felt obliged to reciprocate by asking the Bruce about his career.

'After Highers I left school and went into social work as an unqualified assistant – aye, you could do that back in the late 1960s.'

The late 1960s? Christ, how old was this fellow? Difficult to gauge under the beard. If he'd left school that long ago he must be near to my age. Why wasn't the beard grey?

'But after about five years,' he continued, 'I realised I needed qualifications if I were to get anywhere. So I applied to university, to do Sociology.'

'Which university? Edinburgh?'

He laughed. 'No. I wanted to get away. I went to York.'

York. *York*. Just to hear the name of the town was a punch in the guts. Oh God.

'When were you there?' I think I managed to make the question sound casual.

'From 74 to 77. After I graduated I lived there for a while, got my first job there. That's where I met my wife – not at university, she was a town lassie.'

'How long did you stay there?'

'Oh, till 85, or was it 86? Then my career took me elsewhere. I fancied specialist trauma counselling rather than generic social work. Meant I had to join the NHS. Haven't climbed the career ladder though. I prefer contact with clients. I don't think – '

'Have you ever been back? Do you still go back?'

'Back? Back where?'

'To York.'

'Yes, a lot, to visit my parents-in-law, when they were

118

alive. My wife still hankers after the place and – '

'When did they die? Your wife's parents, I mean?

He hesitated, looked at me quizzically. I heard Susie clear her throat, no doubt prior to stepping in.

'Her father died in 88. Her mother lingered on 'till 96, poor wee lady. She had dementia towards the end.'

'Did you go up to see her often?'

'Dave,' Susie broke in. 'what's all this about? Look, I think it's time we sorted out the arrangements for future visits, don't you, Robert?'

The Bruce began talking, but I wasn't listening. I was thinking - his wife's parents, residents of York, no doubt avid readers of the local press. But if the mother had dementia before 1996 …

'Dave? Are you with me?

'Eh? Sorry?'

'I was saying, would you like to continue with a visit every month like you've had with Susie?'

'Oh. Yes, Whatever. I mean, if that suits you …'

They left soon after. Susie ceremoniously handed her keys to my front door to the Bruce, who shook my hand again and said he'd see me in a month, and then they were gone, without so much as a smile from Susie.

I went back to the kitchen and slumped in my chair. The Bruce's revelation about his association with York had shattered me. Of all the ghastly coincidences – or was it a coincidence? Might the management of the Counselling Service have deliberately chosen him to replace Susie? But if so, why? They'd learn nothing more than they probably knew already, and hadn't Susie said such details were never revealed to practitioners? No. I was falling prey to a ludicrous conspiracy theory.

And, thinking rationally, if Bruce's mother-in-law had died in 1996 and had dementia before that, then he and his wife would have had little interest in local press reports when in York. And of course the woman may well have died before August, the month in which my life-changing

119

event had occurred.

There was probably nothing to worry about. No, there wasn't, I convinced myself. I got up, rinsed the empty coffee mugs, and went up to the study. Frank's e-mail awaited me. It would act as a welcome diversion.

I read Frank's email twice, then sat rigid. It was certainly a diversion, but not a welcome one. Buried amongst the outpourings of angst concerning his forthcoming retirement and the strained relations with his wife was the revelation I'd been waiting for. For a fraction of a second I experienced the arousal that comes from being party to salacious gossip, but this was immediately overtaken by shock and then by deep burning anger.

Initially it was directed at Pete. From what I'd learned about him from Frank, it was only to be expected. Then, as my mind ran through the scenario again, it was Judy who became the focus of my wrath. How could she? It was me, her first lover, whom she'd betrayed. The fact that she'd married Jack mattered not: he was a safe pair of hands to whom she'd probably turned merely for comfort once I'd left the area. He was a virtuous dullard, had probably got religion: he was always a bit that way inclined, sanctimonious probably.

And thinking about it, had he been a proper husband to her she would probably never have been tempted to stray. No doubt she'd got bored with him, who wouldn't? What must it be like for an attractive vivacious woman to be married to a God-botherer like him?

No, I couldn't really blame her. As for Pete, my anger towards him had diminished to mere irritation. It all came down to Jack: it was he who was responsible for what had happened. It was all his fault.

Was I being irrational? I tried to analyse my feelings. If I'd been around at the time, wouldn't I have done the same as Pete? Probably. But it wouldn't have been just an opportunistic shag. I'd have laid claim to her, and things would have turned out differently for both of us. I wouldn't be as I was now. No, Jack's inadequacies were responsible for all that had happened, for shattering the perceptions I'd had of my youth. Fuck rationality: he should be made to pay for it.

Buckinghamshire

Pete

She must be at Sarah's, he decided. But he was buggered if he was going to give her the satisfaction of him phoning her, the stupid bitch. She'd done this sort of thing once before, after he'd lost his temper. No doubt she'd come home tomorrow, tail between her legs.

So he settled himself in front of the TV with a bottle of Scotch and a packet of fags. He found himself drinking quickly, glass after glass, and the gameshows and soaps had become merely a background irritant. So, slightly pissed, he went to bed. It was something of relief to be alone, knowing he'd not be disturbed by Marion's snoring. And her farting. She'd become a noisy farter when she began piling on weight. And when she wasn't farting her guts were rumbling. Christ, she was becoming an old woman before her time: how long would it be before she added belching and dribbling to her repertoire?

He woke, with a headache, at six o'clock after a night in which he'd dreamed about Judy. The dreams were elusive, but they'd been arguing. She'd said she never wanted to see him again. As he stumbled out of bed he was hit by the realisation that the dream was founded on fact. This had the effect of intensifying his headache.

On weekdays, he was used to eating breakfast alone – Marion rarely rose until ten – but the actions of boiling the kettle, cutting the bread, inserting the slices in the toaster, usually undertaken without thought, seemed weighted with a new significance now they were being performed in an empty house. It occurred to him that for those who lived by themselves, early mornings were probably lonelier than their evenings when at least they could go out, socialise, or at worse have the company of the TV or a CD, or even a book.

He set out for work in a sombre mood. It was overcast and drizzling, a likely foretaste of the five gloomy months ahead. Bloody hell, the clocks would be going back in two weeks. He found the short winter days depressing. They never used to worry him when he was a young man, he never even noticed the dark mornings and evenings when a teenager. Was this awareness brought about by his advancing years, he wondered? Who was it who'd spoken about raging against the dying of the light? Some poet, probably. Pete didn't like poetry, never read any, thought poets were a bunch of wankers, but the line about the dying light he'd heard once on the radio and it had grabbed him.

At least his business premises in Wendover were light and spacious. He had his own office of course, a much more intimate room, but furnished according to the fashion of the day, though he'd had to seek the advice of his secretary about that. He still enjoyed his work, except when he ran up against the objections of those tossers in the County Planning Department. It kept him very busy, and this morning was no exception. He was having to prepare for a meeting with one of his developer clients, and needed to chivvy his staff so they had all the designs completed and ready to run off paper copies.

Thus engrossed, he gave very little thought to Marion, until he took a break for lunch. He was chewing through a ham sandwich bought for him by his secretary when he remembered she still hadn't contacted him. He decided to call her on her mobile. But there was no reply. There was no point in leaving a voicemail message: she never answered them. So he fished out his Blackberry and sent her a text – *Assume you're at Sarah's and you'll be back this afternoon. Please confirm. We can go out for a meal tonight if you want.*

His afternoon was equally busy. There was a lot of correspondence to deal with. He didn't like answering letters. He used to try to dictate his replies to his secretary, but gave this up because she was an articulate woman and he was embarrassed by his lack of verbal fluency. So most of the time, she composed the letters and gave them to him to sign. But she couldn't handle the more technical correspondence, and for that he had to draft out replies on his PC which he then forwarded to her to amend and print out. This was equally embarrassing because there were always a lot of amendments, mostly corrections to his grammar and punctuation. English had been his worst subject at school. Frank Grayson and Tim Bailey used to mock his essays, the sods.

So it wasn't until five-thirty when he was preparing to leave when it occurred to him: Marion hadn't replied to his text. Not surprising. It would be just like her to ignore it and to have returned home, there to greet him casually when he came in as though nothing untoward had occurred, and then grudgingly prepare a meal.

But when he got home, her car wasn't in the drive. He went inside: everything in the kitchen and lounge was just as he'd left it. What the fuck was she playing at? He picked up the phone and tapped in Sarah's number.

'Hello?'

'Sarah, it's Dad.'

'Oh, hi Dad.'

'Will you put your mother on, please?'

'Mum? She's not here.'

'What time did she leave?'

'What d'you mean? She hasn't been here at all. What's going on?'

'Oh. Oh, God, sorry. Just remembered. She was meeting a friend this afternoon. Said she'd be back after six. She'll probably be here any minute. Forgot all about it. Sorry, Sarah.'

'Dad, are you okay?'

'Yes, of course, why shouldn't I be?'

'It's just you sound a bit strange. Is everything all right?'

'Yes, yes. Just tired. Had a busy day. I'll speak to you again soon. 'Bye, Sarah.'

'But Dad – '

He turned off the phone.

He wandered into the kitchen, rummaged in the fridge for a ready-meal to heat up. Mingling with his anger was a slight trace of worry. Had she got pissed and crashed the car? He'd give it until sevenish and if she hadn't turned up by then he'd better start phoning the emergency services. Cursing to himself, he extracted a pizza and put it in the oven. As he was doing so, his Blackberry buzzed.

He pounced on it: a text from Marion. *Am staying at Angela's tonight, will prob stay for a few days. Got to sort myself out, then we must talk. Don't try to contact me. Don't tell Sarah I'm not at home.*

He drove towards Aylesbury. He couldn't face staying in. He had to do something, though God knows what, anything to stop his brain constantly recycling that text message. Bitch. Stupid bitch. Yeah, she needed to sort herself out, but what was there to talk about?

He drove through the sprawling estates on the edge of the county town, taking care to avoid the street where he and Marion had once lived, the local shopping arcade they'd frequented, the primary school which Sarah had attended. They'd been happy then, he an enthusiastic young architect in a local practice, she a doting young mum and a loving wife. It had all started to go wrong when he'd accepted the financial backing provided by Marion's father. Marion then had the whip hand, had insisted on Sarah going to private school, had demanded they move out to the house in the country. That bitch never let him forget that he was where he was today because of daddy's help. Bollocks. He could have made it by himself, given time, couldn't he?

He found himself approaching the inner ring road. The

County Hall loomed over it, a brutalist concrete structure completed back in 1966, when Frank was still articled to the firm in his home town. He'd caught a bus to Aylesbury especially to see it. He'd thought the building was great, the sort of thing to which all modern architects should aspire. But now he found he felt ambivalent about it. Why? He couldn't articulate the reason. It was yet another example of the uncertainty he'd recently begun to feel about everything. Uncertainty was a sensation unfamiliar to him.

A drink. He needed a drink. Not a drink for its own sake of course, but to be part of the bonhomie to be found in a pub. He didn't know anyone in the town, but maybe he could get chatting to some of the locals. Trouble was, he didn't know any of the pubs. When he socialised his with clients or business associates it was always in the lounge of a hotel. He didn't want to run into any of them tonight, not in his present mood. He decided to wander round and see what the place had to offer.

He parked his car in the multi-storey and walked into the Market Square. At least it had stopped raining, but it was overcast and gloomy, already starting to get dark. The only people about were young teenagers, well, he assumed they were teenagers, it was hard to tell these days. They lounged around in groups, the lads and the girls in separate gangs, eyeing each other up, the lads guffawing, the girls screeching. He could overhear snatches of conversation and was shocked by their language: every remark was punctuated by the likes of 'fuck' or 'slag' or 'wanker'. Christ, we hadn't spoken like that, had we? Not when girls were around, anyway. Now, it seemed to be girls who swore most. Perhaps it was for the best he'd sent Sarah to a private school if these girls were typical of those at the local comprehensive – no, hang on, Bucks was still had a selective system: they'd be pupils at the local Secondary Modern or whatever it called itself these days.

He found himself adjacent to a group of girls. They were so engaged with each other that they paid him no attention. He loitered, started to observe them closely. Bloody hell, they couldn't be more than thirteen or fourteen. Pubescent breasts, boyish hips, thin legs – apart from the three or four who were overweight. Despite the cold their clothes were skimpy, figure-hugging. Was it because the wearers were little more than children that made it so disturbing? It brought to mind his schooldays when he used to ogle the girls in their gym-kits.

Then he noticed some of the boys were eyeing him. Bloody hell, he didn't want trouble. What was he doing, staring at girls young enough to be his grand-daughter?

He hurriedly walked away, full of self-disgust. What had got into him? More than ever, he needed a drink.

There was a pub across the Market Square. It looked unlikely to be the sort of place frequented by young teenagers, though hadn't he been only sixteen when he'd had his first drink in the *George*? What the hell. He went in.

The place was almost empty apart from a few blokes of indeterminate age standing by the bar. The room was large and packed with empty tables, not the sort of cosy place he'd been seeking, but he went to the bar and ordered a pint and a whisky chaser.

'You're a bit quiet tonight.' he remarked to the young woman who served him.

'It's Tuesday, innit? It'll fill up a bit later. You wanna see us on Fridays when we have bands in. That'll be six pounds fifty.'

He carried his drinks over to a table near the bar and sat down. He took a swallow from his pint, but it was the whisky he really needed, so he downed it in two gulps. So much for it being a chaser. He was tempted to go and order another one immediately, but didn't want to draw attention to himself: the blokes at the bar had stopped talking and eyed him suspiciously when he'd placed his order. Why? There was nothing wrong with him, was there?

Then it came to him: he hadn't changed when he'd got

home and was still wearing his suit and tie, the sort of gear that made him conspicuous to the clientele of a pub like this. They probably thought he was posh. Posh! If only they knew his origins! He sneaked a glance at the men, who were laughing uproariously at a joke one of them had cracked. They were younger than he'd first thought. Their clothes were casual, of course, and gave no indication of their social status. These days everyone seemed to dress the same. It was hard to know how to speak to young strangers, whether to be polite and use standard English, or address them as 'mate' and adopt the strange cocknified accent that most people under thirty now used. He was suddenly reminded of his grandfather, who'd had the old Bucks accent and pronounced Aylesbury as 'Owlsbury'. 'I'm just a-goin' stiddy over to Owlsbury,' he used to say.

Remembering that made him smile, and he said the word 'Owlsbury' several times, out loud, to see if he could still mimic the pronunciation. He wasn't aware the young men had stopped chortling. He was still smiling when a fist thumped on the table in front of him. He jumped, looked up.

'You takin' the piss, mate?' The speaker wasn't big and burly, indeed he was almost emaciated. His sharp features were misshapen, his thin lips screwed into a scowl.

'Eh? Sorry?'

'You 'eard.'

'Look, I'm sorry, but I've no idea what you're talking about.' He smiled ingratiatingly.

Weasel features were thrust close to his face. 'Wipe that fuckin' grin off yer face, you ol' fucker.'

'But look, mate, you've misunderstood – '

A hand reached out and grabbed his lapel, started dragging him up from his chair.

'Kevin! That's enough!' It was the young woman from behind the bar. She came over. 'Cut it out! You've been warned about this sorta thing. If you don't want Albert to ban you, yer'd better drink up and get out.'

Pete was released and received a shove which thrust

him back in his chair. His assailant, muttering, turned back to the bar and reached for his drink. His mates gathered round him and there was a muted conversation, punctuated by glances directed at Pete.

The young woman said 'Sorry about that' and returned to her post. 'Right, you've finished your drink, Kevin. Now get out. Otherwise I'll call Albert.'

More mutterings ensued, then the whole group swaggered towards the door, each member glowering at Pete. The door closed behind them: Pete exhaled in relief. His heart was pounding. He reached for his whisky, forgetting he'd emptied the glass what now seemed like hours ago. He needed another. When he got up to walk to the bar he found his legs were trembling.

'A double Scotch, please. And one for yourself. Thanks for rescuing me.'

He was served the drink, and he downed it in one.

'If I was you, mate,' said the woman, 'I'd stick around in here for a while. Give Kevin and his mates time to get well clear.'

That provided the excuse he needed. He asked for another double Scotch. The woman obliged. She peered at him.

'Look, mate, why don't you take your drink over to the lounge area?' She indicated an area furnished with easy chairs and settees on the other side of the island bar. 'It's, like, comfier there and the people who use it are more like your sort, if y'see what I mean. Young, though.'

It was meant well, Pete supposed. He thanked her, picked up his glass, and made for the lounge.

It was certainly more comfortable in the lounge area, but he was not at ease. His encounter with the teenagers in the street and the men at the bar had shaken him to the core. Was this how life was among the underclass? Pete had read about the country's underclass in the *Daily Mail*, but had always assumed it was confined to the large conurbations. But in Aylesbury? Of course there'd been an influx of London overspill; that might account for it, and there was also a sizeable Asian community, not that he was prejudiced of course. But it wasn't the place he'd once known, and certainly not the Owlsbury his granddad used to visit.

He'd been gulping at his Scotch: the glass was nearly empty. Perhaps he ought to go easy, but then he remembered why he was here. It was to get away from an empty house, to try not to obsess about Marion's betrayal, that bitch, leaving him to go and stay with Frank's wife … *oh Christ*! She wouldn't just be with Angela, would she? Frank would also be there, in the evenings. A vision came to him of the three of them eating dinner together, discussing him, no doubt. Frank would be loving it. And he might … yes, he *would*, the bastard, he'd let slip, oh so innocently of course, about Judy, and then Marion would have the excuse to leave him, and she'd take half the money with her, and …

He leapt up, stumbled, righted himself, and went to the bar.

'Another double Scotch, please.'

'Are you all right, my friend?' It wasn't the woman. She'd been joined behind the bar by a man, not a young man, but built like brick shit-house. Albert, maybe.

'Yes, course I'm all right. I'll have a half of bitter to go with it.'

The drinks were served, somewhat grudgingly. He carried them back to the lounge, where he was no longer alone. A group of young people had entered while he was being served and were settling themselves down round a table opposite him. One of them was standing, asking each of the others what they wanted to drink. Pete noticed he was quite well spoken, by the standards of the day. That was a relief. No likelihood of any bother from them.

He reached for his whisky glass, emptied it in three swallows. At last, a welcome warmth began to spread through him. The thought of Marion, Angela and Frank sitting together still produced anger, but it was muted

129

because other thoughts intervened, disconnected thoughts. Then the animated chatter of the young people opposite swept over him in waves: he studied them, how old were they, late teens, early twenties? Were they dressed smartly? Couldn't really say. Nothing to indicate what tribe they were in. Did young people have tribes these days? Like the Teds and the Mods and Rockers, and the Hippies, and the Punks, and who were that lot who were around when Sarah was a kid? New Romantics, was it? Sarah. Oh God, she might blame him, 'cos her mother would get to her. Maybe he'd phone her when he got home, get his oar in first.

Hilarity from the group opposite. Hard to focus on them, but the girls looked nice. One in particular: slim, long dark hair, lovely smile, great legs. Just like Judy used to look. Bloody hell, she really did look like Judy. Did she know how gorgeous she was? The bloke sitting next to her wasn't paying her much attention. Silly bugger. He'd lose her if he wasn't careful. She ought to be told she was lovely. No harm in that, surely?

He got up and walked with great care over to their table.

'Excuse me.'

Conversation ceased. All eyes turned to him. He leaned over the table towards the girl.

'Just wanted to tell you. You look like a girl I used to know. Judy, she was called. She was gorgeous, just like you.' He hiccupped. 'Hope you don't mind me saying so.'

There was a moment's silence, then the lad sitting next to the girl stood up.

'Yes, we *do* mind. You're pissed, you lecherous old sod. Go away. '

'But I was only – '

'You heard what he said.' This came from beside Pete. He turned to face the speaker, staggered, and fell across the table. The sound of overturned glasses, female screams, male shouts of anger. Dazed, Pete lay prone across the table.

He was hauled to his feet. 'Right, my friend, you're not welcome in here.'

It was Albert. Pete was frogmarched to the door.

He fell over twice on his way to the multi-storey. On the second occasion, when he found it hard to get up, he admitted to himself he was drunk. Pissed as an owl, in fact. Not up to driving home: he didn't want to damage the car. It would have to be a taxi.

He limped back to the Market Square. It had started to rain, heavily. His ankle was hurting and it was getting worse with every step. Where would he find a taxi? He couldn't see one. There was nobody about whom he could ask. He'd have to phone for one. He pulled his Blackberry from his pocket, dropped it, and nearly fell over again when he bent to retrieve it. He turned it on, but there were no local taxi firms in his list of contacts. He began to feel not only drunk, but ill, and breathless. He had to get home, had to go to bed. What could he do?

Salvation: he noticed a phone booth on the corner of the Square. Taxi firms advertised in phone booths, didn't they? He managed to reach it without falling over, but got soaked in the process. Once inside he was assailed by the stench of urine. The bloody underclass again. But there were several adverts for taxi firms on the wall. He selected one, and tapped out the number on his Blackberry.

The bloke who answered seemed to find it hard to get what he was saying. He sounded Asian: all the taxi companies were run by Asians these days. The buggers never seemed to understand plain English. It took a long time to sort out where he wanted to go and all the while he felt progressively more ill.

The fellow insisted that he'd be picked up outside the pub in the square. The last place he wanted to be, and it meant another trek across the square in the rain. By the time he got there he was exhausted, his heart thumping, and the pain in his ankle was agonising. He had to sit down. He lowered himself carefully, squatted on the kerb and was seized by a fit of coughing.

Eventually, a taxi pulled up beside him. The driver remained seated. Pete tried to get up, but couldn't. The driver got out and stood over him.

'Are you ill, sir?'

'Not feeling too good. Give me a hand up, would you?'

After a moment's hesitation, the driver obliged. Once on his feet, Pete turned to thank him. As he spoke, the driver recoiled.

'Are you drunk, sir? I don't carry drunks in my taxi.'

'No, no, not drunk. I've hurt my ankle. Give me a hand to get in, please.'

The driver made no move to help him.

'Look, I'll pay you double the fare. Just get me home.'

Another long hesitation, then he was helped to clamber into the back seat, and the taxi set off.

He was so relieved to be on his way that it took a while for him to register they weren't going along the main road. He started to tell the driver, but he couldn't be heard over the wailings of Asian music being played on the radio.

'Hey!' he shouted. 'This is the wrong way!'

The radio was turned down. 'This is the most direct route, sir. The cheapest for you.' The radio was turned up again.

He sank back in his seat, peered out of the cab. It was pitch black, rain was streaming down the window. They were in open countryside, but he wasn't sure where. The taxi was jolting over the rough surface of the country lane, and he began to feel very ill indeed. There was a pain in his chest and upper arm. Waves of nausea assailed him.

'Stop! Stop the car!'

The taxi came to a halt. He fumbled to open the door, but it was locked. He vomited copiously over the upholstery.

The driver leapt out, yanked open the rear door.

'Get out! Get out! You drunk! You dirty my taxi!'

Pete, his hand clenching his stomach, was unable to move. 'Sorry, sorry. I'll pay you triple the fare.'

'Not enough! When you home, I wait while you clean my car.'

The anger which had been assailing him at intervals throughout the evening rose to the surface, redoubled.

'Clean your car? Who the fuck d'you think you are, you Paki bastard?' he bellowed, then vomited again.

Next minute, he found himself sprawled on the grass verge of the lane.

'Find your own way home!' the driver shouted at him. The taxi drove off.

He lay on the verge, unable to rise. He was aching all over; the pain in his upper arm had intensified. Then his guts began to churn. Oh God, he was going to shit. Couldn't shit here, not by the road in full view of any car that might pass. He raised himself on one elbow, looked around. Behind him was a hedge, but a few yards to the right was a farm gate. It wasn't fully closed. If he could get to it, go through into the field, get behind the hedge... He managed to get up on all fours and crawled towards the gate, got through it, crawled a few more feet so he was behind the hedge, unzipped his trousers. But he couldn't stand up to pull them down. His bowels emptied.

He collapsed back on the sodden ground. Panic overtook him. He groped in his jacket pocket for his mobile – must phone Judy, no, not Judy, Marion. But before he could grasp the phone, a weight began pressing on his chest, an intolerable weight.

Angela and Marion

Frank had phoned to say he'd be late home from work. Angela was unsure if she was relieved or disappointed.

On the one hand, it meant there'd be fewer hours in which she'd be required once again to prompt him to exchange at least a few civil words with Marion. The situation the previous evening had been as though she were an arbitrator between two estranged parties, one

133

desperately seeking rapprochement, the other on the verge of initiating hostilities. Over dinner, Marion, once three glasses of wine had been imbibed, had tried to engage Frank in conversation – how was his business? Wasn't a bit boring being a Councillor? Had he ever thought about taking up golf? Was it he who'd chosen the décor for this room? How did he like his Cabriolet? Did he change his car every year? Although each question was answered at best monosyllabically, at worst with a grunt, this had not deterred Marion. She'd carried on the interrogation, until eventually Angela had had to repeat each question while frowning at Frank in the hope this might elicit a response. Arbitration had eventually broken down when Marion had said 'Now Frank, what was that silly quarrel you had with Pete all about?' which resulted in Frank getting up and asking to be excused: he had a headache and was going to bed.

But on the other hand, Frank's delayed return from work meant she'd be exposed alone to more of Marion's company, and this was not something she relished. As soon as Frank had left the dinner table last night, Marion had changed her record and began to recount a catalogue of all Pete's sins which included not only frequent slaps and the odd punch, but near-alcoholism, several incidents of rape, and threats to prevent her seeing Sarah. Angela had pointedly not produced a second bottle of wine after Marion had emptied the first, and said she had to get to bed. After escorting an unsteady Marion to the spare room, she'd gone to her own room to find Frank fast asleep. Or pretending to be.

This morning, Marion still hadn't appeared for breakfast by ten o'clock. Angela cleared the table of cereals and fruit juice and got on with the housework. At eleven-thirty Marion emerged, still in her nightdress and wearing the dressing-gown Angela had loaned her. She was not a pretty sight.

'Oh God, coffee, coffee!' she moaned, her voice rasping.

'Instant coffee in the cupboard behind you, milk in the fridge. Help yourself.'

'Rather fancied proper coffee. Can you make me one, Angie? Not sure I'm up to it.'

It was then that Angela felt a twinge of something more than irritation.

'Sorry, Marion. I'm a bit busy as you can see. You're welcome to proper coffee after lunch, if you can wait that long. I usually have a snack at one.'

There was the hint of a scowl, but Marion made herself a cup of instant, scattering coffee grains over the floor and slopping milk over the kitchen table in the process. She made no attempt to clear up.

She remained silent after that, went into the lounge and sprawled on the settee, reviving only when Angela served up a snack lunch. In the afternoon Angela wondered how she might broach the topic of how long Marion intended staying, but in the event it was just a matter of sitting and listening to her monologues about Pete and what a bastard he was. Angela had heard enough, got up and went to the kitchen. But Marion followed her, and said she'd be getting very hungry if dinner was going to be delayed because of Frank's late return from work and she didn't like eating much after six because it played havoc with her digestion, and did Angie suffer from bloating and trapped wind by any chance?

So it was a relief, at seven o'clock, to hear Frank's car pull up in the drive. When he entered, Angela registered the guarded expression he'd been wearing for days now, and his kiss of greeting was perfunctory. He went straight upstairs to change and didn't return until Angela called him to say dinner was ready.

Angela braced herself for a re-run of the previous evening's tense session of non-communication, and indeed Marion once again began to attempt to engage with Frank, but she was interrupted by the buzzing of her mobile phone, which, to Angela's irritation, she always placed on whichever table she was sitting at.

'Oh, it's Sarah. You won't mind if I take this?'

She didn't wait for a reply.

'Hello! Sarah, darling!'

'No, I'm staying with Angela and Frank for a few days …'

'Just felt like a change of scene, that's all …'

'I don't know. Why should I? He's often late home …'

'Oh, did he? Well, he's probably gone out again to eat, 'cos I wasn't there to cook for him, was I …'

'What d'you mean, sounded strange? Don't waste your sympathy on him, he doesn't deserve it …'

'Look, I'm in the middle of a meal. I'll phone you tomorrow. Bye, darling.'

She turned off her phone. 'That was Sarah,' she said unnecessarily. 'Getting in a stew because Pete isn't home. She keeps phoning him. She always was a daddy's girl.'

'But Marion,' said Angela, 'you're going to have to tell Sarah what's happened between you two, aren't you?'

'Well, I'm wondering about that. Maybe I won't go and stay with her after all, so there's no need for her to know.'

'But if you and Pete are going to separate …'

'Oh, it probably won't come to that. He knows which side his bread's buttered. But I'd like him to stew for a few more days. It's okay by you if I stay here for another week, I suppose?'

Angela sensed Frank turn rigid. She daren't look at him.

'We'll have to think about that, Marion.'

Frank went to load the dishwasher, then returned to tell Angela he was going up to his study and would probably be going straight to bed afterwards. He didn't say goodnight to Marion, and Angela didn't blame him.

Marion went straight into the lounge. Angela followed her, sat down and told her they needed to establish precisely how long she intended to stay.

'Can we talk about it tomorrow? I really don't feel up

to it tonight.' Then, without asking if it was okay, she switched on the TV.

Part of Angela was relieved. She felt very tired, not up to what would inevitably be an emotionally charged discussion. It could wait until tomorrow: yes, she'd do it over breakfast, assuming Marion would be up in time. She ought to be, because she hadn't drunk any wine tonight. Angela had told her they'd drunk the last bottle. Perhaps it was because of her enforced abstinence that she was less loquacious this evening, and as time went on she spoke hardly at all, appearing to concentrate on the mindless game-show on the TV. She even sat through the ten o'clock news bulletin, something she'd yesterday dismissed as being boring.

'Right, Marion,' Angela said, after they'd watched the weather forecast, 'If you'll excuse me, I'm off to bed. Why don't you get an early night as well? You look as though you could do with it.'

'Eh? Oh, no. There's a film on now I'd quite like to watch.'

'Okay. Don't forget to turn all the lights off in here when you've finished, will you? Goodnight.'

The bedside light was still on when she went in, but Frank appeared to be asleep, curled up on his side, his face towards the edge of the bed. She undressed quickly and got in beside him. He didn't stir.

She lay on her back, mulling over the events of the evening. But it wasn't Marion she began thinking of, it was Frank. Poor old Frank: she hadn't been very attentive to him over the past few weeks, had she? She'd been totally wrapped up with Marion and her problems, and now she was wondering why, because Marion was no longer the ebullient, affectionate friend she'd been when the two couples used to meet as a foursome. There was no denying it, she'd turned into a selfish, inconsiderate, rather sad woman. Okay, Pete had hit her, but had she really suffered the years of abuse she claimed? And if he had, maybe she'd invited it by her behaviour? God, what a heretical thought: there was no excuse for abuse. Thank the Lord she was married to a gentle, affectionate, thoughtful man who loved her.

And she loved him, very much. She turned on her side. The duvet had slipped down, and Frank's naked back was exposed. It wasn't the well-toned, muscled back it had been when they first married, in fact it was obese; the flesh around what had once been his waist was drooping. She felt a wave of affectionate sympathy for him, placed a hand on his shoulder.

He snorted, gave a half snore, then resumed his steady breathing. She ran her hand down his back, then up again, then began caressing it, increasing the pressure gradually.

He turned onto his back, eyes still closed.

'Frank.' she whispered.

His eyes opened. 'Angie? Wassa matter?'

'Frank. I'm sorry.'

'Sorry? What for?'

She put an arm round him, and her mouth close to his ear. 'Sorry for the paying so much attention to Marion,' she whispered. 'Sorry I invited her to stay. Sorry she's here. She's a pain in the bum. But she won't be here tomorrow night, I promise.'

'You mean you've told her to go?'

'Not yet. But I will, first thing tomorrow. I'll tell her she's got to go and stay with her daughter.'

'Oh, thank God for that.' He pulled her to him, kissed her. It was a long kiss. 'Bloody hell, Angie, I've missed you. It's good to have you back.'

He pulled her over him. 'Why don't you take off your nightdress?' he whispered.

***

Next morning. Marion lumbered back from the bathroom, wondering again why the hell Frank and Angela hadn't installed an en-suite facility in their guest bedroom. It wasn't as if they were short of a bob or two, after all. She

138

was tempted to get back in bed, but it was nine o'clock and yesterday when she'd got up late Angela had been a bit sniffy. In fact, she'd been a bit off most of the time, not the fun-loving Angie she remembered. It was probably living with Frank that had caused it: he'd turned into a miserable old bugger, could hardly exchange a civil word.

She rifled through her overnight bag to find clean underclothes. Shit, she'd only packed enough for a two-night stay. Maybe, if she felt up to it, she'd drive into Aylesbury to buy some more, enough to last for a week, maybe also buy another dress or two. Then she'd get round to unpacking her bag and storing things in that bloody antiquated chest of drawers.

Then she remembered. Last night Angie had said they needed to talk about how long she was intending to stay. That was strange, because she'd already mentioned she wanted to stay for a week, hadn't she? Had Angie's remark been a hint she was no longer welcome? If so, bloody Frank would be to blame for that, of course.

But there was no way she could go and stay with Sarah, not while her face was still bruised. Sarah would press her to tell her what had happened. She didn't want Sarah to know. Sarah was always inclined to take Pete's side in any dispute.

She'd better get downstairs while breakfast was still on the table. That might improve Angie's mood. She dressed hurriedly, put on a bit of make-up – the bruise was beginning to be less obvious – grabbed her mobile phone, and set off down the stairs.

Angela was sitting at the breakfast table, reading the *Guardian*, a strange paper for the wife of a Tory councillor to take, Marion thought.

She looked up.

'Oh, you're here. Just in time. I was about to clear the table. Help yourself to cereals and toast. There's still some coffee in the pot.'

There was a distinct lack of warmth in her tone, Marion noticed. She also observed that though it was only nine-thirty, Angela was smartly dressed, her hair immaculate, and she somehow managed to look twenty years younger than her age. She also looked … what was the word … replete? Marion was reminded of a line from a film or a book, she couldn't remember what it was, where a character had said – *She has the air of a woman who's being slept with. And slept with very well.* She felt a gripe of envy, and then, remembering that Pete had once described Angela as a very sexy woman, a twinge of dislike.

She didn't speak while she ate her breakfast. Neither did Angela. But once she'd finished eating and was drinking her coffee – it was lukewarm – Angela said 'Now, Marion. We need to talk about how long you're staying here.'

'Oh. Right. Well, you see, the problem is – '

Her mobile phone vibrated. Saved by the buzzer.

'Sorry, Angie, this is from Sarah. I'd better take it.'

She picked it up.

'Hello, Sarah, darling. This is – '

'Mum, listen. Dad still hasn't come home. I phoned him as soon as I woke, he didn't reply. Tried his mobile, it went straight to voicemail. So I – '

'What's the panic, darling? He probably – '

'No, *listen*, will you. I drove straight over to your place. He wasn't there. And his car wasn't there either, so – '

'He'd probably left for work.'

'For Christ's sake *listen*, mum. This was before eight o'clock. He never leaves that early, does he? So I went home, waited till just after nine, then phoned his office. Spoke to his secretary. He hadn't arrived. She said she'd ask him to phone me as soon as he did. But he didn't. So I rang his office again a few minutes ago, he still hadn't arrived. I tried his mobile again, but it's gone dead. I'm worried, mum.'

'I'm sure there's nothing to worry about, Sarah.'

'But there is! He sounded strange when I last spoke to

140

him. What's going on, mum? Why aren't you at home? Have you had a row? Don't you *care* what might have happened to him?'

'Well, I suppose –'

'Look. I'm going to phone the police. But you're going to have to go home, mum, because I'll have to tell them that's where dad lives. I can't go all the way over there. It's half term, can't leave the kids. You need to be there in case the police go round. Okay? How soon can you get there?'

'Well, in about an hour, I suppose, but –'

'Good. Ring me when you get there. I'm phoning the police now. I'll tell them you'll be home by eleven.'

'But – '

Sarah had rung off.

Damn him. This was a ploy, of course. Just like him. He was trying to make her feel worried, feel guilty. And Sarah had fallen for it.

'Marion? Are you all right?'

'What? Yes, of course. But I've got to go home. It's Sarah; she's in a bit of a state. In fact, I've got to leave now.'

She stood up. 'I'll get my coat. I'll leave the rest of my things here.'

'But … does that mean you'll be coming back? To stay, I mean?'

'Oh Christ, I don't know, Angie. I hope so. If you'll have me, that is.'

She went to collect her coat before Angela had a chance to reply.

Judith and Jack

It was Friday afternoon, and Judith had ambivalent feelings about Fridays.

Over recent years, she'd begun to get tired at the end of

141

the working week. She knew she was slowing up, mentally as well as physically, finding it harder to keep on top of the plethora of correspondence, phone calls and emails from worried or angry clients, and the constant requests from her boss to stop what she was doing for a moment, please Judith, and could she attend to this new case because it needed to take priority? And it was becoming harder to manage the junior staff. Some of them had begun to question her instructions because, they claimed, what she was telling them to do ran counter to what she'd told them to do the day before. She hated to admit it, but her brain worked more slowly than those of the youngsters in her charge, found it harder to assimilate new information and easier to forget things it had learned. And she often had a headache, brought on by constantly having to switch from reading-glasses to mid-range ones as she peered alternately at hard-copy documents and her computer screen. So by Friday afternoons she found she was looking forward to the prospect of two stress-free days.

But on the other hand, being at work gave her a focus. At the weekends she would be exposed to Jack's presence and the irritation it brought because, let's face it, he was such unstimulating company. And this week there was also guilt, because of the way she'd lied to him the previous Sunday.

Superimposed on her irritation and guilt was worry and uncertainty. Would Pete call for Jack on Sunday? If he did, how could she face him? If he didn't, what would Jack make of it? Might Pete perhaps phone Jack beforehand to make some excuse for not playing golf? Please God let it rain so no excuse would be needed.

But she couldn't face the prospect of a Saturday spent worrying about the following day. She came to a decision. There were ten minutes to go before she left the office. Time to send an email.

Pete. Please don't delete this before reading it. Let's try and put behind us what happened last Sunday for Jack's sake. I need to know if you'll be coming to collect him on Sunday, and if not, what reason you'll give. Please reply to my home address asap. I very much regret what happened between us and I hope you do too. Judith

As she walked home, it occurred to her that all this business had started because she'd been searching for Tim on *Friends Reunited*, but had only found Pete. She realised she hadn't given Tim a thought for weeks.

***

Saturday morning in the Library as usual, but Jack hadn't been engaged in family history research. He nodded to his fellow classmates as he left the computer room. It was good to know he wasn't the only one who'd been left behind by the advance of modern technology, and gratifying to discover that he seemed to be quicker than some of them at picking it up. The young man who took the class was very patient, far more patient than Jude had been with him. He hadn't told Jude he'd been attending the classes – she thought he was doing his family history researches – and was looking forward to telling her he'd now be able to go on-line. On second thoughts, perhaps he'd better wait until after next week's lesson before he told her. In any case, today might not be a good time. Jude had been in a strange mood all week, distracted, not really listening to the things he said.

When he got home he found her sitting at the computer. She was just staring at the screen. He said 'Hello, Jude' She jumped, and hurriedly logged off.

'Oh, hello. Are you going for a bike ride this afternoon?'

'Dunno yet. See what the weather's like. Looks like it might rain again.'

'What's the forecast for tomorrow?'

'Haven't heard it. Why?'

'I just wondered if you'd be off with Pete playing golf.'

'Why? Have you got something else planned for me?'

'Don't be so ridiculous! Of course I haven't!

Sometimes you do say the silliest things.' She got up. 'I suppose you'll be wanting your lunch now.' She walked past him, without looking at him, on her way to the kitchen.

Jack was crushed by her outburst. What had he said to deserve that? He'd genuinely thought she might want them to do something together; go for a walk maybe, or even go for a drive, though she'd once said she was ashamed to be seen in their old banger. But perhaps it wasn't what he'd said that had caused her flash of temper. There was obviously something worrying her. He knew better than to question her. No doubt she'd tell him when she was ready.

After lunch, which was eaten in silence, he went for his afternoon bike ride. He was relieved to be out of the house, but the ride didn't bring its usual sense of uplift even though the beech woods were at their spectacular autumn best, the leaves a melange of copper, russet and gold. Perhaps his mood resulted from the overcast skies? Rain looked imminent. No, it wasn't that. It was Jude.

I'm lucky to have her. Wasn't that always something he told his friends? They didn't know the half of it, didn't know how close they'd come to splitting up during the terrible time after she found she couldn't conceive, and the even worse time afterwards when he had to accept he could never be a proper husband to her. He'd always had problems in that respect, starting on their wedding night, and it had worsened after Jude's diagnosis. At first she'd thought this was because she'd lost her looks, and had been distraught. But then their prolonged, anguished conversations in which he'd managed to persuade her the problem was all his, had eventually brought them together again, but in a different relationship, one of mutual affectionate support. And so it had been for the past twenty-five years. He was content with that, and assumed she was also. Surely this was how it was for most couples of their age? So what could be the reason for her recent strange behaviour?

She seemed a bit more cheerful when he arrived home,

asked him if he'd enjoyed his ride, and over dinner chatted about her on-line friends. This, he thought, might provide him with a good opening to tell her about his computer classes, but she suddenly rose, went over to the radio, turned it on.

'It's time for the weather forecast,' she said.

Why the sudden interest in meteorology? He listened: the forecaster had the usual cheerful tone adopted when the outlook was indifferent, trying to emphasise the positive – sunny intervals but mainly cloudy with some outbreaks of rain.

She turned off the radio. 'Doesn't look like the weather for golf tomorrow, does it?' she said.

'Oh, I dunno. So long as it's not pouring it'll be okay. Pete never lets the odd shower put him off.'

'Why don't you phone him?'

'No need. He always rings me if he's decided not to come, doesn't he?'

She didn't reply, and began clearing the table. That was usually his job. He leapt up and said he'd do it, why didn't she go and relax in the lounge? She didn't reply to that either and began piling the dirty dishes onto the work-surface by the sink.

'You wash, I'll dry,' she said.

He pulled on his Marigolds and turned on the tap. It always took an age for the hot water to come through. Judith positioned herself by the draining rack, drying-up cloth at the ready. In the age of dishwashers, how many couples still went through this ritual, he wondered?

'Jack, listen.'

Her voice sounded strange, lower pitched than usual. He looked at her: she didn't return his glance. What was coming? An explanation for her behaviour? He felt a sense of foreboding.

'What is it, Jude?'

'I'm sorry. Sorry I snapped at you this morning.'

'Oh, that's all right, I reckon –'

'No, listen. When you asked if I had something else

145

planned for you tomorrow afternoon, something other than going out with Pete, I mean … well, I've been thinking. It'd be nice if we did something together for once, wouldn't it? If the weather's as bad as forecast, we could go out for a drive, couldn't we? Why don't we make a day of it? Maybe have lunch in a pub? You could give church a miss for once. Phone the vicar and tell him something's cropped up.'

Relief swept over him. So that was what had been troubling her, the fact they spent so little time together outside the house. She had *her* friends, he had … well, Pete. He turned, put his arms on her shoulders, pulled her towards him, made to kiss her.

'Take your Marigolds off, Jack! You're dripping all over me.'

He wrenched them off, grabbed her again, and they kissed. A fleeting kiss.

'That'd be great, Jude. I'll phone the vicar now.'

'And you'd better phone Pete as well, just in case he's intending to play golf.'

'Yes. I'll do it as soon as we've finished the washing up.'

'I'll finish it. You do your phoning now.'

***

As she continued with the washing up, Judith was only too aware her tactic would only bring a temporary reprieve. Tomorrow was sorted, but what about next Sunday, and the ones following? All the dreadful possibilities remained. And why hadn't Pete replied to her email? Harbouring a grudge about last Sunday, no doubt.

It was only when she began putting away the clean crockery she became aware Jack was still on the phone – she could hear his muffled remarks coming through the living room door. Why was it taking him so long? Oh Lord, what was Pete saying to him? It hadn't occurred to her until now that Pete might be … no, Pete wouldn't be so vindictive as to tell him about last Sunday.

Jack was putting down the phone as she entered.

'All sorted?'

Jack stared at her, his expression unfathomable. 'No, it isn't.'

'Why? What d'you mean?' *What's Pete told him?*

'I spoke to Sarah, Pete's daughter. Pete's in hospital, in Aylesbury. He's dangerously ill. Marion's with him. Sarah was just leaving to go there.'

Judith grabbed the side of the settee for support: the ground had seemed to shift beneath her.

'What's wrong with him?'

'Heart attack. A bad one. And that's not all. He was found early in the morning in a field just outside Aylesbury, by a dog walker. He'd been there all night, apparently. It was touch and go for a while.'

'In a field? But why?'

'Nobody knows why. His car wasn't nearby. It was found later that day in a car park in Aylesbury.'

'But … when did it happen?'

'He was found on Wednesday morning. They reckon he'd had the heart attack the night before. He'd had a lot to drink, apparently.'

Judith sank back onto the settee.

'Jude, It wouldn't seem right for us to go out tomorrow now, would it? In any case I'd like to go to church, offer up a … well, you know. It's a good job I didn't phone the vicar first. Would you like … would you consider coming as well?'

Now, more than anything else, Judith would have welcomed a comforting embrace, but all he had to offer was a seat in a pew. Had anything been to hand, she would have thrown it at him.

Staffordshire

The phone rang at last.

'Hello? Susie?'

'Yes. Are you okay for today, Dave? The weather's not so good, is it?'

'I don't mind a bit of drizzle if you don't.'

'Not at all. I'll be with you in about half an hour, then. See you.'

In fact, I welcomed the drizzle. It meant I could put up the hood on my anorak. If anyone approached I could look down - my face would be scarcely visible. Not that I anticipated meeting many people, not in this weather out in the empty countryside on the Shropshire border.

Had she chosen to call off our date – that's how I thought of it – I would have been devastated. She'd phoned only the day after her visit with the Bruce to suggest this Saturday for our walk, and I'd been in a state of fevered anticipation ever since. It was as though a long-broken link with myself as I'd been ten years before had suddenly been restored. There was an adrenaline buzz that came from the feeling anything was possible, however unlikely. It was as if my body had begun to exist again, that I was more than just a whirlpool of emotions trapped inside a battered container. Try as I might to damp down my expectations – it was only a walk with a friend, after all – I had a spring in my step, a song in my heart, and all the other clichés which describe the long-forgotten exhilaration that comes from the prospect of hours to be spent in the company of an attractive woman. And it wasn't even quite as I used to feel in my philandering, confident middle age – no, I felt more like a teenager, for whom the outcome of an assignation is often uncertain, the very uncertainty adding to the excitement.

And there was something else. Something I wanted to ask her to do after our walk. Something so personal, so weird even, that I was unsure whether a few hours in her company would be enough for our friendship to have deepened sufficiently for her to agree to it.

I paced about in the hall in my walking boots, back-pack and anorak ready to hand, impatient for her arrival.

148

When her outline appeared through the frosted glass I waited for the three long rings at the doorbell, but they didn't come. Instead she banged on the knocker. Of course! She no longer had a key! I stumbled over my backpack in my haste to reach the door.

'Hi Dave! All ready?'

She was wearing a sweater and loose-fitting jeans and her hair was tied back. A new, off-duty Susie. Almost a new acquaintance. Would we, I wondered, have to go through a new getting-to-know-you procedure now we'd be together in an unfamiliar environment unsupported by the rituals of the counselling process? I wasn't sure how to handle it.

'I'm ready. Why aren't you wearing boots, Susie? It'll be pretty muddy.'

'Can't drive in boots. They're in the car. Have you got some shoes in that back-pack?'

'No. Why?'

'Cos I don't want your muddy boots in the car when we've finished the walk, that's why.'

'Oh. Right. I'll get some.'

Cursing to myself, I charged upstairs to get some trainers. It was so long since I'd been in a car I'd forgotten the rules of passenger etiquette. Not a promising start to the day. I felt like a chastised child.

I got in the car, flung my back-pack in the back seat.

'Belt up, Dave.'

'Eh?'

'Seat belt.'

Bloody hell, something else I'd forgotten. I was no longer the chastised child, more a forgetful old man on the verge of senility. Was this how the day was going to be, constantly trying to remember how life was lived outside the confines of my home? Would I exhaust Susie's patience?

She drove through the estate and out onto the main road. I found I was gripping the seat. Travelling at more than walking pace was another thing I'd forgotten. And the roads were far busier than I remembered, and Jesus, surely people hadn't always driven at this speed? Susie seemed totally at ease, in fact to my mind she was driving aggressively, tailgating cars in front of her, executing snappy gear changes before accelerating to overtake, cursing under her breath when confronted with a queue of traffic. I'd never been a confident driver, hadn't liked petrol-heads, had disparaged those who behaved as Susie was behaving now. I was tensed-up, concentrating on potential hazards ahead, and would have found it hard to chat to Susie had she been talking to me. But she wasn't. The journey was being undertaken in silence.

At least she observed the speed limit while driving through Baldwin's Gate, and then had to drive sedately as the road wound through the hills on the other side. I'd always loved this stretch with the tree-covered red sandstone outcrops and the emerging view of pastures as the road descended. It still looked good, even in the November drizzle.

'Susie, I haven't been here for years. Would you mind driving a bit more slowly? I want to take in the countryside.'

'Of course. Sorry Dave, I wasn't thinking. Did you used to come out this way a lot?'

'Yes, quite a bit. It was when I was researching local landscape history.'

'Landscape history? You mean geology, that sort of thing?'

I thought I'd told her before about my research, but she probably hadn't taken it in. So I proceeded to put her right, told her about man's impact on the landscape, how present day scenery was a palimpsest of what had gone before, told her about how I'd been inspired by the work of WG Hoskins, pointed out we were driving through the landscape of eighteenth century parliamentary enclosure, started to tell her about my own research – then I stopped, realising I was back in the lecture theatre, on my hobby horse.

'Sorry, Susie. I'm being boring.'

She glanced at me. 'Not at all, Dave. It's nice to hear you being enthusiastic about something.'

Silence descended again as we drove through Loggerheads. Bloody hell, what had I been thinking of, giving her a history lesson? But what else could I talk about? Apart from our counselling sessions we had no shared experiences, and it struck me how little I knew about her and her history. I knew she was a Stokie – her education hadn't quite ironed out her Potteries accent – but I didn't know exactly where she lived, what her social life was like, what her interests were, what sort of music she liked, how she'd spent her youth. I didn't even know if she was married – I thought probably not, she didn't wear a ring. Divorced maybe? Was she in a relationship? Did she have kids? She'd never mentioned either a partner or children.

Just before we reached Market Drayton I told her to turn off the main road. I directed her along the narrow lanes which meandered through the undulating countryside of the Staffordshire-Shropshire border. We were heading towards Tyrley Locks on the Shropshire Union Canal, my intention being that we'd walk along the towpath before heading back through the fields and woods.

'Bloody hell, Dave, it's like the back of beyond out here.'

'Haven't you ever been here before?'

'Never.'

That didn't surprise me. I'd found Potteries folk rarely ventured out into the countryside to the west.

'What know they of Staffordshire who only Staffordshire know?' I said.

'Eh? What d'you mean?'

'Oh, I was quoting Kipling, or rather, misquoting him.'

She glanced at me. 'Bit of a clever bugger on the quiet, aren't you?'

Oh God, had I offended her? I tried to make amends by saying it was good that so few people knew of the area; it resulted in its remaining unspoiled, unaffected by tourism. She didn't reply to this, and we drove on in silence. The day wasn't panning out as I'd hoped. Clever bugger? Silly bugger, more like.

We parked by the lock and began walking along the towpath. It was muddy in places, which often necessitated walking in single file. Not conducive to conversation, but this didn't worry me too much: I was content just to experience a landscape other than that of my regular morning walk. The drizzle had eased so I pulled off my hood: as I'd anticipated there was nobody else around. Susie made the odd appreciative remark about the scenery and I took care to reply in similar fashion rather than treating her to another lecture.

When we left the towpath and set out across the fields we were able to walk side-by-side. I began a gentle interrogation about her past and her interests, steering clear of anything she might construe as prurient curiosity about her personal life. I learned she was born in Tunstall of working-class parents, had gone to the Polytechnic in Sheffield, had moved back to the Potteries after completing her post-diploma training and had lived and worked in the area ever since. She enjoyed her job. She'd made a wide circle of new friends but was closest to her old school mates, most of whom had never left Stoke. She liked rock music and dancing, attended yoga and Pilates classes, and went to the gym twice a week.

'You must be pretty fit,' I observed.

'Just trying to keep middle age at bay.'

'D'you mind my asking how old you are, Susie?'

She glanced at me. 'How old do you think?'

'I'm not much good at young people's ages. Mid to late thirties, perhaps?'

She stopped walking, turned to face me. 'It was worth coming on this jaunt just to hear that. I'm forty-seven.'

'Christ! You look nothing like it! And it's not just because you're slim – you have a wonderful figure if you don't mind my saying – it's your skin texture; not just your face but your arms and le-'

I stopped, probably too late. But she was grinning. 'I bet you say that to all the girls.'

We started walking again. Occasionally when the path narrowed we were forced close together, our upper arms touching, and twice our hands brushed, and the second time I gave hers a brief squeeze. She didn't respond in kind. We reached a stile, a high one with two steps on each side. I clambered over first, and stood to offer her a helping hand as she climbed down. But she didn't take it. Instead she stood on the lower step, placed both hands on my shoulders and jumped. After she landed she remained facing me, her hands still on my shoulders.

'Are you enjoying your walk, Dave?'

'Oh yes. Very much.'

'Good. I told you it would be therapeutic.'

She removed her hands and we set off once again. I found I'd become totally relaxed, a sensation long unfamiliar to me. Usually I veered between dull, nagging discontent and acceptance of my fate and, very occasionally a burst of elation such as I'd experienced when Susie had suggested today's outing. But this was how life should be, being outdoors in the company of an affectionate friend knowing there was a possibility, admittedly a faint possibility, that the affection might deepen into something more. I noticed it had stopped drizzling and the sky, though still cloudy, was much lighter.

'How d'you reckon you'll get on with Robert?'

Her question jerked me back to reality. I hadn't given the Bruce a thought all day.

'Oh, okay, I reckon.'

'Dave, why did you grill him about his time in York? Did you live there once?'

'No. But I used to lecture at Open University summer schools at York University.'

'But you kept quizzing him about the precise time he

was there, in the town, I mean. What was so important about that?'

I decided to tell her the truth, but be very economical with it.

'My … my injuries were sustained while I was in York. I just wondered if the Bruce had read about the incident, that's all.'

'The Bruce? You've lost me. What are you talking about?'

'Robert. Robert the Bruce.'

There was silence for a couple of seconds, then evidently she twigged. She yelped in appreciation, then chortled, a real belly-laugh, something I'd not heard from her before.

'You're a silly sod, Dave! Sometimes you're like a teenager!'

'I wish, Susie. I wish.'

As we continued on our way, our conversation became light-hearted: playful banter I suppose you'd call it. I teased her about being a true Stokie, never wanting to leave the area. She countered by saying I was a posh bloody southerner, but not so bad when you got to know me. She said she'd bet I liked classical music; I said yes, of course, because I was posh wasn't I? At that, she poked me in the ribs. I confessed to liking rock as well, but probably the stuff that was popular before she was born because I still couldn't believe she was more than the thirty-five.

And so it went on. I was so engaged with her that it came as a surprise when we got back to the car. Not only does time fly when enjoying oneself, but distance seems to diminish as well. We'd been walking for over two hours. She had to remind me to take off my boots and change into my trainers before she allowed me to get in.

We sat side-by-side in the front seats.

'Are you hungry?' she asked.

'Now you come to mention it, yes, I am.'

'I don't suppose you'd consider calling in at a pub for a

late lunch?'

For a fraction of a second I was elated by imagining sitting in a pub with her. But then, for the first time today, I remembered what I looked like.

'I'm sorry, Susie, I'd love to, but I can't. Couldn't cope with people's reactions on seeing me.'

'Okay, Dave. Just a thought. Good job I've brought a packed lunch. It's in my rucksack. Reach over and get it, could you?'

I groped in the back seat for her rucksack, and as I swung it over I glimpsed myself in the driver's mirror, the first time I'd seen myself in months. I was shaken. What, I wondered, was it like for Susie, being in constant close proximity to a freak? Or had she got so used to it that it was something she no longer noticed? My thoughts raced towards possible future scenarios. If we ever got to the stage where ... well, she'd want to have the lights off, as would I, but what would it be like for her, waking in the morning to be confronted with a gargoyle on the pillow beside her? I dismissed the idea. The whole scenario was impossible. There was a slow ebbing of the contentment I'd felt on the walk.

As we ate our sandwiches my replies to Susie's remarks were brief and abstracted. She leaned across and opened the glove compartment in front of me and extracted a CD.

'Fancy some music?' she said.

'Yes, okay.'

I didn't care what her choice of music might be. The distraction of whatever she played would be welcome, because I didn't know how to revert to our affectionate exchanges.

'Think you might like this,' she said as she inserted the CD in the player.

The very first guitar chord and the harmonious voices which followed were instantly recognisable. 'The Everlys!' I shouted, 'September 1957!' Susie grinned and nodded, began tapping to the rhythm on the dashboard. I began to sing along – *'There goes my baby, with someone new; she sure looks happy, I sure am blue.'*

The track ended. I began to ask if this was a compilation CD made by her for my benefit, but another track began. It was also by the Everlys and it was 'Wake Up Little Susie'. Susie started singing.

'God,' I shouted over the music. 'Surely you can't remember this? Even if you're as old as you say you are you'd have only been about been four when it came out.'

'Of course I remember it! Me mum used to sing it to me all the time.'

The CD was of all the Everlys' hits, in order of release. In between bites at our sandwiches we sang along the disc, and soon found ourselves harmonising, Susie taking Don's tenor part, and me Phil's baritone, all through 'All I Have To Do Is Dream' 'Let It Be Me', 'When Will I Be Loved' and 'So Sad', right up to 'Cathy's Clown' after which I asked Susie to eject the disc.

'I thought you were enjoying it, Dave.'

'I was. But for me The Everlys were the 1950s, the soundtrack to my adolescence. But in the 1960s my tastes changed. I've got that CD in my collection, but I never play it.'

'Why not?'

'Too painful to listen to by myself. What was it Noel Coward said about the potency of cheap music? Old records evoke happy past times and old friends who used to sing together. But how come you're an Everlys fan?'

She hesitated a moment before replying.

'My ex-partner re-introduced me to them. So I'm like you, I've not listened to that disc since we split up. As you say, too painful.'

So she was without a partner! Was there hope for me?

'What happened, Susie? How long ago did you split up?'

'Irreconcilable differences I suppose you'd call it. We'd grown apart. We'd been together for nearly ten years. We split about six months ago.'

156

'Christ, I'm sorry Susie. Only six months ago! And there was me whinging on about my problems while you were going through it. Why didn't you tell me?'

'Wouldn't have been professional. Anyway, you were a welcome distraction – along with my other clients of course.'

The moment was right for me to reach out and grab her hand. I was sorry she was unhappy, yes, I was, really, but what an opportunity it gave me to offer comfort! And she didn't shake off my hand, well, not immediately. Might I perhaps make another move, put my arm round her, maybe?

But if my advance were to be rejected, if she took offence, I would lose the opportunity to ask her for the personal favour I needed. This required careful thought. I had to maintain the equilibrium we'd reached in our relationship, one of affectionate friendship. So I suggested it was time we set off back to my house.

As she drove I was searching for a way in which I could lead into asking her my favour, and then, by a remarkable coincidence which gave a whole new meaning to the term serendipity, she asked me how far I'd got in making contact with my old school friends. Perhaps it was all our talk about the Everly Brothers and the 1950s that had reminded her.

'Well, I exchange regular emails with Frank Grayson – you remember, you helped me track him down by finding his company's website. And he's told me a lot about another old friend called Pete, and I intend contacting him sometime. But I can't yet.'

'Why's that, then?'

'Because there's another fellow whom it's essential I make contact with first.'

'Sounds very convoluted. Are you playing one off against another by any chance?

Jesus, what had given her that idea? Was it something I'd said in our therapy sessions? I was sure I'd never divulged my intentions, because it was only recently I'd become sure of them myself. Had her years spent counselling me given her an insight into my character such that she saw me as being manipulative?

'Well, *are* you?'

'Am I what?'

'Playing one off against another.'

'No, course I'm not. It's just I was never very close to Pete, but I was with the other fellow, Jack's his name, and I'd like to find out how he's getting on first. But he's not online, so I can't email him. I do have his phone number, but I can't call him.'

'Why ever not?'

'Because … look, never mind why at the moment. Susie, it's just occurred to me: you could be a great help in solving a dilemma. Can I ask you a very great favour?'

'Try me.'

I opened my front door and let Susie in first. Out of force of habit no doubt, she went straight into the kitchen.

'Hey, no need to sit in there. Come into the lounge. D'you fancy a glass of wine? And later I'll rustle up a light meal. Let's make an evening of it.'

'Hang on, Dave. Before we do anything else I'd like to get this phone call out of the way. And you know I'm going to do it against my better judgment.'

On the journey home I'd explained what I wanted her to do, to phone Jack, and if a woman answered to say sorry, she'd got the wrong number, but if it was a man, to hand the phone straight over to me. As I'd anticipated, this had prompted a lot of questions – who was the woman? Why didn't I want to speak to her? Why didn't I want her to know who was calling? What sort of game was I playing?

I'd told her it wasn't a game, it was just that I'd known the girl to whom Jack was now married, but we hadn't liked each other and she probably wouldn't want to speak to me, might even put the phone down. I was glad I'd told her this in the car: she'd been concentrating on her driving and wouldn't have noticed what passed for a blush on my ravaged face. I'd never been able to lie without turning red. Her response had been that it all sounded a bit dodgy and she didn't really want to be party to it. It had taken a lot of persuading before she finally agreed.

Now, back at the house, I could see she was right in one respect. It would be best to make the phone call immediately, so we could then relax with a glass of wine or two. So I picked up the phone, tapped in the number, and handed it over to her.

How long was it before the connection was made? Twenty seconds, maybe? But it was enough time for me to panic, to remember the stammer that afflicted me whenever I had to converse with someone unfamiliar. When talking to Susie my diction was clear.

She handed me the phone and nodded to me.

'H..hello. Is that J..Jack?'

'Speaking, Who's that?'

'It's Tim, Tim Bailey. Do you remember me?'

There was a long silence, then -

'Blimey! Of course I do! It must be nearly fifty years since – '

I had to interrupt him before he spoke my name. I asked if he was alone.

'Alone? Well, Judy's here. You remember Judy, don't you? I married – '

I interrupted again, asked if she was in the same room.

'Eh? No, she's in the lounge, but – '

'Jack, sorry if this sounds s..strange, but don't tell her it's me who's phoning.'

He asked why not. I told him I'd explain when we next spoke, and asked when he'd be alone in the house. He said he rarely was, and began to sound exasperated, asked what all this was about.

'Long story,' I said. 'Here, I'll give you my ph..phone number.' I dictated it slowly. 'Give me a ring when you get a chance. And remember, not a word to Judy. Bye, Jack.'

'But –'

I switched off the phone. I found I was breathing heavily, and perspiring. I turned to Susie, now sitting at the kitchen table. She was staring at me, her expression hard to read.

'Christ, I could do with a drink now,' I said. 'How about you? Wine? Red or white?

'White please, and just a small one.'

I busied myself collecting corkscrew, bottle and glasses. I was conscious she was still staring at me.

'Tim Bailey, eh?' she said. 'Is that your real name?'

'No. It was my original name before I changed it by Deed Poll. I thought you knew that. David is my real name now, I can assure you.'

'Good. Tim doesn't suit you.'

I didn't ask her why. I put the wine bottle and glasses onto a tray.

'Let's go into the lounge,' I said.

My lounge was sparsely furnished, apart from the bookcases lining the walls. In front of the TV was a large reclining chair which I'd purchased for comfortable viewing when I'd been discharged from hospital. It had an orthopaedic look to it, not inviting to a guest. So, as I'd hoped, Susie sat on the two-seater settee. I put the tray on the coffee table in front of her, and sank down beside her.

'That was a wonderful day, Susie. Thanks so much for taking me out. And thanks for helping with the phone call.'

'Well, I enjoyed the day out.'

I poured out the wine.

'Hey, I said I only wanted a small one.'

'You don't have to drink it all.'

But of course I was hoping she would, and then maybe have another. It was time to embark on my mission to give comfort, and she'd be more likely to be receptive if she had a few drinks inside her. I moved closer to her.

'Susie, today's been all about me, hasn't it? What about you?

160

'What d'you mean?'

'Are you still unhappy? About breaking up with your partner, I mean?'

'I'm beginning to get over it, but I can't say I'm happy, not yet.'

Now was the moment to grasp her hand, but the one next to me was holding her wine glass. I moved even closer to her. Did I detect a slight movement away from me?

'You've been a life-saver to me, Susie. Now I hope I can help you.'

She looked at me. 'And how do you think you might do that?'

'Well, for a start, you can talk to me about it. What was your relationship like? What was your partner like? Was he older than you?'

She continued to look at me. I leaned towards her.

'She, Dave.'

'What?'

'She. My partner was a woman.'

PART FIVE

November 2002

Staffordshire

My usual morning walk. The meteorologists would have us believe November is an autumn month, but for me it heralds the start of the winter of discontent which lasts until April. A few tattered leaves still clung to the trees, but the incessant rain had turned the paths over the hill to quagmires and the pastures across the valley were unfit for beasts: the cattle were now confined to their winter quarters. Even the birds had taken shelter, apart from a sparrow hawk which glided over the meadows in search of prey. To the east, Stoke was hardly visible, shrouded by low cloud, and the distant Pennine edge might not have existed. The landscape was colourless, grey.

I was in limbo. Susie's revelation had come as a shock of course, but what she'd gone on to say had shaken me even more. Now, two days later, I was not feeling the deep despondency I thought I might. According to Susie, there was still the possibility of our being friends, whatever that might mean. But as it would be a friendship which held no expectations, there was now no possibility of disappointment. So there was not the potential for the blackness of despair, just the greyness of mild discontent.

I'd been so taken aback by Susie's almost casual statement that her ex-partner had been a woman that I'd been unable to respond.

'What's the matter, Dave? Have I shocked you?'

'No, no, not shocked, just very surprised. You never gave any hint … I mean there was no indication …' I'd trailed off limply, not wanting to give offence. This was uncharted territory for me.

162

'What are you saying, Dave? Did you expect me to shout my sexual preference from the rooftops? Or behave in a way you assume gay women behave? Have you actually known any Lesbians?'

I'd not answered her immediately. Yes, I had known a few Lesbians: one had been a colleague at Keele, and she'd made her predilections very clear to the extent of proudly referring to herself as a Dyke. She'd also been a radical feminist and had strongly disapproved of my bedding students. To say we didn't hit it off would be an understatement: we'd loathed each other.

'There was a colleague of mine once,' I'd said eventually. 'But I didn't know her well. Susie, I'm sorry if you think I'm unaware. Look, let me be honest. You're a very attractive woman. You dress to make the best of your assets. To be frank, you dress sexily, as if to attract men. So I had no reason to believe - '

She'd interrupted me with a burst of laughter, but it had sounded forced.

'You're stereotyping women, Dave! I dress the way I do because my partner liked it, and because I think it suits me.'

'But weren't you aware of the effect it had on me?'

Up until then our conversation had been conducted with us slumped side-by-side on the settee, occasionally making eye contact. But as soon as I'd asked this question Susie sat upright, and turned to face me, her expression suddenly serious.

'We're getting to the nub of things now, Dave. What I'm going to say now I ought perhaps to have said before our day out, but I couldn't while I was still your counsellor. So hear me out, will you?'

'I'm all ears.'

'Look, over the years I got fonder of you than perhaps a counsellor should, but it was just friendly affection, and I assumed it was the same for you. But that day we went up to your study, to work on the computer, it was then I realised you ... well, had inappropriate feelings for me.

Once I'd left you I knew I'd been unprofessional, sitting next to you, giving your shoulder a squeeze, with you being so vulnerable. So I was faced with the problem of how to extricate myself from the situation without causing you too much distress.'

At that point I'd interrupted her to offer her another glass of wine, but she'd placed her hand over her glass.

'I wondered about telling you I was gay, but that would also have been unprofessional. We're not supposed to tell clients about our personal lives. So I decided at our next meeting I'd go back to a very formal approach, but that didn't work, did it? The only way forward was to sever our professional connection so I could tell you I was gay and at the same time maybe strike up a real friendship, because friendship is what you need. And I thought today was showing we're good friends.'

'Well, it has, hasn't it?'

'Up to a point.'

I think it was then I'd realised things might well not be panning out the way I'd hoped.

'What d'you mean?'

'Look, Dave. I wasn't happy about making that phone call for you in the first place. And having listened to what you said to your old friend, I'm even less happy now. Despite what you say, I get the impression you're playing some sort of game, trying to manipulate people.'

I'd denied it of course, had reminded her that it was she who'd first suggested I make contact with old friends, indeed had advised me on how the internet could help to do so. She hadn't responded, and changed the subject.

'There's another thing, Dave. I enjoyed our walk today, and the chat, but ... but, well, it's your obvious need for physical contact that concerns me. You took every opportunity to try and touch me – oh yes, I know it was just hand-touching, but you must realise I can't give you what you obviously need, even if I wanted to.'

'But Susie – '

'I'm not criticising you, Dave. I know you're desperate

for touch. Everyone needs to be touched. My mum told me one of the worse things about getting old and ill was there was no one apart from me who held her hand. Maybe one day the NHS will set up teams of licenced touchers.'

At that we'd both laughed, but this time the forced laughter had come from me.

I'd offered her another glass of wine, but she'd refused, said she had to go. When she reached the front door she'd turned to me.

'Dave, I think I need a bit of space to consider where we go from here. I'm beginning to wonder… well, if I'm doing you any good. I'll give you a ring as soon as I've decided what's best.'

I'd had a day to consider all she'd said. Her continued friendship would be welcome, of course, but I had a lingering worry that her only motive for continuing to see me might be pity.

The main reason for my uncertainty was the matter of my disfigurement. We'd spoken about it often in the counselling sessions – it was after all the reason for my isolation – but it was something we'd never discussed in terms of our relationship. On our day out I'd intended to ask her if, given our frequent contact, it was something she still noticed, and if she secretly found me repulsive. Now any prospect of a deeper intimacy had disappeared, the issue was less important.

No, the problem was this. On our walk she'd asked me if I fancied having lunch in a pub. I couldn't face it. I never would be able to face the stares of other people. And what would it be like for her, sitting in a pub or café alongside a freak? Surely such a situation would be embarrassing for her? So all future meetings would have to be walks in the country, alone together, avoiding others. How long would it be before this began to pall for her? Could a friendship survive without the stimulation of jointly socialising with others?

Such was my immersion in my relationship with Susie

that over the past two days I'd hardly given Jack a thought. But now, back home, busying myself loading the dishwasher, it occurred to me – the bastard still hadn't phoned.

Buckinghamshire

Marion

When she arrived, Marion could remember nothing of how she'd got there. The woman at the main reception desk brusquely told her how to get to the Intensive Care Unit, then resumed her conversation with her colleague. Bloody NHS: those sort of bad manners weren't found in private hospitals. She managed to negotiate the maze of corridors which led to the unit, and was received much more sympathetically at the nurses' station, but the compassion in the voice of the nurse who addressed her, far from providing comfort somehow added to her distress. She was ushered into a visitors' waiting room and told the consultant would be with her in a few minutes. After half an hour she was still waiting – bloody NHS again – and numbness had begun to set in. This wasn't happening to her;

When, accompanied by a nurse, the consultant finally entered, he shook her hand, apologised for keeping her waiting, introduced himself as Mr Ganesh, and sat down beside her.

'Mrs Kennedy, I'm afraid your husband is dangerously ill. He suffered a major heart attack, we think on Tuesday night, but as you know he wasn't found until this morning. You'll understand the delay in his receiving treatment hasn't helped his condition.'

'Yes. I understand.'

'And I'm afraid the fact that he was unconscious for so long, out in the open, in the rain, has exacerbated the problem. Does he have breathing issues? I mean, did he

166

suffer from shortness of breath before this incident?'

'Well, yes, I suppose he did, I mean, when he exerted himself he got breathless, wheezed a lot.'

'Was he a smoker?'

'Yes.'

'And was he a heavy drinker? You see, Mrs Kennedy, there was a high level of alcohol in his blood when he was brought in.'

'Well, we … he had a few drinks every evening after work, but he wasn't ever drunk, not really, if that's what you mean. Doctor, can I see him now?'

'Yes, of course. But you must prepare yourself for what you'll see. The equipment in intensive care units unnerves many visitors when they first see it attached to their loved ones. Let me explain …'

But she was unable to concentrate on what he was saying. She could hear his words but was unable to grasp their significance. Eventually, he ended his lecture and touched her hand briefly before standing up.

'Nurse will take you in now, Mrs Kennedy. Don't hesitate to ask her anything you don't understand.'

On entering the room, she was assailed by a scene that might have been from a science-fiction movie – tubes and cables festooned over the room, a screen with wavy lines of various colours tracking across it, and the noises! Bleeping from the screen, a ghastly sucking sound from the bed. And on the bed – something with electrodes on its chest, a peg attached to its finger with a cable extending from it, tubes coming out of its nostrils. It was an alien: shrunken, lifeless, shrouded in a white robe with only its arms, chest and face exposed. The face was contorted and ashen, apart from the rosacea on the nose. It was those red swellings which jolted her into the realisation that this was indeed the husband whom she'd recently mocked when she'd discovered he was using her make-up to try to disguise them. Hesitantly, she reached to touch his hand. It was cold. Tentatively, she squeezed it. It was unresponsive. How long had it been since they'd squeezed each other's hands? Twenty years at least.

'You should try talking to him, love,' the nurse said. 'He won't respond but he might be able to hear you, might recognise your voice. Talk about the good times you've had, like holidays, or times with kids, or friends.'

But if squeezing his hand had been difficult, talking to him would be impossible. What could she say? What good times had they had together recently? After what had recently passed between them, to have murmured endearments would be not only embarrassing but hypocritical. She sat in silence. The nurse eventually retreated behind a screen.

She had no sense of time passing, and started when a nurse, another nurse, suggested that she go home and get some rest, and not to worry, he was in good hands, and if there was any change, well, we've got your phone number, haven't we?

So she went home. She phoned Sarah to give her a brief report, and ignored an answerphone message from Angie. For the first time in years, she didn't seek the solace of alcohol. The thought of it made her feel sick. In any case she needed to be alert for a phone call which she knew would only bring bad news. Exhaustion finally overcame her at about five in the morning.

The days merged into hours of discomfort and tedium. She was no longer distressed: exhaustion served as an anaesthetic. The bedside chair was plastic, one of the stacking variety, its only advantage being that it gave her an aching bum which prevented her from nodding off. She abandoned all attempts to talk to him. The nurses suggested she try reading aloud articles from newspapers and magazines, but she just felt foolish. The kindly remarks of doctors and nurses were the only oases in the desert of her isolation. But sometimes their presence was less comforting, such as those times when they needed to attend to changes in his condition, times when she was asked to leave the room. Yesterday she'd returned to find the tubes in his nostrils were covered by a ventilator mask. It had been impossible to relate to something which was an inanimate object, so she'd gone home early, ignored yet another answerphone message from Angie enquiring how things were, phoned Sarah to give her a brief report on how nothing had changed, and had then gone to bed, resigned to another sleepless night.

But today, thank God, the mask had been removed. And did he look less gaunt than he had been?

'His breathing's improved a bit, and we're reducing his sedation,' the nurse said, 'He's not out of the wood yet, but we think he could soon be moved out of here to a High Dependency Unit. We've got to make a few adjustments first. Why don't you go and have a coffee out in the foyer? Give yourself a proper break.'

It was good to have someone making a decision for her. Usually she retreated to the unit's visitors' lounge which was often occupied by other relatives, like the tearful young couple whose son had run into the path of a speeding car, and the dignified old lady whose husband had suffered a massive stroke.

She walked along the corridor and passed the nurses' station at the entrance to the Unit. Most of the nurses she now knew – the young, cheerful black woman who called her darlin', the gaunt one with greying hair whose sympathetic manner belied her rather sour face, the startlingly attractive brunette who could have been a fashion model, the young man who looked no older than a teenager and was deferential when he spoke to her. As she passed they greeted her; how was she today? Had she managed to get any sleep last night?

How did they do it, she wondered: how did they return to this place day after day to cope not only with sickness and death, but with distraught or grieving relatives? Was this ordinary life, for them? Did they become inured to it, go home at the end of their shift and laugh and drink or watch TV or make love, and think no more of what they'd witnessed? As she automatically washed her hands before leaving the unit it occurred to her that for the first time in days she'd been thinking about people other than herself and Pete. And Sarah, of course. She'd thought a lot about her daughter during her vigils, and they weren't kindly thoughts.

When she entered the hospital foyer it struck her that it was like being in the normal day-to-day world. She'd passed through it many times before, of course, but had not registered her surroundings, for on entering and leaving the building she was either in dread at what might confront her in the ICU, or upset by what she had witnessed. Now, it revealed itself to be more like a shopping mall than a hospital entrance, spacious and airy, with shops and coffee bars around its perimeter. The people thronging it seemed relaxed, carefree even, at home in the place. No doubt some had been visiting patients undertaking minor operations, soon to be discharged, or perhaps they were outpatients themselves, elated because they'd been given the all clear.

For the first time in days she felt hungry, and craved coffee, proper coffee, not the foul concoction delivered by the machine in the ICU nor the endless cups of bland Instant she made at home but emptied into the sink after a few sips. There was a Café Nero nearby. She went in, ordered an Americano and a cinnamon whirl, and took a seat near the door.

Away from Pete but knowing he was nearby and being tended, her thoughts turned, as she knew they would, to Sarah. It was obvious, from their exchanges over the phone when Pete had gone missing and then after his being found, that her daughter held her partly responsible for his condition. 'Mum, what the hell were you doing anyway, leaving him to go and stay with Angela?' she'd said, and then 'Why didn't you go home immediately when I told you he hadn't arrived at work?'

All very well for Sarah, Marion thought: *she* didn't know what Pete had put her through. And if she was so concerned about him, why hadn't she dumped the kids on someone and come to visit him? She'd texted on Thursday to say she'd come on Saturday – *oh God, that's today!* Marion hadn't checked her phone before leaving the house this morning, and mobiles had to be turned off in the ICU. She scrabbled in her bag to find it; it wasn't there. She checked her pockets – not there either. She tried her bag again, emptied the contents on to the table – *oh no! Have I left the bloody thing at home?*

Had Sarah already arrived, perhaps? Was she even now sitting beside Pete in the ICU, thinking that she, Marion, was again failing in her wifely duty?

She had to get back. She jerked to her feet, spilling what remained of her coffee over the table and half-ran across the foyer; then, short of breath, hurried along the corridors leading to the ICU. She turned a corner, and collided with a woman coming the other way.

'Mum! What do you – '

'Sarah! Oh Sarah, the nurse suggested I had a coffee in the foyer while they attended to your dad. I only – '

'I know all that. A nurse told me. I was on my way to find you, wasn't I?

'Have you seen your father?'

'No. Didn't get further than the nurses' station. How is he?'

'Better today than yesterday, but not good. You see, he had to have – '

'Spare me the details. I want to see him for myself. Come on, let's get back to him.'

She turned and hurried off. Marion was unable to keep up with her.

When Marion entered Pete's room Sarah was already sitting by the bed, holding his hand, and weeping. 'Dad, dad,' she kept repeating through sniffs. Marion grabbed another chair and sat beside her. Sarah didn't look at her but just asked 'Why didn't you tell me he was like this?'

'But Sarah, I tried to, but … I wanted to spare you the

details. I was hoping he'd improve by the time you got to see him.'

'Does he know what's going on? Can he hear us? Have you tried talking to him?'

'Well, I've read things to him, you know, from the paper, but he didn't – '

'Read to him? *Read*? For God's sake, mum, what bloody good would that do?' She leaned over her father, spoke into his ear, 'Dad, it's Sarah. Squeeze my hand if you can hear me.'

'He can't hear you, Sarah.'

For the first time, Sarah turned to look at her mother.

'Well, I'm not giving up. I'm going to keep talking to him. You can go and have another bloody coffee if you like.'

Marion was taken aback by the vehemence of the statement. Then her shock turned to anger. How dare she! To imply that she could work some sort of magic in the few minutes she'd been here! But Marion said nothing, stayed sitting in her chair.

After ten minutes she began to wish she *had* gone for a coffee. Sarah was delivering a monologue at Pete, peppered with endearments, about her memories of her childhood, how much she'd loved it when he'd played with her, how she'd enjoyed the trips he'd taken her on. Then she started talking about her kids, how much they loved their granddad, how he must get better soon and come and stay with them. Marion wasn't mentioned. It was as though she didn't figure at all in their family history.

Evidently having exhausted her store of memories, Sarah began to sing to him. Sing, for God's sake! Marion was embarrassed for her – she'd never had a good voice. But she recognised the songs: they were the hits of Pete's youth which he'd taught his daughter when she was a child: songs by Presley, the Everly Brothers, Buddy Holly. Marion had never liked rock'n'roll, had been bored when Pete had enthused about it. Was Sarah was deliberately

172

doing things to exclude her?

Then the singing stopped abruptly.

'Mum! He's moved!'

'What? Are you sure?'

'Yes. Look!'

Marion peered at him and yes, his head was shifting slightly from side to side. Then, a sound: his breathing more laboured perhaps?

'I'll go and get a nurse.'

'No! Wait! I'm sure he's trying to say something.'

They both leaned over him. At first they heard only meaningless rasping grunts, devoid of consonants. But the sounds were repetitive, and eventually became two-syllable words. Marion recognised them first. '*Judy. Judy.*' Then two more words which followed the repeated name – '*Judy, I'm sorry.*'

'Mum? Who the bloody hell is Judy?'

Jack and Judith

Okay, it was bad news about poor old Pete, and Jack was concerned about his old mate, but why was Jude taking it so badly? It wasn't as if they'd been that close, was it? Blimey, for God knows how long the two had only seen each other briefly when Pete called to collect him on Sundays, and they hardly spoke more than a few sentences to each other.

But when he'd passed on Sophie's news that Pete was in hospital, dangerously ill, Jude had collapsed back on the sofa as though she'd been clobbered. For a long time she'd said nothing at all, hadn't seemed to be listening when he tried to reassure her. Then she'd started crying, not aloud, but an occasional tear had trickled down her cheek, and on one occasion her shoulder heaved. What had got into her? She hadn't been like that when her mother died, and Pete was still alive, wasn't he? But she'd been in a strange mood for weeks now. Was she ill, perhaps?

Then she'd said she was going to lie down in the bedroom. He'd asked her if she wasn't feeling well, if there was anything he could get her; she'd replied that she'd got a headache and needed to sleep it off; she'd take a couple of paracetamol.

That was three hours ago. He'd looked in on her once; she was lying curled up, her face half buried in the pillow. He'd whispered 'Jude', but there'd been no response. He'd decided to let her sleep it off.

Now, alone in the living room, and with nothing to occupy him, his mind turned to Pete. The news was only just sinking in, and he realised that he, like Jude, was not merely concerned, but upset. Pete. His oldest friend. He could be a bit of a boaster, could old Pete, but he was good company, and the thought struck him how important their Sundays together were to him, how much he'd miss their trips to the *George*, if, God forbid, Pete were to die. It was a shame Jude and Marion hadn't hit it off. But for a while Pete had continued to be friendly with Jude, affectionate even, though they no longer seemed to have much to say to each other. Blimey, that coolness between them had started years ago: how time had flown. She'd never really explained why it had happened. Strange she seemed to be so upset now.

After about an hour, Jude emerged from the bedroom and, without saying anything, sat down opposite him.

'Are you feeling better, Jude? Has your headache gone?'

'Almost.'

'Would you like a cup of tea?'

'Not just now, thanks.'

'Well, I was just going to make myself a cuppa. Sure you wouldn't like one?'

'I said no, didn't I? Don't *fuss* Jack.'

He went into the kitchen. Bloody hell, was she was going to be like this evening? He thought about going on to the computer, but as it was in the living room he wouldn't be able to concentrate with Jude sitting there.

174

Nothing for it but to go and sit with her, and try not to fuss.

She looked up when he went in with his tea.

'Why don't you try phoning Marion again?' she said. 'See if there's any more news?'

'But it's only five o'clock, Jude. Sarah said Marion never gets back from the hospital until after six.'

'Well, maybe Sarah's back home.'

'But – '

'Oh just *phone*, can't you? If there's no one in, you can try again later.'

He'd better humour her, he supposed, and supressing a sigh he went over to the telephone.

***

Judith wasn't sure if she wanted Marion to be in, in case the news was bad. But she could no longer stand the suspense of not knowing. Was it all her fault? Pete had been so angry last Sunday when he'd left her at Lee Common. His face had been purple. She knew he had high blood pressure; Jack had told her. Had the way she'd behaved to him caused his heart attack? Was it on Tuesday he'd had it? Had he been building up to it since their argument?

When Jack picked up the receiver and began punching in the number, she realised she didn't want to listen. She covered her ears: she'd learn the news soon enough when the phone call ended. Then Jack spoke: she heard him say 'Marion'. So she was in! Judith clamped her hands more tightly to her ears. Jack wasn't saying much, but the call seemed to be lasting for ages. For pity's sake, all Marion needed to say was if he was better or worse or stable. What was taking so long?

At last, Jack replaced the receiver. Judith uncovered her ears.

'Well? How is he?'

There was no reply. Jack remained standing by the

175

phone, staring at her. His expression was unreadable.

'For God's sake, is he worse? He ... he hasn't ...'

'He's not worse, far from it. He's been talking.'

'Oh, thank heavens. That must mean – '

'Yes, what does it mean, Jude?'

Jack's expression hadn't changed. She noticed his posture was rigid. What was up with him? What did he mean by that strange question?'

'What's the matter?'

'Marion was hysterical. Amongst other things she told me not to phone her again.'

'What? But why?'

'Maybe you can answer that question. Marion said Pete only spoke a few words. One of them was your name. He said your name several times. Then he said "Judy, I'm sorry." What was he apologising for? What the fuck's been going on?'

The shock at hearing Jack use the 'f' word was almost as great as hearing what he'd told her. Of all the possible scenarios resulting from Pete's heart attack this was one she'd never considered. Her head was reeling; she had to say something, but what?

'So ... so is Sarah still at the hospital with Pete?'

'How the hell should I know? For God's sake woman, is it important?'

He started pacing round the room, muttering to himself. Judith had never seen him like this. Desperately searching for something to say, she hoped he'd say something first, something, anything, to which she could respond. But he didn't. After a few more circuits of the room he slumped into the chair opposite her, covered his eyes with his hands. The lengthy silence in the room was tangible. Then he took his hands from his eyes and stared at her.

'Well? What's been going on between you and Pete?'

She'd had time in the silence to concoct a story of sorts. No, not concoct a story, but tell as much of the truth as might seem feasible, and to leave unsaid things he didn't need to know, and to hope he'd never find out. Economy with the truth, wasn't it called?

'Nothing's been going on, Jack, honestly. Y'see, a couple of weeks ago I discovered *Friends Reunited*; it's a website that can put you in contact – '

'I bloody know what *Friends Reunited* is.'

'Well, I started looking at it to see if there were any of our old school friends on it. There weren't many, but Pete was one of them. I wanted to test how the website worked, so I posted a message on it for Pete, just to see if he'd reply.'

'And did he?'

So soon into her story, and already the need to lie! What hole was she digging for herself?

'No, he didn't. You see, when you post a message on the site you leave your email address so the person can reply by email. Pete didn't send me one. So I can only think that's what he was apologising for.'

'So what was in your message that you expected him to reply to?'

'Only to say I was trying out the website and asking him to email me to confirm he'd got the message.'

Jack was silent again, no doubt considering the plausibility of her story. Judith suddenly felt a craving for a strong cup of tea.

'But why?' he said eventually, 'Why did you want to try out *Friends Reunited?* It's for old friends who've lost contact, isn't it? Well, we're still in contact with our school friends, aren't we? Apart from those we were never really friendly with in the first place.'

She had to give a reason. Anything to divert his attention away from Pete.

'You see …Look, Jack. D'you remember that strange phone call we had months back, from the fellow who asked to speak you but he wouldn't give his name? Remember, you were in the bathroom, so he said he'd phone you back?'

She risked looking at him. His face was contorted, but

with what emotion she couldn't tell.

'It was only sometime after that call I realised I recognised his laugh. I thought it might have been Tim Bailey, so that was why I went on *Friends Reunited*. Just curiosity.'

'Oh, I see.' The three words were heavy with sarcasm. 'Tim Bailey. The one who tried it on with you in the Sixth Form. At least, that's what you told me. Sure it wasn't more than that? Still got the hots for him after all these years, have you?'

'No, Jack! No! It was –'

'Well *I've* got something I haven't told *you*. I was going to, but bloody Pete's heart attack put it out of my mind. Just after we got that news, I had a phone call. From your precious Tim. And d'you know what? He asked me if you were at home, and when I said you were, he asked me to phone back when I was alone.'

'But why –'

'That's not all. He said I wasn't to let you know he'd called. What was all that about? What bloody secret life have you been leading?'

Judith got up. 'I'm going to make a cup of tea. D'you want one?'

'Tea? *Tea*?

All Judith could think as she escaped into the kitchen was that this sort of thing shouldn't be happening to a woman of fifty-nine.

Angela and Frank

It was now five days since Marion had left, summoned by Sarah's insistence that she come home. Angela hadn't heard from her since. She'd almost forgotten how irritating a house-guest Marion had been. She'd tried phoning her on numerous occasions, but only ever got the answering service. Each time she'd left a message, saying she hoped everything was all right, and would Marion phone back when she had a chance, please? But she hadn't. Angela didn't have Marion's mobile phone number – their restoration of contact had taken place too recently, too hurriedly, for them to have got round to exchanging numbers.

What in God's name had happened? When she'd left, Marion had given no indication anything was seriously wrong, other than that Sarah was in a bit of a state. Was it something to do with Pete, perhaps? Maybe Pete had told Sarah about Marion leaving him, and Sarah was blaming her mother for it? Marion had always complained Sarah was a daddy's girl.

She'd decided to try calling Sarah, had started searching the telephone directory, until she realised she didn't know Sarah's married name. So much had happened in seventeen years she and Marion had been estranged – children marrying, grandchildren arriving, parents dying – all the experiences they should have shared, experiences that strengthen the bond between friends in their 40s and 50s. Only it hadn't been they who'd been estranged, had it? It was their husbands.

'Hello Ange! Something smells good!'

Angela started. She hadn't heard Frank come in.

'Oh, hello! Yes, dinner's nearly ready. Had a good day?'

'Not bad. I'll just go and change out of this clobber.'

Things had been good between them since Marion had left: their loving relationship had been fully restored. More than restored, it was almost as though they were newly-weds. 'Randy old buggers, aren't we?' Frank had said after a session on the settee which had surprised them both. Angela had not shared with him her concerns about Marion's silence, in fact she'd taken pains not to mention Marion at all. Frank hadn't referred to her either, except obliquely when he'd said how good it was to have the house to themselves. Angela felt the odd twinge of guilt about not telling him of her attempts to phone Marion, but that wasn't something he needed to know, was it?

After dinner, over which they'd chatted amiably about their respective days and consumed two large glasses of wine each, Frank winked at her and said he fancied an early night. That suited Angela: coupling on the settee had been exciting, like being a teenager again, but teenagers don't suffer from backache the next day brought on by badly sprung cushions.

They were loading the dishwasher – Frank pinched her bottom in the process – when the telephone rang.

'Leave it,' said Frank.

'Can't do that, it's only eight o'clock. It might be one of the kids.'

She picked up the phone, said her name, and was immediately assailed by a hysterical tirade which gave her no opportunity to respond until Marion, for it was she who was calling, asked her the question to which she could only answer 'Yes, give me half an hour.'

She replaced the receiver, and turned to face Frank.

'Frank, that was Marion.'

'Oh yes?'

The guarded expression in his voice was evident, but Angela had no alternative but to tell him.

'Pete's in hospital, dangerously ill. A heart attack. Marion's beside herself.'

'Oh.'

'Their daughter's with him. Marion's at home.'

'Well, she's got some support, it seems.'

'Yes, but she's distraught. She was going on about something I didn't really understand, she was sobbing so much. She wants me to go over.'

'Oh, Christ, no, Ange. You didn't say you would?'

'I had to, Frank. Apparently Sarah's spending the night at the hospital, so she's alone. I'd never forgive myself if – '

'But you've had a lot of wine. You'll be way over the limit.'

'I'll get a taxi.'

Frank seemed to be giving this suggestion a lot of

180

thought: he was rubbing his chin.

'No, Ange. I'll drive you. I'm more used to night-time driving. With four eyes on the road we should be ok.'

'But ... how will I get back?'

'I'll stay there with you. *You* might need some support, knowing that bloody woman. In any case I don't want her persuading you to let her come back here. Come on, get your coat on.'

***

Frank drove slowly along the dark country lanes, more slowly than was strictly necessary. It wasn't so much that he was fearful of an accident, rather that the nearer they got to Marion's house the more he knew how reluctant he was to undertake this mission. It had been bad enough having Marion as a guest, but at least in that situation he'd been on home territory, had been able – admittedly to a limited degree – to dictate the rules of engagement, and to retreat to his study, or to bed, when he'd no longer been able to bear her company.

But now they'd be on Marion's home turf, imprisoned there by the requirement to be polite and listen to her hysterical ramblings. He and Angela hadn't been in the Kennedy household for God knows how many years, and after the enmity with Pete had begun he'd resolved never to cross their threshold again. But what concerned him most was that Angela might once again become sympathetic to that bloody woman and be sucked into spending more time with her and less with him, just as they'd started enjoying a belated second honeymoon. Talk about an unwarranted intrusion into the bridal suite.

Angie was saying very little except to forewarn him of road junctions and sharp bends. What was she thinking, he wondered? Was she as reluctant an aid-worker as he? Was she doing this only out of solidarity with a woman who'd been abused by her husband? If this was the case he could understand. Pete was a bastard, a disgrace to his gender.

Frank caught himself hoping his heart attack would prove fatal: it would solve a lot of problems.

He pulled into Marion's drive. He hadn't even turned off the engine before the front door opened and Marion ran out. She made straight for the driver's door. When he opened it she immediately started gabbling and several seconds elapsed before she evidently grasped she was addressing him and not Angela.

'Where's Angie?' she demanded.

He turned on the interior light.

'She's here, Marion, see?'

She immediately ran round to the passenger side. She didn't give Angela time to climb out before launching into another tirade which only stopped when Angela extricated herself, stood facing her, and grabbed both her arms.

'Okay, okay, Marion. I'm here now. Calm down; let's get inside.'

As they walked towards the door Frank heard Marion say 'What's Frank doing here?' He was wondering the same thing himself.

He decided to give Angela a few minutes to try and pacify Marion before entering the house, but could think of nothing to occupy himself other than tidying the glove compartment. For the first time in more than twenty years he regretted he no longer smoked. It wasn't that he craved nicotine, just that he would have welcomed the activity the manipulation of a cigarette would have provided. He was both bored and anxious – two of life's least desirable emotions. And the anxiety stemmed not from concern for Marion, and certainly not for Pete, but from a worry that Angie would again become enmeshed with their problems. Was he becoming a selfish old bastard? As you got older you think you've stayed the same as you always were, but there are occasions when you are aware change has crept up on you, you've become a different person, with new attitudes, beliefs, prejudices.

Enough of this. He jumped out of the car, slammed the door, locked it. The front door to the house was still open.

As he entered the hallway he was immediately struck by what he'd forgotten about the place – the minimalist décor that characterised Marion's taste. Bare parquet floor, ice-white walls, a single spotlight on the ceiling, no furniture, no umbrella stand, not even any hooks on which to hang coats. He realised how comfortable was the outdated, rather shabby shambles that characterised his own house, and remembered how disparaging Marion had been about it.

He could hear voices, well, one voice, coming from behind the door which led to the lounge. He opened it and entered. Angela was sitting on the settee beside Marion, holding her hand. Marion was still in full spate. Angela looked up at him, raised her eyebrows. Marion hadn't seemed to register his presence, or perhaps had chosen to ignore him. He sat down on the easy chair opposite them, recalling as he did so how Pete had told him what a battle he'd had with Marion when he'd insisted on having something comfortable to sit on.

He looked round the room – Marion was still talking to Angela – and was struck by what a mess the place was in. The austere décor served to emphasise the clutter – overflowing ashtrays, unwashed cups, glasses and an empty wine bottle on the occasional table and another on the floor, discarded clothing on the settee, dust on the ceramic mantel-shelf of the fireplace. Surely Marion had a daily cleaning lady? Perhaps she'd given up the unequal struggle and resigned. If so, he didn't blame her.

He had to force himself to look at Marion. She was even more of a mess than her living room – hair lank and evidently unwashed, no make-up, bags under her eyes, sucking greedily at a cigarette between sentences; no, not sentences but half-formed slurred phrases which made little sense. She looked, not to put too fine a point on it, like a fat drunken old slag. Was one allowed to think of a woman in those terms these days? Why not, if they were true?

He managed to gather that Pete, after a brief time when

183

he seemed to be rallying, had relapsed again. He started to make a comment of commiseration, but Angela looked at him and shook her head. It was apparent any intervention on his part would be unwelcome. How much longer would he be expected to sit here, a mute observer of a scene akin to some cheap soap-opera on the TV? He was on the verge of getting up, telling Angie he'd wait for her in the car, when he heard the front door slam shut, footsteps in the hall and a female voice shouting – 'Mum? Mum? Whose car's that outside?'

The door to the lounge opened. A woman entered. She was youngish, tall, and blonde. Of course: the Kennedys' daughter! Sarah, was it? She'd been on the cusp of adolescence when Frank had last seen her.

She ignored his presence, and that of Angie. She approached Marion, squatted down in front of her.

'They've sent me home. Said there's no point me being there, I'd be in the way. He's got worse, mum, he's got the mask back on. They said they'd phone if there was any change. Mum? Oh Christ, have you started drinking again?'

'She's not had anything since we've been here, Sarah,' said Angela. 'You do remember us, don't you? Frank and Angela Grayson? You were hardly more than a child when we – '

'Oh yes, I remember you. Not likely to forget you, am I?' She stood up. 'What are you doing here anyway?'

'Marion phoned me, Sarah. She sounded desperate. So we came to see if we could help.'

'Well you can't. And I'm here now, so there's no need for you to stay, is there?'

Throughout this exchange, Marion had been silent, but she suddenly burst into wails. It reminded Frank of the keening of bereaved women in African countries.

He stood up. 'Right, we'll be off then. Sorry to hear the news about your father. Come on, Angie. Sarah can look after Marion now.'

Angela got up, and after bending over to touch

Marion's hand, walked over to join him. 'Goodbye, Sarah,' she said. 'Keep me informed about … well, everything, won't you?'

'I'll see you out,' said Sarah, and led the way to the door. Once they were in the hall, she turned to Frank. Her features were screwed into a mask of loathing.

'Christ, you've got a bloody nerve, coming here, pretending you're sorry about Dad.' Her voice was low but the words were spat out with venom.

Frank recoiled. 'But your mother asked Angie to come.'

'Well, Angela's capable of driving here herself, isn't she? It's you I never want to see here, not after what you did to Dad.'

Frank heard a sharp intake of breath from Angela. He felt as shocked as she obviously was. How much did Sarah know? He didn't want to wait to find out.

'Come on, Angie,' he said. 'Let's be off.'

As soon as they were through the front door it was slammed behind them.

Frank drove for at least a mile without speaking. Angela also said nothing. It was as though they needed to distance themselves from the melodrama they'd just witnessed before being able to comment on the performance.

'My God, Angie,' he said eventually. 'What did you make of that? D'you reckon Pete might have told Sarah about … well, you know; what I threatened to reveal?'

'From what Marion told me, Pete's in no condition to tell anyone anything.'

'But he might have told her years ago. Didn't you say she'd always close to her father? Maybe he felt able to confide in her and swore her to secrecy.'

'I doubt it very much. Would a father really confide to a daughter about his infidelity, especially a daughter he doted on? It's not that, Frank. There's something you don't know, something Marion told me before you came in.'

'What's that, then?'

'Apparently, the night before last, Pete rallied a bit. It was during Sarah's first visit to him. Marion was there as well. He spoke a few words. He seemed to think it was Judy he was talking to. He kept saying her name, and then kept saying he was sorry.'

'Oh bloody hell.'

'That's why Marion was so upset. It wasn't because his first words were addressed to someone else. It was because although she'd spent hours with him, it only took one visit from Sarah for him to start talking.'

'What was Sarah's reaction to being called Judy?'

'Marion said she just kept asking her who the hell Judy was. She told her Judy's married to one of Pete's old school friends. But apparently Sarah keeps asking her why Pete kept apologising to her. That's another thing upsetting Marion; the fact she doesn't know. Oh, slow down a bit, Frank.'

Frank glanced at the speedometer. Christ, he was doing 60. He decelerated, but it wasn't enough. The conversation, and the emotions it engendered, required total concentration. He pulled up alongside the entrance to a field.

'Why have you stopped?'

'I need to think, Angie. All this business – Pete and Judy. I thought it was all in the past. D'you reckon it may have started up again?'

'I doubt it. Who knows what goes through a person's mind when he's semi-conscious? Probably Pete's life was flashing in front of him. Anyway, it doesn't concern us now, does it? It's between Pete and Marion. What you did all those years ago won't be important to Marion now.'

'I just wish to God you hadn't got involved with Marion again.'

'So do I, Frank.'

He turned to face her. 'What? D'you really mean that?

'Yes. I'd begun to realise she'd turned into a different person when she stayed with us. I only went to visit her tonight because … well, quite honestly I thought she might

186

do something silly if she was alone. But now Sarah's with her – well, it's not my responsibility any longer, is it?'

'No, it's not. Oh, give us a hug, Angie.'

Their embrace was clumsy, encumbered as they were by seat belts.

'Let's get home,' said Frank. He started the engine.

As he drove off a tide of relief washed over him. He'd got Angie back again. Pete and Marion could be consigned to history. As could Jack and Judith: in any case he hadn't seen either of them for years. He and Angie could get on with their lives.

Echoing his thoughts, Angela remarked that they'd both been silly to get so wrapped up in the past. 'And after all,' she said, 'it's not as if you've told anyone else about that business, is it?'

Frank was about to agree. Then he remembered – oh bloody hell, he'd told Tim Bailey about it. His feeling of well-being ebbed away, to be replaced by uncertainty. He'd have to tell Angie. And tell her why he'd done it.

PART SIX

November-December 2002

Staffordshire

It was obvious the useless bastard wasn't going to phone. Just like him: at school he'd always had been indecisive, always waiting for others to take the lead, always falling in with others' plans. Now it seemed he'd got worse, couldn't even comply with a request. It was a simple enough matter, wasn't it? To phone me whenever he was alone? Surely Judy wasn't always with him all hours of the day and night? Maybe he was so useless that he relied on her for everything – maybe he was losing it, a victim of early-onset Alzheimer's? That would be typical of him. If that was the case he might not even understand what I was going to tell him.

But he was going to be told, of that I was determined. The only benefit from his failure to ring back was that I'd been able to rehearse my lines until I was word perfect. I wouldn't come out with it as a sudden revelation; no, I'd lead into it gently, ask if he still saw anything of Pete, express surprise if he still did, and if he didn't, commiserate with him and say I could understand why. Then explain the reason for my surprise (or for my commiseration), and ask if the affair had lasted long, say I admired him for sticking with her. What might then transpire would depend on his reaction. But I would of course let slip it had been Frank who'd told me all about it. That really would put the Staffordshire cat amongst the Buckinghamshire pigeons.

And I had to do something positive to stop me thinking about Susie. What a fool I'd been about her. She hadn't phoned since we parted on the day of our walk. So much for her promise of friendship. Only to be expected from a bloody dyke.

So today was the day. I was going to phone him. If Judy answered the phone, I'd disguise my voice and say 'Sorry, wrong number', then hang up. I doubted they'd have a modern phone that listed incoming call numbers – far too 21st century for the likes of Jack. Anyway, it was a risk I was prepared to take.

I was in my study, just about ready. I was free of distractions, for once unencumbered by the nagging awareness that I really ought to clear up all the detritus in the room. All my clothes had been put away, books and magazines consigned to their proper places on the shelves, the desk-top freed from its usual covering of clutter – except for the ashtray, no longer hidden behind the computer screen but occupying pride of place in front of it, ready to do what it had been designed for. In fact … yes, I'd roll a ciggie first, take a few drags before phoning, then save the rest for when I'd achieved my objective.

I tapped in the number. The dialling tone went on and on. Of course, Jack wouldn't have an answerphone, would he? I was about to disconnect when –

'Hello?'

'Jack! It's Tim here.'

'Oh.' He sounded distinctly unenthusiastic.

'Had you forgotten you were going to call me?'

'Yes. Had other things on my mind. What is it you want?'

That sounded unfriendly. It wasn't said aggressively, but rather as though the prospect of talking to me was unwelcome because he had better things to do.

'Just wanted to catch up with you after all these years, Jack, to hear how life's treated you. And are you still in contact with any of the others who were in our class? I'd love to – '

'Others in our class? Is this some sort of joke?'

I was taken aback, not so much by the indignation in his voice as by the fact he'd interrupted me. Jack never

189

used to force himself into a conversation: it was usually he who was interrupted.

'Joke? Why should it be a joke, Jack?'

'Oh, well, I suppose you haven't heard.'

'Heard what?'

'About Pete: you remember Pete Kennedy, I suppose?'

'Of *course* I do. What about him?'

'He's dead. He died last night, in hospital. Heart attack.'

'Bloody hell, Jack. Christ.'

Yes, I was shocked by the death of a contemporary, even one I'd never really liked: who wouldn't be? But immediately after the shock came disappointment, anger even. My carefully rehearsed script could not now be delivered. Events were slipping from my control.

I became conscious that Jack was talking.

'… so if you don't mind, I'd better attend to her. She's in a hell of a state. I'll let you know when the funeral is. You'll be coming, I suppose?'

'Sorry, Jack, didn't quite catch that. Who are you talking about? Who's in a hell of a state?'

I was dissembling of course. I knew who he was referring to. Great! It gave me the opportunity to take control again.

'I was talking about Jude. She's taken the news about Pete very badly. So I'd better go and try – '

'No! No, Jack, don't go, not yet. There's one thing I need to say.'

'What's that?'

'Just that I know how hard this must be for you, Jack. Having to pretend you're upset about Pete. And on top of that, having to comfort Judy. You've obviously forgiven her. That's very generous of you: I don't think I could have.'

'What? What d'you mean? What are you going on about?'

'Judy's fling with Pete, of course. Oh, I know it was a long time ago, but I gather it was pretty common

190

knowledge at the time, down in your part of the world.'

There was a prolonged silence. What wouldn't I have given to have seen the expression on his face! I hoped to God he wouldn't hang up: he needed to be skewered by my second revelation.

'You … you dunno what you're talking about.' His voice was decidedly shaky and I detected a trace of his former sub-cockney accent. 'How can you? You en't lived here for forty years, en't been in contact with any of us…' His voice trailed off.

'But Jack, I have been in contact with one old friend. Frank Grayson.'

'Frank? En't seen him for years.'

'I know that, Jack. But it was Frank who told me about your Judy's little fling with Pete – oh, must be getting on for twenty years ago now, wasn't it?'

I was hoping he'd ask the leading question, but there was no response. I'd best land the killer blow before he had a heart attack of his own.

'Didn't you know that Frank knew, Jack? Well, he did. And d'you know how he found out? Pete told him. Are you still there Jack? Did you hear that? Yes, it was Pete who told Frank. Boasted about it, apparently.'

It was then the line went dead. Mission accomplished.

I sank back in my chair, breathing heavily. Why was that? Exhilaration, perhaps? But I didn't actually feel as exalted as I thought I would. Perhaps it was because I couldn't witness the anguish I hoped that pathetic loser was now experiencing, his long-deserved punishment for being such a wimp that this wife sought comfort with Pete. Neither of them deserved her. If only she'd agreed to my request for a second date after we'd got it together at Lee Common. Life might have been different for both of us had she done so. I would certainly have rescued her from a lifetime of tedium: she might even have kept me on the straight and narrow. Why is it that one has to be approaching old age before one appreciates the significance of events in one's youth?

I reached for my fag – one advantage of roll-ups is they don't continue to burn when left in the ashtray. I re-lit it, took a deep drag. And then another. But as I continued smoking, I began to feel a sense of anti-climax. Okay, I'd sown the seeds of discord, had been involved in the first scene of the drama, but what next? I needed to see how the plot developed, what the climax would be, and to relish the denouement. But how could I?

A wild notion entered my head. I'd attend Pete's funeral, keep my distance from the mourners, observe how they behaved. Would Jack be talking to Judith, would Judy be talking to Frank? Would Pete's widow be talking to any of them, not that I'd ever met the woman, but she'd be easy to identify, wouldn't she? She'd be first in line behind the coffin.

I fantasised about the scene for several seconds before remembering that a journey down to Bucks by train would be impossible, being stared at by fellow passengers, commented on by their kids, mocked by yobbos. All that before I even got to the ceremony! Travel by taxi, maybe? No: far too expensive.

In any case, what would the reaction of the mourners be if they caught sight of me? *Who's that freak? Pete never mentioned knowing anyone like him.* And Jack and Judy and Frank – would they recognise me? Did I even want them to? I couldn't cope with their pity. Imagine being pitied by that loser Jack!

It had all gone wrong. In the space of fifteen minutes after ending my phone call to Jack, it seemed nothing had been gained. I wasn't even sure now what it was I'd hoped to achieve. I was just as alone as I'd been before setting out on this fruitless journey – no, more alone, because I no longer had Susie in whom I could confide.

Susie. For Christ's sake, why was I wishing for company, her sympathy? It was she who'd set me on this path to despair, wasn't it? She who'd helped me find the addresses, and she who'd then decided she wanted no more part of it and no more contact with me. Probably it was all pre-planned, a dyke's revenge on my heterosexuality. The bitch. The fucking bitch. All the future held now was a visit from Robert the Bruce.

I knew I couldn't face that. There was only one way out. But I needed to prepare for it carefully.

Buckinghamshire

It was only a short journey from Chesham to the crematorium in Old Amersham, but Judith hadn't driven for years. Jack had refused point blank to attend the funeral. Judith had considered hiring a taxi, but decided she needed an activity to distract her from thinking of the moment when she'd be reunited with people whom she wasn't sure she wished to see.

And she was having to concentrate, hard. The car had never been easy to handle, and she'd forgotten its idiosyncrasies. But worst of all was the blinding December sun, low in the sky, glinting at the edge of the visor. Why was it that so many of the funerals she'd attended in recent years had taken place in beautiful weather?

She left the town and drove up Chesham Hill. It was the road she'd travelled on the bus twice a day for seven years when she'd been at Grammar School. Jack and Pete had been fellow passengers for five of those years – no, she mustn't think of that. Concentrate on driving.

When she reached Amersham-on-the-Hill she realised her route was taking her past the Grammar School. She didn't want to be reminded of her school days. After leaving she'd never returned to the place, had never attended school reunions. Only a few years after she'd left, a new selective school for girls had been opened in a nearby village, and the old school had become boys only. As she drove past the school entrance she found she was thinking – if only the girl's Grammar had been in existence when she was a teenager! Pete and Jack at primary school would soon have been forgotten, and she would probably never have met Tim and Frank. And she wouldn't be making this journey today.

She entered Old Amersham. The crematorium was located on a hillside on the other side of the town, set in large grounds landscaped and extensively planted with trees, no doubt to spare motorists on the main road the sight of the furnace chimney. Judith had attended a few funerals here, mostly those of aged relatives but more recently those of a few contemporaries. No doubt she'd end up here – in twenty-or-so years, maybe, if she was lucky. Or thirty or forty, if she was unlucky. She'd probably see Jack out. He of course would want to be buried in Chesham churchyard after a Christian ceremony.

She was early, deliberately so. She parked close to the building's entrance and sat in her car waiting until the hearse arrived. The last thing she wanted was to stand in the cold having to talk to people. She'd wait until the coffin had been wheeled in and the mourners had filed in after it, then she'd slip in behind them and stand at the back. Any conversation she might have with people would best be left until the ceremony was over. She was still unsure what she was going to say, and apprehensive about what might be said to her.

People began to arrive. After parking, they had to walk past her car on their way to the covered waiting area in front of the entrance. None of them noticed her. She peered at each in turn, but failed to recognise any of them. Many were middle-aged men unaccompanied by female partners: Pete's business associates, probably. Men of a certain age in dark suits all looked the same. There were quite a few women of a similar age, unaccompanied by men. They clustered together near the entrance, exchanging air-kisses of greeting. Of course! Pete had told her that Marion was a member of her local Women's Institute. It occurred to her that the mourners, if such they could be called, represented the two halves of the Kennedys' separate lives.

A Golf Cabriolet drew up in a bay opposite to where Judith was parked. A woman got out from the passenger side. From the way she moved Judith guessed her to be youngish – there was no clutching at the car roof, no pushing on the seat. She was very slim. But she wasn't dressed like a young woman, apart from high heels, and her short dark hair was greying. She closed the car door and stood by it, waiting for the man in the driver's seat to get out. He was taking a long time to undo his seat belt.

Eventually, he heaved himself out, staggering before he achieved an upright posture. He was very overweight, almost completely bald, with puffy cheeks and sagging dewlaps. Judith judged him to be in his seventies. But when he moved slowly round the car to join the woman – his wife, presumably – Judith thought there was something familiar about the way he walked. He reached out to his wife and they walked hand in hand towards the entrance. Seen from the rear, his walk was unmistakable, even after forty years. It was Frank Grayson. The person to whom she most wanted, and most dreaded, to speak.

Her thoughts were diverted by the arrival of the hearse, and behind it a limousine. She watched the attendants reverentially lift the coffin out of the hearse and onto a wheeled trolley. Could it really be Pete in that box? It was hard to believe. There was never such a problem with aged relatives – after all, they'd always been old, hadn't they? But the lump of decaying flesh in the coffin was the child she'd played with, the teenager she'd been wary of, the young man who'd become a friend, and later so nearly something much more. But it had only been the once. He'd betrayed her, hadn't he? And she'd managed to convince herself that his heart attack was the consequence of his life style, not the result of their recent acrimonious parting.

When the coffin had been wheeled into a side entrance, she turned her attention to the limousine. The occupants were getting out, and went to stand alongside the other mourners. She recognised Marion, though she'd put on weight – but then she'd been chubby even back when

195

Judith and Jack had paid their rare visits to the Kennedy house. A slim, blonde woman was standing beside her. Could that be Sarah? She'd been a little girl when Judith had last seen her: she must be in her thirties now. If it *was* Sarah, she seemed to be making no effort to comfort her mother, who was dabbing her eyes. Strange. No doubt the man standing the other side of Sarah was her husband. He had his arms on the shoulders of two little girls, who looked overawed. Pete had told her, the last time they'd met, how he doted on his granddaughters, but even so, fancy their mother bringing kids of that age to a funeral!

Marion turned and led the mourners into the crematorium. Judith got out of the car, and joined the end of the procession.

***

Frank didn't enjoy funerals: they were getting to be too frequent, and, not being a believer, he always felt uncomfortable having to mouth the words to hymns and prayers. Once he and Angie were seated, halfway towards the back, he looked towards the lectern and the noticed the fellow standing behind it wasn't dog-collared or cassocked – thank God, it looked as though it was going to be a Humanist ceremony. Immediately, he realised the irony of his thanking God for that.

But a church ceremony would at least have provided the distraction of the scent of candles maybe, and certainly the sight of stained-glass windows, carvings, and memorials to the great and good of previous centuries. Crematoria were too austere, and they always had a faintly antiseptic smell. Their plain, brightly lit interiors meant there was no escaping the bleak view of a coffin standing on its plinth, ready for its descent into the furnace, though come to think of it, hadn't he heard that the actual incineration took place at night, lest people be upset by the sight of smoke rising from the chimney? No doubt all the bodies from each day's ceremonies were fried together.

Were the ashes of each of the deceased kept separate, he wondered?

Angie leaned towards him. 'Do you know any of these people?' she whispered.

'Recognise a few from Planning Committee meetings. Developers. Pete's clients. Don't know who the women are. Strange music for a funeral, isn't it?'

The entry of the mourners was being accompanied by a record of a guitar band playing an instrumental piece. The sound was rather tinny – why couldn't crematoria invest in proper speakers? Angie nudged him and pointed to the front page of the Order of Ceremony she was holding. It listed the music to be played. It seemed he was listening to *Wonderful Land* by the Shadows. Bloody hell, yes, he vaguely remembered Pete enthusing about that. He looked down the list – pop hits from the 50s and 60s. Could it be that Pete had given instructions about how he wanted his funeral conducted? It certainly wouldn't have been Marion who'd chosen that music. He remembered an incident back when he and Angie were still friends with the Kennedys, when, over dinner, Marion had derided Pete's love of rock'n'roll. He, Frank, had joined in the derision.

The last guitar chord faded away. Frank sneaked a look behind him – yes everyone was seated. Not exactly a full house. He was looking to see if any old school friends were present, in particular Jack and Judith, though he doubted he'd recognise them even if they were here. He couldn't spot them. He'd almost forgotten the complex details of who, apart from himself, and now Tim, knew about the Pete/Judith fling – maybe Marion perhaps? But did Jack? And in any case, would Judith want to attend?

Come to think of it, why was *he* here? Whatever friendship had existed between him and Pete had long gone, and as for Marion … He was here to support Angela, he supposed. But it came to him that there was another reason. It was generational solidarity, a sense that people like him who remembered the world as it once was would soon all be memories themselves.

The Officiant moved towards the lectern. Frank felt Angie touch his hand: she squeezed it. Bless her, she hadn't been upset when he'd revealed that he'd told Tim about Pete and Judith. She understood what had led him to do it. Things were still good between them. Please God – God again! – let it be many years before one of them stood in a crematorium in front of the other's coffin.

***

Marion couldn't take anything in. Bits of the day were still vivid – the argument she'd continued to have with Sarah about her choice of music, the difficulty she'd had in struggling into the black suit which had seemed to fit her well enough in the shop, the slow ride through the sunlit Chilterns to get here. But now, sitting listening to the Officiant but not hearing what he was saying, she couldn't grasp what all this was about. Pete was dead, certainly. He was there in the box in front of her. But what should she be feeling? Grief? Relief? Anger? She veered between the three, and occasionally felt all simultaneously.

The Officiant finished his address and stepped back. Marion started when Sarah rose and made her way to the lectern: she'd completely forgotten that Sarah had insisted on giving the … what had she called it? Eulogy, yes, that was it. It had been another source of conflict between mother and daughter: surely a relative oughtn't to do that? Shouldn't it be one of Pete's old friends?

'Who do you suggest, then, mum?' Sarah had asked. 'Frank Grayson, the bastard? Or that Judith woman?' At that, Marion had clammed up. She still had no idea why Judith should have been the last name on Pete's lips, and she didn't want to know. Why the hell did Sarah keep going on about her?

Sarah began her address. It was punctuated by sniffs. Marion knew it off by heart because she'd had to listen to her rehearsing it aloud, on at least four occasions. It went way over the top. What a wonderful dad! What super times they'd had! How he'd loved his grandchildren! How they loved him! She, Marion, wasn't mentioned. The address ended with Sarah saying how much dad used to love this next song, and how appropriate it was that he'd died in December, whereupon the speakers crackled into life and Marion was forced to listen to Elvis singing *Blue Christmas*. She blanked it out by forcing herself to recall Pete's last abusive actions. Anger was the best antidote to schmaltz. But bloody hell, she could do with a drink.

***

Angela was finding the ceremony mawkish beyond belief. The music was bad enough, but even more painful was Sarah's sentimental panegyric. And not a word about her mother! From where Angela was sitting she could see the back of Marion's bowed head: what on earth should she say to her when the service was over? To say the trite words *I'm sorry for your loss* to someone who'd once been a close friend would be far too formal, but what expression of sympathy, if any, would be appropriate for a widow who'd been abused by her husband? Perhaps she'd just give Marion a hug. But then there was Sarah, of course. Angela had no idea what she would say to her, but a hug was out of the question.

Sarah's address was apparently nearing its end: she'd turned to face the coffin. 'This last record was another one of Dad's favourites,' she said. 'It says everything about how I'm feeling. It's called *So Sad*.'

Angela could remember that song. Although she'd soon outgrown the music of her teens, she'd always enjoyed the keening harmonies of the Everly Brothers. But again, more mawkish sentiment! She found herself listening to the words *–We used to have good times together, so sad to watch good love turn bad.* Had Sarah deliberately chosen this record to make a point about her parents' marriage? Or was it just an example of her apparent gross insensitivity? This funeral seemed to be entirely about

Sarah's own agenda.

The coffin began its rather jerky descent. Once it had disappeared, the Officiant stepped to the lectern, said a few valedictory words, then reminded everyone they were invited to join the family for refreshments at the *Kings Arms* in Old Amersham. The assembly began to file out, led by Marion and Sarah. Angela's relief at the ending of the ceremony was tempered by the knowledge that she and Frank now had to join the queue to offer their condolences.

***

Outside the exit, Sarah took up position next to her mother. Marion was nearest to the door, so those leaving would be required to speak to her first. This suited Sarah, given that she knew so few of the attendees. And it was about time mum contributed something to the proceedings; she'd done precious little so far. But Sarah was relieved that things had gone so well, just as she'd planned it. Dad had been given the send-off he deserved, and he would have loved the music. The kids had behaved themselves as well, but they were excused this duty. Their dad had taken them to the car.

The unaccompanied women were the first out. Most of them kissed Marion's cheek and muttered a few remarks in her ear, but Sarah noted that her mother had little to say in return. Obviously, not close friends then. Probably acquaintances from the Women's Institute. Each of them smiled at Sarah as they passed her, but few of them spoke. Miserable bitches, Sarah thought – didn't it occur to any of them to complement her on her eulogy?

Then came the men. They all looked ill-at-ease as they waited to greet Marion. Sarah watched as the first one shook her mother's hand, then said 'Robin Tyler, Tyler Construction. I'm sorry for your loss.' He then shook Sarah's hand and said exactly the same thing to her. The men who followed all took their cue from the first, each announcing his name, the name of his company, and then

200

expressing his sorrow. Sarah said 'Thank you' to each, but she noticed her mother remained silent. It was obvious that Marion hadn't met any of them before. She'd always complained that dad had never included her in whatever social activities accompanied his business. For the first time that day, Sarah felt a flicker of sympathy for her.

While she was thanking the last of the businessmen, she saw, out of the corner of her eye, bloody Frank Grayson and his wife. What a nerve that man had. Angela walked straight up to Marion and flung her arms round her. Marion returned the hug. The embrace lasted a long time, but Sarah was unable to hear if any words were exchanged. When it was over, Angela approached her and made to kiss her cheek. Sarah dodged it. How dare the woman presume such an intimacy! After having, no doubt, been party to whatever her husband had done to dad!

Sarah couldn't face being greeted by Frank. He shook her mother's hand, said a few words, but Sarah turned her head away as he made to speak to her. For a moment he hesitated in front of her, then moved on. A scattering of suits followed, the odd one accompanied by a skirt. Sarah could sense that her mother was getting restless: longing for a gin and tonic probably.

Then, at the very end of the procession, a woman. Smartly dressed in a black suit, slim to the point of being too thin, short grey hair, a face scored with lines which couldn't disguise the fine bone structure. She also, Sarah noticed with a flash of envy, had very good legs. She approached Marion and the two stood facing each other. The woman spoke first.

'Marion. Do you remember me? It's ages since we last met. I'm Judy, Judy Kennedy, Jack's wife. I'm so sorry about Pete.'

Sarah grabbed her mother's arm and led her away.

***

Judith was the last to drive out of the crematorium car

park. She'd waited until Marion and Sarah's limousine had left before she'd walked to her car.

What had all that been about? Why had Marion's daughter been so rude? As for Marion, it was hard to judge what her reaction had been to seeing her: a hint of hostility on her face perhaps, before she'd been hustled away? Of course, back when she'd first married Pete, her attitude to Judith, and to Jack had been patronising at best, dismissive at worst. But she'd never shown outright rudeness. So why now? Surely Pete hadn't confessed their fling? No. Impossible. If so, surely Pete would have said so when they met three weeks ago? Only three weeks? It seemed like years.

She had difficulty in finding a space in the *King's Arms* carpark. It was the first time she'd been there. It was a half-timbered hotel on Amersham High Street which, back in the 60s wasn't the sort of place the youth of Chesham would have wanted to frequent, even if they'd had cars in which to get there. Even Tim and Frank, both Amersham lads, had described it as stuffy. And now, although a well-dressed respectable lady in her late-50s holding a responsible job, she felt slightly intimidated when she walked in.

The lounge bar was decorated for Christmas, tastefully of course. She was greeted by a uniformed young man, who, when told she was a member of the funeral party, directed her to a function room leading off the lounge. A hum of muted conversation came from people standing in groups and holding glasses of wine and plates of nibbles. Judith didn't feel like eating, but took a glass of white wine from the tray held by a waitress, then moved over to the side of the room where she stood observing the interaction between the guests. She could see Marion talking to a group of four women. A few feet away Sarah was surrounded by men. There was no sign of her husband or children. It occurred to Judith that Sarah was the only young person present: everyone else was late-middle-aged or older. As glasses of wine were consumed, conversations were becoming more animated. It wouldn't be long before someone laughed loudly. She'd noticed this often happened at funeral wakes. Did people subconsciously become aware they were survivors and should celebrate the fact?

As soon as she'd entered the room, she'd noticed Frank, standing with his wife – God, she looked more than twenty years younger than him – over by the large patio window. Now and again Frank was approached by some of the men, and a few words were exchanged. Some were introduced to Frank's wife. But the conversations were short, and it wasn't long before the couple were left standing by themselves. Unusually for a couple of that age, they seemed to have a lot to say to each other.

Oh for God's sake, why couldn't the woman go to refill her plate, or seek out the wine waitress, or go to the loo, anything that would leave Frank by himself for a few minutes? But Judith realised that the longer she waited, the more her resolution would dissolve. She'd have to do it now, regardless of his wife being present.

She put down her wine glass, walked over to them and stood in front of Frank. He stopped talking to his wife and looked at Judith. It was a quizzical look, with no sign that he recognised her. Close up, his physical deterioration was even more apparent.

'Frank. Hello. Remember me? It's Judith. Judy Mason as was. Judith Kennedy now: I married Jack. Remember him?'

He stared at her. Then –

'Judy! Good God, Judy!'

For a moment, Judith thought he was going to hug her. But he turned to his wife.

'Angie, this is Judy. We were at Grammar School together. Haven't seen each other since just after we left. Judy, this is Angie.'

The two women exchanged hellos.

'Judy, you look wonderful!' Frank said. 'How are things with you? And Jack: isn't he here? Is he all right?'

'No, Jack isn't here, and he isn't all right. That's something I want to talk to you about.' Judith was surprised that her voice sounded so calm.

'Oh, he's not ill, is he?'

'Not ill. Just very distressed. So am I.' She noticed a flicker of uncertainty pass over his face.

'Distressed? I'm sorry to hear that, Judy. But how can I help?'

This was the point of no return. She'd just state the facts, bluntly but calmly, in the hope of shaming him into an abject apology. If his wife was an innocent party in all this, then too bad.

'Listen to me Frank. I know that you know I had a fling with Pete, a very long time ago. It was a one-off and I'm not proud of it. I also know that you threatened to tell Jack about it. It was Pete who told me all this, only a few weeks back – yes, I saw him that recently, and no, our relationship was purely platonic. I'm not interested in your motives, Frank. I don't care about whatever it was Pete did to make you threaten him. All I want to say is this: how could you even think of ruining the life of a man who never harmed anyone? Yes, I mean Jack '

She paused, not for breath, but to try to swallow. Her throat was dry. Frank was staring at her open-mouthed. She noticed that Angela was holding his hand, looking at him not in surprise, but with concern. Obviously, none of what Judith had said had been news to her.

'But Judy – '

'I haven't finished yet. I said Jack was distressed, didn't I? That's because he *knows*. He knows I had that fling, and he knows that Pete told you. He only found out a few days ago. Any idea how he found out, Frank? I'll tell you. Tim Bailey phoned him and told him. And how did Tim get to find out? I think you know the answer to that, don't you, Frank?'

Frank was shaking his head, then he put his hands to his temples. Judith realised that she didn't need to hear the answer to her last question, and no longer wanted to wait for an apology – what good would it do? She'd had her say: that was enough. She didn't want to be here anymore. She must get home to Jack, to try once again to get him to talk to her.

She turned abruptly and began to walk to the door. She heard Frank say 'Judy, wait!' and at that her pace quickened and she pushed her way through the guests. In her haste she brushed against Marion, but didn't stop to apologise. As she ran towards her car she was conscious that she'd burned her boats, that by her actions she'd now severed all connections with her school friends. Except Jack, of course.

'Judith! Please wait!

Judith had climbed into her car and was about to slam the door shut when the call came from across the car park. A female voice. She looked out to see Angela running towards her in her stockinged feet, her high-heeled shoes in her hand.

Judith wondered - should she stay? She had no quarrel with Angela, at least she assumed she didn't. Her hesitation was enough to allow Angela to reach the car and bend down so her face was at the window. She looked distraught. 'Please let me talk to you, Judith,' she heard her say.

The manners drilled into Judith by her parents took over. To have ignored the plea and have driven off was something her conditioning didn't allow; she was conscience-stricken at the very thought of it. She wound down the window. 'You'd better get in.' She opened the passenger door.

'Oh God, my feet are wet, and muddy too,' Angela said as she got in. 'Sorry to mess up your car.'

'You couldn't make it more of a mess than it is already.' Judith realised she was apologising. Why? Because, she realised, she was assuming that Angela probably drove a flashy modern car. Frank had presumably inherited his father's wealth, and in any case was a businessman as well as a county councillor.

Angela smoothed down her skirt. It was a demure skirt, slightly old-fashioned, and not obviously expensive. Judith found herself warming to her.

'Angela. I don't know you. I've got no quarrel with you. I'm sorry if what I said upset you. I wanted it to be for Frank's ears only, but … well, you never left each other's side, did you?'

'We tend not to, at affairs like funerals. Judith, I can understand how you're feeling – oh hell, what a stupid thing to say. I can't possibly understand, can I? I've never been in your position. Look, would you mind just listening to me for a few minutes? I just want to explain how all this mess came about.'

'Would it make me feel any better?'

Angela appeared to be considering this.

'Probably not,' she said eventually. 'If I'm honest, Judith – look, can I call you Judy? Yes? Well, if I'm honest what I really want you to realise is that Frank isn't the bastard you think he is. He just made one mistake. Without going into details, he acted unprofessionally as a councillor in a way which disadvantaged Pete's business, and the only way he could think to stop Pete spilling the beans was to threaten to … well, you know.'

'I call that two mistakes. Did he tell you about it at the time?'

'Yes, he did. We've never had secrets from each other. I thought what he did was wrong, and told him so. But he already knew that. He's spent the rest of his life regretting it. He's not a bad man, Judy. We all make mistakes.'

'Does he regret the other mistake he made?'

'What d'you mean?'

'Telling Tim Bailey all about it. So that Tim could tell Jack.'

Angela didn't reply. Judith looked sideways at her: she was staring through the windscreen. Her mouth was working slightly. Judith began to feel sorry for her: she was trying to defend her husband against the indefensible.

'Look, Angela,' she said. 'You don't need to put yourself through this. I don't hold you to blame in any way. Let's just forget it, shall we?'

'I can't forget it. You see, what you just said, about Frank telling Tim Bailey. I feel partly responsible for that.'

Then she turned to face Judith.

'This isn't really the place for this conversation, is it? People'll start coming out to their cars soon. And my feet are bloody freezing. But there's still lots to talk about, isn't there? Look, I'm going to give you my mobile phone number. If ever you do feel like meeting and talking, text me.'

Judith laughed. 'I don't have a mobile phone.'

'You're kidding!'

'No, I'm not.' She was about to add that she thought they had nothing more to say to each other, then it occurred her: she'd handled her conversation with Frank badly, hadn't asked him for the one piece of information she needed. Maybe Angela could provide it?

'But you can give me your number,' she said. 'It'd be okay to phone you on it from my landline, wouldn't it?'

'Yes, of course. Hang on … oh damn, I don't have pen or paper with me. Have you?'

'No, I haven't. What would I want with pen and paper at a funeral?'

They looked at each other and grinned.

PART SEVEN

December 2002

Buckinghamshire

Judith

Saturday morning. Judith and Jack were walking together down the High Street on their way to Costa. Such a joint excursion was rare, but now they were, for the first time in decades, going to have coffee with another couple. Most surprising of all, and Judith still couldn't quite believe it was about to happen, it was Angela and Frank whom they were to meet.

She was still dazed by the events of the past few days. It had all happened so quickly – her phone call to Angela the day after the funeral, Angela's plea that Frank be given a chance to apologise to her, Frank coming on the line and saying he wanted to explain and apologise to both her and Jack in person, and couldn't they all meet somewhere? Then her attempts to get Jack to talk to her, success being achieved only when she'd told him that she wasn't prepared to carry on living with him like this, and, when this threat worked sufficiently for him at least to start responding to her remarks, her two-day campaign to persuade him to meet Frank.

They'd set off early for Costa, at Jack's insistence. 'I want to get there first,' he'd said. 'Don't like the idea of seeing bloody Frank sitting there looking like he owns the place when I walk in.' Judith wondered why he was so possessive about a coffee bar.

Christmas was only a week away and the pedestrianised street, usually echoingly empty, contained more people than Judith remember seeing for years. She rarely visited the High Street on Saturdays, preferring to shop in her work lunch-hours. Her circle of acquaintances shopped at the weekends in the large Tesco store in Amersham.

It was as well they were early, because their progress along the High Street was slow. A number of people, mostly men but also a few women, hailed Jack, stopped to talk to him. Judith knew a couple of the men, but the rest had to be introduced to her. This brought home to her again how she and Jack led largely separate lives. 'How do you know all these people?' she asked, after Jack had wished a Merry Christmas to the sixth or seventh person who'd spoken to him.

'Oh, you know, the library mainly, and the choir of course.'

'And what about the young women? Why didn't you introduce *them* to me?'

'Oh, they're just people I run into now and again. Don't know their names.'

'Your secret life, eh?' she said in an attempt to be ironic, then immediately regretted her choice of the very words he'd used about her during their recent acrimonious conversations.

In fact, she was grateful for the exchanges of Christmas greetings because it meant that Jack's attention was, if only temporarily, diverted from the forthcoming meeting with Frank, something that was still possible he might walk away from. He'd fought hard against seeing Frank, apparently blaming him for everything that had gone wrong. In an effort to convince him otherwise, Judith had done what she'd always known she'd have to do – been totally honest about everything that had happened in the past. She'd managed to convince him that Pete had been a one-off, and in the discussion that followed about that, they'd spoken more intimately about their marital problems than they ever had at the time when they most needed to. But not intimately enough.

It was when she'd started talking about Tim that she found she was being honest not just with Jack, but, for the first time, with herself. She'd always tried to blank out what had happened forty years ago at Lee Common because she was ashamed. 'Leading him on' was the phrase that would have been used at the time to describe her behaviour, and she supposed she had, because he'd aroused feelings in her that she'd never experienced before. But when she'd asked him to stop, he hadn't. When she'd insisted that he stop, he still hadn't. And when she'd resisted, he'd used force. So she'd felt guilty not just for encouraging him, but for changing her mind at the last moment.

When she'd explained all this to Jack, he'd reacted with anger – why hadn't she told him this before? And why hadn't she reported Tim to the police? It had taken her a long time to make him understand that back in the 1960s things were different for girls. She couldn't have stood the shame. And she wouldn't have been believed.

But she no longer felt shame, nor guilt. Now, the meeting with Frank was even more important. Any apology that Frank would offer to her and Jack would just be a small bonus. Most vital was that he give her Tim's email address. She would insist on that, as a condition of her accepting his apology. She wanted to lambast Tim, not just for his malicious phone revelations to Jack, but for the way he'd abused her, no, use the right words, raped her, when she was eighteen.

Jack had always been courteous, so it surprised Judith when instead of holding the door open for her, he barged ahead into Costa then stood, blocking her entry. He peered round the room, then, evidently satisfied, led her to a table near the window.

'Let's sit here Jude, so we can get advance warning before Frank walks in. Right; straight coffee for you I suppose? What d'you want to eat? The carrot cake's pretty good in here.'

Judith opted for an Americano but said she didn't want anything to eat. She was feeling nervous. She watched

Jack as he walked to the serving bar. As he made his way there he turned his head on three occasions and grinned at people who were waving and smiling at him. They were all young women, accompanied by infants. It was evident he was a regular and popular customer here. And now he was being chatted to and smiled at by the girl taking his order. Judith was seeing her husband in a new light: her mind's eye view of him was that of the sober, almost dour man who shared her house and whose only social contact was with members of the church choir and the old men whom he met in the library. And Pete, of course, until a few weeks ago.

Watching him as he stood waiting for his order to be delivered, it struck her that for his age he was a good-looking man, in fact much more attractive than he'd been in his youth when he'd been a rather shambling uncoordinated figure. He still had his hair, his bone structure was good (she'd always envied his straight nose), he was slim and he carried himself well. Strange how she'd never really appreciated this before. Perhaps it was the result of having seen Frank a few days ago: she still found it hard to believe that the obese old man at the funeral was the handsome sixth-former who'd chaperoned her on her visits to the *George* with Tim.

Jack, her husband, an attractive man! The idea was novel. Did he know he was? If this was so, did that mean he found his personal problem the more hard to bear? To know that even if he wanted to take advantage of whatever a woman might offer him, he would be unable to take it up? No: he probably never even considered it. He had reached the age where his problem was, so she'd read, common amongst men, and many men apparently accepted it. She assumed Jack had, as had she, almost. But it had taken nearly forty years for her to come to terms with it. She sometimes congratulated herself on only once having fallen from grace, but in her guts she knew her regrets were not for the things she'd done, but for the things she hadn't. Her curse was to have had an active libido in constant conflict with the values drummed into her by her upbringing.

Jack advanced toward her carrying a tray, smiling as he approached, not at her, but at the young women. He put down the tray, then sat, facing the window.

'Thanks,' she said, then 'How much time d'you spend in here?'

'I call in every Saturday after I finish at the library, don't I? Why?'

'It's just you seem to know a lot of people here.'

'Well, it's a bit like pubs used to be, isn't it? You know, regulars, and you get to –'

He stopped and stared out of the window.

'Bloody hell, is that Frank?'

Judith turned. Frank and Angela were approaching.

'Yes, that's Frank. I told you he'd put on weight. Try not to stare at him too much, and please be polite, won't you?'

'I'm always polite.'

Jack and Frank shook hands. Frank said that Jack looked very well, Jack returned the compliment. There followed an embarrassed pause, mercifully broken by Frank having to introduce Angela and Jack to each other. Jack shook her hand, said he was pleased to meet her. Angela turned and hugged Judith – a bit over-effusive, Judith thought, given they'd had only one previous meeting, but she returned the hug, and the actions served as something of an ice-breaker. Frank took Angela's coffee order and went to the service bar.

The three of them sat down. Angela took charge of the conversation. Judith noted how she took care to involve Jack in the chat. She asked him about the town, how long he'd lived here, said how Frank always spoke fondly of his times here. Jack responded politely, though, as Judith expected, he couldn't resist pointing out that Frank had lived in Amersham, a much posher town.

Frank returned with two coffees, a cinnamon whirl and

a slice of carrot cake, both on one plate. He sat down and began greedily devouring the cinnamon whirl, which he finished before starting on his coffee. Judith noticed that Angela was watching him, a slightly exasperated expression on her face, but she said nothing. If Frank's eating habits were the only cause of strain in their marriage, then lucky them, she thought.

'It's strange to be back in the old town,' Frank said after taking a swig of coffee. 'I never get to come here now. Is the *George* still going, Jack? D'you still go there?'

'It's still open, but it's not what it was,' said Jack, 'but I go every Sunday with …' He tailed off.

Frank looked at him quizzically. Judith decided to intervene.

'Jack used to go there with Pete,' she said. 'But even if Pete hadn't died, Jack wouldn't want to go with him now, would you Jack?'

Jack shook his head. Frank looked embarrassed. Angela put down her coffee cup and grasped his hand. 'Come on, Frank,' she said. 'We all know why we're here. Why don't you just say what you've come here to say?'

Frank sat back in his chair, put one arm across his swollen belly and rested the elbow of his other arm on his hand. With his free hand he began stroking his chin. Was this an affectation, Judith wondered? He looked as if he was about to pronounce on a public matter of extreme importance. Was it a pose he adopted in Council meetings, perhaps?

He cleared his throat.

'Jack, Judy, thanks so much for coming. Jack, I would have quite understand if you never wanted to see me again. After I came back to Bucks I often thought I'd like to meet up, but then, after what happened I … well, I was too ashamed, I suppose.'

Jack made as if to reply, but Judith put a restraining hand on his arm. 'Let him finish, Jack.'

'Look, the only thing I want to say … well, the only thing I can say, really, is how sorry I am for what I did, well, what I threatened to do. Y'see, Pete had me over a barrel, I'd behaved unprofessionally, Pete was going to spill the beans, so the only way I could stop him was – '

Angela interrupted. 'Jack and Judy know all that, Frank. No need to go all over it again.'

'And if he *had* spilled the beans,' said Judith, 'would you have done what you threatened to do?'

Frank slumped forward, put his forearms on the table. 'I honestly don't know, Judy. I like to think I wouldn't have – after all, it would have just been revenge, too late to have done me any good. But I was angry. All I can do is say how desperately sorry I am. I'm not asking you to forgive me.'

'It all was a long time ago.' The remark, said quietly, came from Jack. Judith wondered if Frank had heard it over the clatter of crockery and the hissing of the coffee machine.

'That's very generous of you, Jack,' said Frank.

Judith wasn't prepared to give Frank such an easy ride. 'But there was something else you did quite recently, wasn't there?' she said. 'You told Tim about it. What on earth made you do that? After all these years? Are you still in contact with him?'

Frank sighed and glanced at Angela. 'I can only apologise again, Judy. As for why I did it, well, I'd find it very hard to explain. It was all down to my own personal problems.'

'Judy,' said Angela, 'it was partly my fault. I'd cut Frank out at a time when he needed to confide in me. I'll tell you all about it sometime. But Frank had been contacted by Tim, who seemed to invite confidences, so Frank … oh God, this is all so complicated. Judy, I know how sorry Frank is. Can't you, and Jack, accept his apology? Please?'

Judith noticed that Angela had grasped Frank's hand while she was talking. They were still holding hands, and Frank was looking at her … how? It could only be described as lovingly. Long-married couples rarely demonstrated such affection in public. It occurred to Judith that the relationship might still be physical. For some reason she couldn't define, this didn't result in envy; instead it made her warm to them. And she was also warmed by the prospect of a growing friendship with Angela.

'All right,' she said. 'I'll accept your apology if Jack does. Do you, Jack?'

Jack nodded. Frank leaned across the table and reached for Jack's hand, which after a second's hesitation Jack took. There was a fumbled handshake. Judith noticed two women sitting at an adjacent table staring at them, puzzled expressions on their faces.

'One thing you haven't answered, Frank,' she said. 'Are you still in contact with Tim?'

'Well, we have each other's e-mail addresses, but I wouldn't say we – '

'Can I have his email address please?'

'Well, I suppose so, but why? Wouldn't it be best just to let things rest?'

'No. Why should he get away with it? I want to tell him – '

'Jude!' Jack interrupted. 'Wait. I'd like to talk to Frank about this. Just me and him.'

Judith was astounded, Jack rarely interrupted her, let alone make an unexpected suggestion.

'That's an excellent idea!' exclaimed Angela. 'You boys must have lots to catch up on. Shall we leave them to it, Judy?'

'Well … yes, I suppose we could. But there aren't any other good coffee places around here.'

'But you live in town, don't you? Can we go back to yours? Can we walk it?'

'Well, yes, we could.'

'Good. Let's go.' She stood up, turned to Frank. 'Take your time boys. We'll see you later.'

Judith was worrying about what Angela might think of their poky little cottage, but her attention was diverted by the sight of Frank greedily devouring the carrot cake which had remained on his plate since soon after he'd arrived. Crumbs were falling from his mouth. It was just how he used to eat in the Prefect's room at school. It always seemed to make him seem less upper-class, less aloof. So if Angela was accustomed to those sort of manners …

She waved a goodbye to Jack and led Angela out of the door.

Motorways Northbound

Jack

For God's sake try and relax, Jack told himself, conscious that his hands were clenched. He'd just glanced at the speedometer: 70mph. Frank seemed not to be concentrating on his driving, he was talking about his job and his impending retirement, and occasionally glancing sideways at him. And the motorway was busy – so many lorries! Frank constantly wove between the middle and outside lanes to overtake them, a manoeuvre that Jack thought was unnecessary: why not just stick to one lane? They weren't in that much of a hurry, were they? After all, they weren't expected to arrive at a specific time: in fact, they weren't expected at all.

Jack never drove on motorways these days: his old banger wasn't up to it, and in any case he'd always been a nervous driver, and his reaction times were starting to diminish. It occurred to him that his last motorway outing was along this very stretch, back in the 1970s when the M40 terminated near Oxford. It was relatively quiet back then, possible to sneak quick sideways glances at the Chiltern countryside.

He remembered now why he'd gone on that journey: he'd wanted to see the recently opened stretch of the motorway that descended through the Chiltern escarpment

216

down to the Vale of Aylesbury. His worse fears had been confirmed: a brutal cutting sliced through the chalk, severing meadows, footpaths and bridleways, a cutting so steep-sided that no trees would ever be able to take root. He'd vowed never to travel that way again. But now here he was, on that same stretch of road.

'It can get a bit busy when we get near Oxford,' Frank was saying. 'Nose to tail sometimes.'

'So I hear from radio traffic reports.'

'Don't you ever come out this way, then?'

'Frank, I haven't driven on a motorway for over 25 years.'

'Good heavens.'

'In fact, I don't mind telling you I'm a bit of a nervous passenger. Would you mind very much slowing down a bit, mate?'

'Of course, I can. Sorry, Jack. Most inconsiderate of me.'

Just as polite as he used to be at school, thought Jack, where his politeness was expressed so formally that it smacked of condescension. It was only after their conversation alone together in Costa that Jack had come to appreciate how emotional he could be. It was that conversation which had resulted in the journey they were undertaking together today.

As soon as Jude and Angela had left Costa, Jack had regretted his insistence that he and Frank be left to talk alone. He'd known what he wanted to say, but hadn't known how to broach it. They'd never been close friends at school: he'd been in awe of Frank, who'd always seemed aloof, even on the rare occasions when he'd joined the gang playing cricket at Lee Common. And when Frank had started coming to the *George*, he'd found him even less approachable, because Frank was by then a Sixth Former.

But Frank had cut straight to the chase, had asked Jack what it was he wanted to discuss without their wives being present, adding that if Jack wanted to get his loathing for Pete out of his system then that was all right by him. Jack had blurted out that it was Tim who was a bigger bastard, and told him what Tim had done to Jude. On hearing this Frank had exploded into a rant, employing the sort of language that Jack had never heard him use before, ending by saying he could appreciate how Jude, even after all these years, wanted to email Tim to berate him for all he'd done. It had then been a simple matter for Jack to explain that he wouldn't be content with an on-line conversation: he wanted to confront the bastard face-to-face. Frank had been quiet for a moment, then had said 'I think that can be arranged, Jack.'

'You still haven't told me how you managed to track him down, Frank.'

Frank slowed down, took up position behind an Eddie Stobart lorry and remained there.

'Well, it took a bit of doing. Then I told Angie what we were planning. She was dead against it at first; said we ought to let things rest. She took a lot of persuading. Then I had to clear my work diary. I wanted to get this meeting out of the way before Christmas.'

'That's what I told Jude. She took a lot of persuading as well.'

That was putting it mildly, but Jack decided against telling Frank they'd almost had a full-blown row about it. Jude had been in tears, and he couldn't understand why. It wasn't until he'd put his arms round her, pleaded with her to tell him what the problem was, that she'd confessed to worrying that Tim might persuade him that she'd been a willing participant. It had taken a lot of affectionate reassurance to convince her that of course it was her he believed, that nothing Tim could say would make him believe otherwise. They'd found themselves cuddling, When had they last done that? Would it happen again?

He pulled himself back to the present. 'Anyway, Frank, how did you find him?'

'Well, he'd told me he lived in north Staffordshire. And I knew he'd changed his name because – '

'Changed his name?'

'Oh, I haven't told you that, have I? He's called David now, David Turner.'

'But why?'

'Don't know for sure. He was a bit vague about it, but it seems to be connected to the fact that he had to retire early – I told you he'd had some sort of accident, didn't I?'

'Yes. Serves the bastard right.'

'Anyway, I'm acquainted with a County Councillor from Staffordshire. Met him at a Tory Party junket some years ago. He did a bit of research for me – electoral register, council tax payment records, that sort of thing. Found his address.'

'So you Tories do have some uses, then.'

Frank laughed. 'Let's just hope Mr Turner's at home. Now, I'm going to have to speed up a bit, Jack. We want to get back home tonight, don't we?'

Yes, Jack certainly wanted to get home that night. He wanted the coming confrontation to be behind him so the matter could be finally consigned to the past, so he and Jude could go back to the way things were before ... but no, that wasn't enough, was it? Having seen the way Frank and Angela were together had brought home to him how he and Jude were just affectionate companions sharing a house, nothing else. Was it all down to his ... problem? Should he have sought help, as Jude had once begged him to? He hadn't, because he was ashamed. Back in the 60s and 70s people weren't encouraged to be open about that sort of personal issue. But God, how he now regretted his refusal. Was he was to blame for all that had happened since, starting with Jude having to seek comfort with Pete? He was tempted to ask Frank to turn back at the next junction, to abandon the idea of confronting Tim or Dave or whatever his bloody name was now. But no: Frank had his own reasons to complete this mission. It would be selfish to deny him that.

But when they met Tim, how should they play it? They hadn't discussed the matter yet. Jack had no idea what he would say; perhaps Frank was in a similar quandary. Should they be reasonable, seek to shame him into contrition? Or go onto the attack, tell him what a shit they thought he was? How would he respond? Might he get violent, even? But hadn't Frank said he was disabled in some way? The thought of three old gits exchanging punches was laughable. In his head, Jack ran various scenarios over and over again. It was like watching a badly-scripted TV soap.

'It'll be slow going for a few miles from now on,' said Frank

Jack started. His head had been so full of what was to come that he'd been paying no attention to the journey, was no longer nervous about the traffic. It seemed they were nose-to-tail in a queue.

'What's all this then? Has there been an accident ahead?'

'No. It's the usual tailback you get before joining the M42. We get on it to link up with the M6. It's usually jam-packed.'

So it proved to be. Jack was astounded: he'd never seen such a complex system of slip-roads and flyovers, traffic at a snail's pace, indicating to change lanes, queuing to leave or join the main carriageway.

'Blimey, Frank. I pity the poor sods who have to do this every day.'

Frank laughed. 'It's getting like this round most cities now. But it should be better here next year, once the toll road opens.'

'Toll road?'

'They're constructing a toll road to link the M42 with the M6 north of Birmingham, didn't you know? Not in time for us, I'm afraid. We'll be joining the M6 at the next interchange.'

A toll road, in England? Jack found the idea hard to take. But then he found a lot of new developments disturbing. When he read headlines in the paper alluding to them, he turned over the page. When mention was made of them on the TV or radio, he turned off – sometimes literally, much to Jude's annoyance. He was beginning to feel like a foreigner in his own country. That was why he tried to restrict himself to the familiar – his home town, the countryside of his youth, where the changes had been more gradual, easier to accept. Bloody hell, he was feeling uneasy being as far away as the midlands, being driven through an unfamiliar landscape. More than ever, he wanted to get home to Jude.

'Frank,' he said, 'd'you mind me asking: did Tim ever talk to you about Jude, back when you two used to bring her to the *George*?'

'Oh yes. He made his intentions quite clear, not just to me, but to Judy as well. In fact, it was Judy who insisted that I join them. She wanted me as a chaperone.'

'So she didn't … well, fancy him?'

'I don't know about that, but I don't need to tell you what a moral sort of girl she was at school. I felt I had to protect her from Tim.'

'Did he ever tell you that he'd … been with her?'

'No, Jack. I can honestly say he never did. Not that we ever spent much time alone together. I never really warmed to him.'

'Really? I thought, you two being in the Sixth Form, and all that …'

'Oh, don't get me wrong, I didn't dislike him. He was just never a bosom pal.'

'Can I ask you something else?'

'Try me.'

'I could never understand how you got to be so friendly with Pete, after you came back to Bucks from London. I didn't think he was your cup of tea at all, when we were at school, I mean.'

'Just circumstances, I suppose, him living so close. But it was the wives who really hit it off. Angie always felt a bit sorry for Marion. She still is.'

221

'She's a lovely-looking lady, your Angela.'

'I know that, Jack. Much too lovely for a fat, bald old codger like me, eh?

'Oh, I didn't mean – '

'Just joking. Jack, we're about to join the M6. I'll need to concentrate on my driving now.'

As they fed onto the slip road, Jack realised they still hadn't discussed what they'd say to Tim.

North Staffordshire

Frank

'Take the next left,' said Jack. 'Yes, here: this is it. Sneyd Close.' He put the map back in the glove compartment.

'This is all very pleasant,' said Frank. 'He seems to have done well for himself, doesn't he?'

The detached houses were in a cul-de-sac and overlooked a spacious area of grass, well-maintained, and planted with trees. Frank had never been to north Staffordshire before, and had assumed it would bear all the hallmarks of an area ravaged by decades of industrial decline. But soon after they'd turned off the motorway they'd entered what was evidently an affluent suburb. Even in winter, with the roadside trees leafless and the beds on the roundabouts devoid of planting, it compared favourably with many of the estates on the outskirts of Aylesbury.

He drew up outside No.13, and with a gasp of relief undid his seat-belt. He could just about tolerate the discomfort on his short commutes to and from work, but long-distance journeys verged on the painful. It really was time he changed his car.

He was conscious that Jack was staring fixedly ahead through the windscreen, as though deliberately avoiding looking at the house outside which they were parked. The poor chap looked tense – well, so am I, he thought. To meet up with someone not seen for forty years would in any circumstances be fraught with uncertainty, but who knew what might transpire from this encounter? The closer he'd got to this destination the more he'd started to worry that all this might be a mistake. Jack no doubt was feeling the same. It was probably the reason why they'd been unable to discuss what they might say. Always assuming that Tim would let them in the house, of course. Frank didn't fancy a doorstep confrontation.

'Well, let's get on with it,' Jack said, and opened his door. Frank did the same and clambered out. Stiff from the journey, he staggered as he walked round the car to join Jack, standing at the passenger side. They walked side-by-side up the short driveway to the front door.

'Will he recognise us, d'you think?' asked Jack.

'Well, you haven't changed that much. I doubt he'll recognise me.'

'Go on then, Frank. Ring the bell.'

Frank pressed the button. A muffled ringing could be heard from inside. He peered through the frosted glass: there was no sign of movement. He pressed the button again, left his finger on it. Nothing.

'He must be out,' said Jack. 'What do we do now?'

'We may as well wait for a bit. Anyway, I'm hungry. We could always eat our packed lunches while we're waiting.'

'Good idea. Pity the girls didn't make us flasks of coffee. I'm gasping for a cup.'

They returned to the car. Jack retrieved his lunch box from the back seat and extracted a sausage roll.

'Hang on, Jack. We don't want to be sitting eating outside his house when he comes home – assuming he does come home. I'll park across the other side of the green.'

They'd been waiting for nearly an hour. Lunches had long been consumed. They'd agreed it was as well that no coffee was available – had it been, both would be wanting a piss by now. It being a cul-de-sac, there'd been no passers-by, apart from a couple of dog walkers who'd let their animals run free and shit on the grassed area. Both owners had assiduously scooped up the mess into black plastic bags before walking off, bags dangling from their hands. Jack had observed that they probably wouldn't have bothered clearing it up if they hadn't been being watched.

It was now 12.30.

'How much longer are we going to wait?' said Jack. 'The bugger might not come home till evening. I didn't plan on being away this long.'

'D'you want to get off home then?'

'Yes. Let's go. We've done enough, I reckon.'

Frank didn't want to give up that easily, but he could sense Jack was getting restless. So he belted up, turned on the ignition and set off round the green. He was about to drive past No. 13 when a car approached, crossed the road, and parked in front of him, half on the pavement, outside Tim's house. Frank had to break sharply. A bearded man leapt out, slammed his car door and hurried up the drive to the front door.

'Looks like our Tim's got a visitor,' said Jack. 'You're unlucky, mate. He isn't in.'

They watched as the man pressed the doorbell. He did it three times, each time keeping his finger on it for several seconds. Then he jabbed at the bell twice, and waited. Anticipating that the fellow would soon give up and walk back down the drive to his car, Frank began to reverse to allow himself space to drive off.

'No! Wait, Frank! He's got a key!'

Frank braked, peered out and saw the man opening the front door. 'Perhaps Tim's moved,' he said. 'Maybe this fellow's the new owner.'

'Well let's go and ask him!' Jack jumped out of the car, ran towards the door.

Frank followed as quickly as he was able. Jack was at the open door, talking to the man who was standing inside. Frank heard the man say that no, he wasn't the owner of the property. 'And what business is it of yours?' he concluded.

'Are you a friend of Tim Bailey's?' Jack asked.

'Never heard of him. What's all this about?'

'No, not Tim Bailey,' said Frank. 'It's David Turner we've come to see. He lives here, doesn't he? Can we come in, please?'

The man took a step towards them and half closed the door behind him. He was tall and well built, and his ginger beard made him the more intimidating.

'Now look here,' he said. 'I don't know what your business is, but I'm here in a professional capacity to see a client. I'm not prepared to let you enter until I've checked that my client knows you and is willing to see you. Is he expecting you? What are your names, and how are you known to him?'

Frank wondered what it was about the Scottish accent that made the speaker sound so authoritative. He decided to be conciliatory.

'I'm sorry, we should have explained ourselves. We're very old friends of David's. We were at school together. We haven't seen him for years. We've travelled up from the south to get here. But he doesn't appear to be in, so when we saw you unlocking the door, we thought – '

'So he's expecting you, is he?'

'Well, no, he isn't. As I said, we wanted to surprise him.'

'Have you been in contact with him at all since you left school?'

'Only recently. By email. It was he who emailed me.'

'And he telephoned me,' Jack interjected.

The man didn't respond immediately: he seemed to be weighing up what Frank had said.

'What are your names?' he asked eventually.

'My name's Grayson, Frank Grayson. And this is Jack Chapman.'

The man's head jerked backwards. 'Are you from Buckinghamshire by any chance?'

'Yes, we are! Has Ti… David mentioned us?'

'Not to me. But he spoke about you to one of my colleagues. It's in the case notes.'

'Case notes? Are you Dave's doctor?'

'Not exactly. Look, I've said too much. I must get inside, Dave'll be waiting for me. He'll know it was I who rang the bell. I'm shutting the door on you. If Dave's willing to see you, I'll come back and let you know.'

He turned, entered the house and closed the door firmly behind him.

Frank and Jack stood outside. 'What d'you make of that?' asked Jack. 'What d'you reckon he meant about case notes?'

'He might be some sort of social worker,' said Frank. 'Remember, Tim told me he'd had a bad accident. Maybe he's confined to the house. If so, he probably needs a social worker to arrange for carers.'

'How long d'you reckon we're going to be kept out here waiting?'

'I expect Tim's bending the fellow's ear about us. Let's give it ten minutes, shall we? If he – '

The door was flung open. The Scotsman charged past them, shouting over his shoulder that he'd got to shift his car. When he'd moved it, he ran back.

'What's on earth's happened?' asked Frank

'I've just called an ambulance. Had to make room for it to park. Dave's ill, in danger I think. Look, you two had better come in. No, on second thoughts, one of you stand by the gate: wave to the ambulance when it appears.'

'I'll go,' said Jack.

The Scotsman turned to Frank. 'You come with me please, I might need your help.' Frank followed him as he entered the hall and began climbing the staircase. He'd almost reached the landing when the Scotsman stopped and turned to face him.

'Did you say you hadn't seen Dave since you were at school?

'That's right'

'Then you'd better prepare yourself for a shock. You probably won't recognise him. Come on.'

The bedroom door was open and Frank could smell shit even before he entered the room. Once inside, he recoiled: there was vomit on the floor, and also on the bed next to a figure lying on its stomach, face turned away from the door.

'Help me get him into a foetal position. He might have choked on vomit. Got to try and clear his airways. Have to get him on his back first. Right, let's pull him. You take his hips, I'll take his shoulders. Ready? Pull!'

Frank had an uncanny sense of being an actor in a horror film, the scene unrehearsed, being told to obey the instructions of the director. They heaved the body – and Frank could think only of it as a body, not Tim – so it was lying on its side, then allowed it to fall on its back. Frank, his face positioned above the body's loins, then knew why the room smelled of shit. His gaze travelled up the chest to the face – *Oh my God! Oh sweet Jesus Christ!*

Confronted with a vision of ghastliness, he wanted to turn away, but he couldn't. He was mesmerised by the gargoyle that stared up at him. He was half-expecting to see the gaping mouth and open bloodshot pupil-less eyes of an unconscious man, but not the shattered remains of what had once been a face. It brought to mind photographs he'd seen of the hideous facial injuries of First Word War veterans, who, despite the best effort of surgeons, were condemned to spend their lives in institutions, unable to cope with the horrified reactions of strangers on seeing them. But this wasn't a stranger lying in front of him, was it? Nausea overcame him.

'Bathroom,' he muttered, one hand covering his mouth.

The Scotsman, bent over Tim's face, glanced up. 'First on the left along the landing. You can leave him to me now, if you'd prefer.'

Frank just made the bathroom in time. After his guts had emptied he found himself shaking uncontrollably. He rinsed out his mouth, then cupped his hands to drink from the running tap. It wasn't enough: he was dehydrated, needed a mug or glass from which to drink. Downstairs in the kitchen, perhaps? He went out to the landing: silence from the bedroom. As he descended the stairs he knew it was not just that he wanted to drink in the kitchen; he needed to physically distance himself from what he'd seen. In that bedroom was something he knew would remain with him for the rest of his life.

The kitchen was untidy, papers strewn over the table, dirty dishes in the sink. He searched in the cupboards, found a mug, filled it with water and drank. Then filled it and drank again. He was still shaking. He sat down at the kitchen table. How long could he sit here leaving the Scotsman to cope alone upstairs? Should he go and tell Jack, still presumably outside waiting for the ambulance, what he'd seen? No; wait until he felt a bit calmer.

He glanced at the stuff scattered on the table. A bottle of Scotch, almost empty, yesterday's *Guardian*, unopened junk-mail, leaflets from pizza houses and Indian takeaways. Prominent at the edge of the table nearest to the door was an A4-sized brown envelope. Written in large letters on it was the legend – *To be handed to a senior police officer.* The writing was in lower case, and Frank recognised it. Even after forty years, Tim's child-like script and his Greek '*e*' were unmistakable.

He picked up the envelope. It wasn't sealed. Should he…? No, of course he shouldn't. It wasn't just curiosity that he felt, but foreboding. Could Tim have been making a complaint to the police? Frank wondered: *might this involve me, or Jack, or Pete? After all, Tim's been in contact with all three of us recently.*

Then, sudden activity. Footsteps in the hall, Jack shouting. 'The ambulance is here!' The Scotsman running down the stairs, telling the paramedics they'd need a stretcher, pushing Jack into the kitchen saying they'd need space, then the rapid descent of the paramedics after only a few seconds in the bedroom. On the stretcher, a body, its face covered. As they approached the front door, one of them shouted to the Scotsman 'You'll need to stay here. I reckon this is a police job. They'll be wanting to speak to you.' Then they were gone. The sudden wail of the ambulance siren made Frank jump. The sound gradually receded.

The Scotsman broke the ensuing silence. 'It's time I introduced myself. I'm Robert McKenzie. I'm Dave's therapist.'

'A sort of social worker, are you?' asked Jack.

'No. I don't work for the Local Authority. I'm with the NHS. If you want my full title, I'm a Cognitive Behavioural Therapist.'

'Why does he need one of those?' said Jack.

Frank was about to chide Jack for the inanity of his question when he remembered that Jack hadn't seen Tim's face.

'I'll tell Jack why later,' he said to McKenzie. 'Is Tim … sorry, Dave, in danger? What did that fellow mean when he said it was a police job?'

'He's more than in danger. I think he's already passed on. These paramedics never like to commit themselves. We'll be told once he's admitted.'

'But why the police?'

'If it's suicide, and it looks very much like it, they'll need to interview me as the first person to find him. And you, probably.'

Frank noticed the shocked expression on Jack's face during this exchange, but he'd said nothing. They were all standing by the kitchen table. For some reason it seemed inappropriate to sit down.

'I assume you know quite a lot about Dave and his life?' Frank asked.

'As much as he was prepared to divulge.'

Frank pointed to the envelope on the table. 'Any idea what that might be about?'

McKenzie picked up the envelope, stared at what was written on it, then put it down again. He breathed in deeply and turned to Frank.

'I'll take you into my confidence because you're old friends of Dave. I'm going to do something highly unprofessional, but it's something I know a colleague who used to be Dave's counsellor would agree with. The police will be here soon, and I don't think it's necessary for them to read what might be in that envelope. I suspect it might be something that would drag up past events unnecessarily, and wouldn't do Dave any good ... well, it wouldn't be something he'd want to be remembered for. So I'm going to open the envelope and read what's in it. Can you both assure me that this is strictly between the three of us?'

'Absolutely,' said Frank. Jack nodded.

McKenzie picked up the envelope and extracted two items. One seemed to be cuttings from newspapers, stapled together. The other was a sheet of paper covered in typescript. Mckenzie glanced at the cuttings, then read the typescript.

'Here,' he said, passing the cuttings to Frank. 'Read those articles first.' Frank took the cuttings and stood next to Jack so they could read them together. They were from *The Yorkshire Post*, the first dated August 1996 which gave an account of a serious assault on a lecturer, Mr Timothy Bailey, who'd been teaching at an Open University Summer School on the York University Campus and who had sustained life-changing injuries. The other cuttings gave updates on the case.

Then McKenzie passed Frank the typescript. It was signed at the bottom *David Turner, formerly Timothy Bailey.* Frank had to read it twice before he could take it in. He passed it to Jack, but almost immediately snatched it back and replaced it in the envelope, because McKenzie was making an extraordinary request.

Motorways Southbound

Jack

Frank had driven only a few streets away from Sneyd Close when he pulled up.

'Why are you stopping?' asked Jack, 'Are you going to tell me what was in that letter? Can't you tell me while you're driving? We ought to get going. The girls'll be wondering where we've got to.'

'That's why I'm stopping. I want to phone Angie, tell her we've been delayed. With a bit of luck she'll still be at your place. If she's left, I'll then call Judy and you can tell her. It's about time you both got yourselves mobile phones, Jack.'

'Maybe. Frank, I hope Angie's still with Jude. If she is, could you ask her to stay there until we get home? It would be easier if we told them what happened while we're all together, don't you reckon?'

'Yes, you're probably right.' Frank pulled his Blackberry from his jacket pocket and punched in the number.

Jack was relieved. After McKenzie had made his strange request and the police had left after questioning them, his thoughts had immediately turned to how he could explain it all to Jude. He knew he wasn't very good when it came to reporting complicated events; he got tongue-tied and listeners could sometimes get impatient. And he had no idea what Jude's reaction might be to hearing of Tim's death. Shock, certainly. Relief, perhaps. But also a glimmer of sadness? Could he cope with that? Far better if Frank did the explaining. In any case, Frank hadn't told him what was in the letter, so he couldn't tell Jude the full story, could he? And …

'Hello, Angie?' Frank had got through. 'Yes, I know. We won't be back until nearly 7 … no, it's too complicated to go into now, and we want to get on to the motorway, it's starting to get dark… Yes… Of course….

Look, darling, could you stay with Judy till we get there?...
Oh, good…No, no, not bad news, well, not for us.… Eh?
That's a good idea. I'll tell him. Must go, darling.'

Frank switched off his phone. 'Okay, Jack. Angie will
stay with Judy until we arrive. Right, let's go.' He started
the car and set off for the motorway junction.

The M6 was even busier than it had been that morning.
After about ten minutes on it Jack had heard Frank mutter
'We've hit the bloody evening rush hour', but after that no
words were spoken, and they were now nearly an hour into
their journey and about to join the M42.

It was dark. Jack was sitting with eyes closed: he
couldn't understand how Frank managed to cope with the
glare of headlights, the flashing of brake-lights and the
winking of indicators, let alone steer through this mayhem.
Maybe the reason for his silence was that he needed to
concentrate: Jack was grateful for that, but on the other
hand, there was so much that needed to be discussed, so
much that he didn't fully understand.

The newspaper reports had been clear enough – Tim,
when he'd regained consciousness, had been unable to
give the police a description of his assailant, had no idea
who it might have been or why he'd been assaulted. In
what was presumably a much later clipping had been a
brief report that although no arrests had been made, the
police were keeping the file open.

But what was in the letter? Why had Frank snatched it
from him? And why did McKenzie want to keep it from
the police? Why had he asked them to take it and the
newspaper cuttings away with them, to shred them when
they got back to Bucks? Why had Frank complied,
hurriedly taken the envelope out to the car before the
police arrived? Was Frank trying to protect him from
something – oh God, might the letter have mentioned
Jude? All sorts of ghastly possibilities flashed in front of
him.

He couldn't stand the uncertainty any longer. If he
interrupted Frank's concentration, that was too bad.

'Frank! Why are you holding out on me? What was in that letter?'

'I'll tell you all about it Jack, but we both need to be calm. I can't discuss it while driving. Can you hang on till we get on the M40? There's a service station just past the turn-off to Leamington. We'll stop there for a while and I'll tell you all. Is that okay?'

Jack concurred.

The traffic on the M42 was even heavier than it had been that morning. Jack resigned himself to a long wait and closed his eyes again. After a while, he felt his head slumping. He jerked upright. Nodding off? How could he sleep at a time like this? He opened his eyes – glare and flashing lights: he couldn't stand it; closed his eyes again. Once more his head slumped forward. He hadn't the energy to pull it back.

Frank

Let the poor old chap sleep, thought Frank. It was probably the effect of stress and shock. Frank wouldn't have minded stopping for a kip himself, but needed to get home as soon as possible, to take that bloody envelope out of the car boot and run it and its contents through the shredder in his study. McKenzie had admitted to being irrational in wanting them to take the envelope as far away from Staffordshire as possible, but he'd said that for him to shred the documents in the office he shared with a colleague would add to his sense of unprofessionalism and could, if discovered, be a sackable offence. All very well, thought Frank, but he now felt he was carrying an illicit cargo: suppose he crashed the car, was taken to hospital, and someone found the documents and passed them to the police as the legend on the envelope directed? Dammit, he thought, who's being irrational now?

It was the urgency in McKenzie's voice when he'd made his request that had made him snatch the letter away from Jack and take the envelope to the car: the police might have arrived at any moment, as in fact they had. Then there'd been the procedure of making statements. He just hadn't had any opportunity to tell Jack what was in the letter. Jack could sometimes be a bit slow on the uptake, and all Frank had wanted to do once the police had finished with him ('You may be called to the station sometime to make a written statement, sir') was to leave and head southward.

It was comparatively quiet on the M40. Frank found himself exceeding the speed limit, something he prided himself on never doing. When he turned onto the service station slip road there was a snort from beside him and Jack's head jerked back.

'Service station, Jack. Quick cup of coffee.'

'Bloody hell. Dozed off.'

'Yes, you were well away.'

He found a parking space close to the entrance to the shopping mall. For once, he was out of the car before Jack, and went round to open the boot. But then he thought – no, he couldn't even risk taking the documents into the coffee bar lest somehow he lose them, or forget them.

He led the way into the mall and then into Starbucks. The smell inside the café made him aware how starved of caffeine he was. He ordered an Americano, double shot. Jack had a latte. Frank's backside had hardly touched his chair when Jack said 'Come on then, what's in that letter that you've been keeping to yourself? And where is it? I want to read it myself.'

It took more time than Frank had anticipated to explain the reasons for his actions. Jack was only satisfied when Frank assured him he could see the letter once it was safely in his study.

'But that doesn't stop you telling me what was in it now, does it?'

'No, I'm about to tell you. But first you need to know what Tim looked like.'

'Looked like?'

234

'Yes. I don't mind telling you, Jack, the sight of him made me feel sick. He was grossly disfigured. Now I know why. His letter explained it was an acid attack.'

'Bloody hell.'

'And he named the man who did it. It was a science technician at York University.'

'Why did the fellow do it? Didn't Tim report it to the police?'

'Apparently not. The letter explains why. Before the fellow threw the acid, he told Tim that if he reported him, he'd retaliate by telling the police why he'd done it. He did it because he'd caught Tim in bed with his daughter.'

'Blimey. Was he raping her or something?'

'I don't know. Tim had met her on the campus, apparently. According to his letter, the girl was a willing participant. But the point is, she was only fourteen. Tim claimed he didn't know that.'

Jack didn't respond, just stared at Frank, his mouth agape.

'It would have meant a prison sentence of course. He changed his name in case his assailant tried to track him down.'

Frank observed that Jack's expression began to change. His eyes narrowed, the open mouth twisted into a scowl.

'Nasty business, eh, Jack?'

'I bet it was rape. He probably did it a lot. He started with Jude, didn't he?'

Frank stood up. 'Come on, let's get going. Remember I want to call in at home to shred the letter before we go on to your place.'

The rest of the journey was undertaken in silence until they were a few miles from Frank's house, when Frank decided to broach a matter that had been in his thoughts since leaving the service station.

'Jack, how much of all this do you think we should tell the girls? Might it upset Judy? Isn't it enough for her to know that Tim's dead?'

235

'No! She needs to know it all!' Jack was almost shouting. 'She needs to know that Tim was a total bastard. She needs to know there's nothing to mourn.'

'Fair enough.' Frank decided not to pursue the matter, but Jack's vehemence gave him pause for thought. Something to discuss with Angie: had she picked up any vibes during her day with Judy, he wondered? That reminded him of another matter.

'Oh, I completely forgot, Jack. When I phoned Angie before we set off, she told me she'd asked Judy if you two would like to come over to us for Christmas. Judy said she'd love to, but she'd have to clear it with you. Would you like to, Jack?'

'Do *you* want us to come?'

'Yes, of course!'

'Well, we have me mum over on Christmas Day.'

'What about Boxing Day then? That'll get us out of having to travel down to Bristol to see our son. Between you and me, I don't get on with his wife.'

Frank began to think that Jack hadn't heard him, or perhaps was searching for a way of refusing the invitation.

But eventually he said, 'Okay. Yes, I'd like that.'

EPILOGUE

Boxing Day

Angela and Frank

'Thanks so much for having us,' said Judith. She and Jack were standing on the doorstep, 'We really enjoyed it, didn't we, Jack?'

'Yes, it certainly made a change.'

Judith and Angela hugged each other. Frank kissed Judith, and after a moment's hesitation Jack pecked Angela's cheek.

'We must get together again,' said Frank, 'and let's not make it too long.'

'Let them go, Frank,' said Angela. 'It's freezing out here.'

They stood watching as Jack and Judith clambered into their car. After a jerky start, the car was driven very slowly out of the drive.

'He seems a bit of a nervous driver, does Jack.' said Angela

'He's a nervous passenger as well. You should have seen what he was like when we were on the motorway.'

They gave a final wave as the car turned into the lane, and went back inside.

'Shall we finish the wine, Angie?'

'Why not? Old Jack didn't seem to be much of a wine drinker, did he? He looked really relieved when you offered him a glass of beer.'

Frank poured two glasses and they sank back on the sofa.

'Well, how d'you think that went?' he said.

'Pretty well, I think, once Jack started to relax. He was pretty tense to start with though, wasn't he? And so formal! The way he kept standing up every time I came in

237

the room! Is he always that polite?'

'He was overawed, Angie. That blouse you're wearing obviously disconcerted him.'

'You're joking!'

'Well, maybe. Actually, the reason he's so formal is because he's so conscious of his working-class roots. He always was, even at school. And of course he's in a dead-end job, and he's a bit ashamed of that. I don't think he and Judy ever get invited out anywhere together.'

'I know. Judy told me. I feel sorry for her. She's so confident; *she* obviously enjoyed our company.'

'Yes, in some ways they're an oddly matched couple, because Judy's so self-assured. They're not exactly comfortable with each other, are they?'

Now might be the time, Angela thought, to tell Frank what Judith had confided during the day they'd spent together when the two men were in Staffordshire. She'd decided against telling him before, because she didn't want it to influence the way Frank might have behaved towards Jack today. He wouldn't deliberately have behaved any differently of course. But if one learns something about an old friend that one never knew before, there are often subtle unconscious changes in the way one converses, the jokes one tells, the subjects one discusses.

She put down her glass and grabbed Frank's hand.

'Frank, I hope you and Jack are going to do what we girls suggested.'

'What was that, then?'

'You know very well. See more of each other, go out together. Jack has no close friends now Pete's gone. And you'll soon be retired, have time on your hands.'

'I hope you're not suggesting I should buy a bike and go cycling with him. I'm not up to that.'

Angela laughed. 'No, I don't want you having a heart attack. But why not go for walks together like Judy suggested? The exercise would do you good. And walking's a good way of getting to know each other.'

'We already know each other pretty well.'

'But there's something you don't know about him. Something Judy told me. It's about their marriage. Jack has a problem; he's had it most of his life. It's made Judy unhappy, Jack as well, probably, but he never talks about it.'

'Do I really want to know the details?'

'I just thought, if you could get Jack to talk to you about it, maybe you could help him, give him some advice.'

***

Frank already had some idea about what Angie was about to say. Problems in a marriage? Jack's problem? That could only mean one thing. When Angie confirmed it, his first thought was 'Poor bugger': it was never a problem that he, Frank, had ever had. Angie's concern, as was to be expected, was more for Judy. She'd been tearful when she'd confided in Angie, had asked whether she was being unreasonable in wanting intimacy at her age.

'And what did you say to that?' he asked.

'I said she was being entirely reasonable.'

'She asked about us, I suppose?'

'No, she didn't. I asked her if Jack had ever sought help. She said he hadn't, even when he was a young man. She reckons he probably thinks it's too late to get help now. She doesn't know, because they never discuss it. They did get near to it when Pete died, but when they got to the nub of the problem Jack just clammed up. That's where you come in, Frank.'

Frank felt the need for more wine. He poured himself another glass.

'I'd like a top-up too, please,' said Angela.

'So how d'you reckon I can help? I'm not a bloody marriage guidance counsellor, Angie.'

'No, but you're a man. Men gossip about these things, don't they?'

'Not if you're impotent, you don't. Anyway, me and

239

Jack have never had that sort of relationship.'

'But if you start seeing each other regularly you might get close enough to talk about these things. Just in general, to start with. You could even mention us – so long as you're not too explicit! Then Jack might start to open up.'

'And if he does, what do I say then?'

'Oh, I don't know, Frank. I can't write a script for you. Why not just suggest he seeks professional help – goes to his doctor as a first step, maybe? He might be prescribed Viagra. Or referred for counselling.'

'Viagra, eh? Thank Christ that's something I've never needed.'

'There's always a first time, old man.'

'Not while you continue wearing blouses like that.'

'Are you pissed, Frank?'

'A bit. But not too pissed. Come on, let's go to bed.'

He pulled her to her feet.

An hour later, Angela asleep beside him, Frank mulled over what they'd discussed. Yes, he'd certainly be seeing more of Jack: Angie was right, he needed the exercise that a walking companion would encourage. But would they ever reach that stage of mateyness when they'd start talking about sex? At their age?

But … poor old Jack. He really did need help. So, if the opportunity arose, he would try to give him some advice. Jack might be outraged, of course, but on the other, hand it might be a means of cementing their friendship.

Frank's final thought as he drifted into a doze was that helping Jack would be a way of assuaging the guilt he still felt for having told Tim about Pete's affair with Judy, and for all that had resulted from it.

He kissed Angela's cheek, turned onto his side, and fell asleep immediately.

Judith and Jack

'It's so cold in here, Jack. Can't we have the heating on just a bit when we're out?

'What would be the point? We'll be going to bed soon, won't we? D'you fancy a cuppa before we go up?'

Judith was about to make a sharp retort to the effect that sitting in the cold to drink it would negate any warming effect the tea might have, but thought better of it. She'd enjoyed her evening, and she thought Jack had as well, once he'd managed to relax. She didn't want to end the day with a disagreement. In any case there was something she wanted to discuss: there was no point trying to talk in bed because Jack always fell asleep as soon as his head hit the pillow. Or at least this was the impression he gave.

'Go on, then. Let's drink it in the kitchen. We can turn on the electric fire in there.'

As Jack busied himself brewing the tea, Judith sat hunched over the electric fire, wondering how she should broach the topic she wanted to discuss. She needed to do it gently, not spring it on him.

'That was a good evening, wasn't it?'

As usual, Jack seemed to be giving his answer careful consideration.

'Yes, it was.'

'They're a nice couple, aren't they? I always liked Frank when we were at school, and I think Angie's lovely. She's got no side to her, even though she obviously had rich parents. Do you like her?

Again, a pause before he replied.

'Yes, I do. I don't know why she had to expose herself so much, though.'

'Well, you know what they say: if you've got it, flaunt it. She's a very attractive woman. Hard to believe she's in her fifties.'

'That's what having money can do, I suppose.'

Judith sighed. This was going to be hard work.

241

'Thanks,' she said as Jack handed her a cup of tea. He sat down at the table beside her.

'Jack,' she said after taking a sip. 'I suppose you noticed that Frank and Angie didn't mention Pete or Marion once all evening?'

'Hardly surprising, is it? Pete's dead and gone.'

'But Marion and Angie used to be close friends. Now that Marion's been left alone I'd have thought Angie would have seen something of her.'

Jack shrugged. 'That's up to her, isn't it.'

This isn't getting us anywhere, thought Judith. She'd just have to tell him straight out, and then ask him the question. She put down her cup.

'Jack, listen. When you and Frank were up in Staffordshire, Angie and I did a lot of talking. In fact, she poured her heart out. She's very upset.'

'What's she got to be upset about?'

'Oh Jack, can't you for once stop judging people because of their backgrounds? Mistrusting people because they're wealthier than you? Rich people can still have sorrows, you know.'

It was rare for Judith to challenge Jack so abrasively. He jerked his head up and stared at her, but said nothing.

'What's upsetting Angie is that Frank is totally against her having any contact with Marion. Apparently he blamed her friendship with Marion for … well, for coming between them. She agreed to sever contact, but then when Pete died … well, it seems Marion's bereft, not just because of Pete, but because her daughter seems to want little to do with her. Marion's all alone. Angie wants to visit her, but Frank won't hear of it.'

'So, what's all this got to do with us?'

It was now she'd have to ask the question, but she was apprehensive about Jack's possible reaction.

'You've come to like Frank, haven't you?'

'Like him? Yes I do. He's not a bad chap considering he's a Tory.'

'And you'll probably get to like him even more when

242

you start going for walks with him, d'you think?'

'Maybe. What's this all about, Jude?'

'Well, I was wondering if, man to man, you might suggest that he lets Angie make contact with Marion.'

'What? How on earth can I do that? Am I supposed to tell him I know what's been going on in his marriage?'

'No, of course not. Just get talking about Pete – that shouldn't be difficult, you both came to hate him – and then lead on to ask about Marion, how she's getting on now she's widowed, and then maybe – '

'No! No!' He slammed down his teacup. 'It was all those secrets and revelations that got us into the mess we found ourselves in, wasn't it? I thought at long last we'd put it all behind us. Let sleeping dogs lie, I say. Frank and Angela must sort it out between themselves. I'm not going to get involved. Did Angela put you up to this?'

'No, of course she didn't. It's entirely my idea.'

'Well, you can forget it.'

'And that's your last word?'

'Yes.'

Well, I tried my best, thought Judith. She was suddenly overwhelmed by tiredness.

'I'm going to take my tea up to bed, Jack. It's too cold down here.'

'Okay. I'll be up in a few minutes.'

***

It took more than a few minutes for Jack's anger to subside. Then he got to thinking. He shouldn't have lost his temper with Jude. She was only trying to help a friend, after all – well, to help a friend to get her husband to allow her to help another friend. Lord, it was all so convoluted.

But he couldn't see how *he* could help. Okay, he'd got to like Frank, but they weren't on the sort of intimate terms which would permit the sort of discussion that Jude had in mind. In any case he'd never been one for conversations of that sort, even with Jude.

243

It seemed that with Angie, Jude had found a soul-mate. He was pleased about that. She needed a close friend, and … oh Lord! Might Jude have discussed their marriage with Angie? What might she have said? Surely she wouldn't have told her … no, impossible. Jude would never do a thing like that.

All his regrets about his failings as a husband rose up to assault him. He owed it to Jude to do things that would please her, didn't he? Even though he might have misgivings about things she wanted? If only this business didn't involve Marion. He'd disliked Marion from the very first time they'd met her, when they were invited to her and Pete's house all those years ago. She was snobbish, drank too much, and blasphemed. But of course she might have changed. If her daughter had rejected her and she was facing life alone, then she was to be pitied. Wouldn't it be the Christian thing to do to what Jude had suggested?

Yes, it would. He still cringed at the thought of having the conversation with Frank that Jude had suggested, but he ought to try. Yes, he *would* try, if only to please Jude. He'd tell her he would, now, unless she was asleep.

He washed and undressed in the bathroom, put on clean pyjamas, and entered the bedroom. The light was out.

He leaned over the bed. 'Jude, are you still awake?'

'Yes.'

'Jude, listen. I'm sorry I snapped at you. I've been thinking. I'll do what you ask. At least, I'll try to.'

Judith sat up.

'You mean you'll talk to Frank?'

'Yes. It might take me some time to get round to it, but I'll do my best.'

'Oh Jack! Thank you!'

She put her arms round him, kissed him, pulled him down beside her. As they cuddled together, Jack felt close to tears. If only the evening could end as she obviously wanted it to. It took him a long time to get to sleep.

Lightning Source UK Ltd.
Milton Keynes UK
UKOW03f0424110517
300908UK00001B/4/P